ALSO BY CRAIG A. ROBERTSON

BOOKS IN THE RYANVERSE:

THE FOREVER SERIES:

THE FOREVER LIFE, BOOK 1
THE FOREVER ENEMY, BOOK 2
THE FOREVER FIGHT, BOOK 3
THE FOREVER QUEST, BOOK 4
THE FOREVER ALLIANCE, BOOK 5
THE FOREVER PEACE, BOOK 6

THE GALAXY ON FIRE SERIES:

EMBERS, BOOK 1
FLAMES, BOOK 2
FIRESTORM, BOOK 3
FIRES OF HELL, BOOK 4
DRAGON FIRE, BOOK 5
ASHES, BOOK 6

RISE OF ANCIENT GODS SERIES

RETURN OF THE ANCIENT GODS, **BOOK 1**
RAGE OF THE ANCIENT GODS, **BOOK 2**
TORMENT OF THE ANCIENT GODS, BOOK 3 (Due early 2019)

STAND-ALONE NOVELS:

THE CORPORATE VIRUS (2016)
TIME DIVING (2013)
THE INNERgLOW EFFECT (2010)
WRITE NOW! The Prisoner of NaNoWriMo (2009)
ANON TIME (2009)

THE FOREVER ENEMY

BOOK TWO OF THE *FOREVER SERIES*

by Craig Robertson

Yesterday, he lost everything.
Today, his list of enemies grows.
Tomorrow, they all want him dead …

Imagine-It Publishing
El Dorado Hills, CA

ISBNS: 978-0-9973073-1-3 (Paperback)
978-0-9973073-2-0 (Ebook)

Cover art work and design by Starla Huchton
Available at http://www.designedbystarla.com

Editing and Formatting by Polgarus Studio
Available at http://www.polgarusstudio.com

Additional editorial assistance by Michael Blanche

First Edition 2016
Second Edition 2018
Third Edition, 2018

Imagine-It Publishing

This book is dedicated to God.
Thank You for all Your love, encouragement, and patience.

PRELUDE

Deep in a war chamber, Warrior One listened intently to the report of his warrior servant, Owant. "Glorious Master Otollar, I bring wonderful news that praises you, as it does Gumnolar." Both men dropped to a knee and knuckled their foreheads after the name of the most holy was spoken. "Our warship *Gumnolar Seeks* has destroyed the infidel craft *Captain Simpson* that violated our existence."

"Details, and be quick. My time is precious. Much is demanded in the service of Gumnolar." Both repeated the ritual bow.

"Yes, Master. Our vessel was initially unable to match the speed of the coward's retreat. A transport craft was stripped bare, fitted with a Fist of Gumnolar, and sent to dispense justice. The pilot, your blessed son Oraner, overtook the unholy and destroyed it."

"And what of *Gumnolar Attacks*?"

"The pilot identified a star system roughly along the direction the enemy craft took. He has altered course to hunt down the scum that boils the hearts of Gumnolar."

Otollar rubbed the back of a fin along a gill slit. "Has he detected signs of the uncleanables there?"

Owant addressed the floor. "No, Master. But in that region of space there are few stars. Offlin is confident our foes cower somewhere in that system."

Otollar slammed his huge tail fin on the table. "If he's wrong, he'll be cast out a water lock into space. To waste the time of one of my prime warships is *unthinkable*."

"Gumnolar will guide his mind, Master. Of this there can be no doubt. He'll have his revenge against the allies of the Beast Without Eyes."

"When does Offlin estimate his arrival in the area?"

"In two, possibly three, cycles."

Again, he stroked a gill. "One ship will not likely neutralize the home world of these servants of the Beast. Launch a Holy Armada at *once*. Half my fleet will make the pilgrimage to end these abominations."

"As it will be, Master."

"How long will it take them to make the journey?"

"At maximum velocity, Master, fifty-nine cycles."

"That is too *slow*. I will not suffer Gumnolar to cry out that long for justice. Do you hear me? They must *obliterate* our enemy in less than fifty-three cycles, or they're never to return to the waters of Listhelon."

Owant doubled over in fear, floating just above the floor. "As it will be, Master. I shall demand the fleet arrive before the Year of Gumnolar 21994."

With a powerful sweep of his tail Otollar darted from the chamber. His servant drifted without moving until he was certain his master was quite gone.

ONE

"Six months until that wacko's ship arrives in our solar system." I tried to stay calm and speak in a measured tone. That wasn't easy. I was *pissed*. "Unless the pilot's a complete moron, he'll have figured out our scout ship, *Ark 3*, had to have come from either Mars or Earth. Long before he gets to the asteroid belt, he's going to know where to point his nukes."

"Our analysis is consistent with your speculations, General Ryan."

I wished to hell she'd stop calling me that. Oh, well, I guessed the UN Secretary General had to be into titles.

"We wonder if there is any benefit from trying to engage him before he can report our exact location to his home world?"

"Minimal," I sighed.

"But not completely meaningless either," added Toño DeJesus.

Thanks, Toño. You might be my oldest friend, but I don't need that kind of love.

"If there is any tactical advantage," Secretary Kahl said, "it must be taken. The lives of every human may depend on it."

"We could send a large fleet," Toño said unconvincingly. "That way we'd all but guarantee victory." He nodded his head slowly. "I just wish we knew more about Listhelon technology. I'd hate to send out a flotilla only to have it lost."

Remind me to strangle you later, Doc. "Or we could send *Ark 1*. She's the only vessel currently equipped with a force field." I had to state the obvious. No one wanted to volunteer me. *That*, I had to do myself.

"That might just be," Toño remarked with a twinkle in his android eyes, "the logical choice." To make me all that more uncomfortable, he leaned his chair back, and cleared his throat. FYI, robots don't get phlegm. "Who would be selected to lead such a mission?"

"There are any number of qualified pilots, Dr. DeJesus." Kahl was in on this, too. I just knew it. I was a tennis ball. They were the tennis rackets.

"No one's going to fly my ship but me. I'll go." There, you made me say it, boys and girls.

"But, you've only just returned from an epic journey." Toño was enjoying this. "We couldn't *possibly* ask you to return alone and unaided to the void of space."

"Maybe," I snapped, "you could come with me, Toño. Then I'd have plenty of company."

"If I didn't have so very much to do," he said, "it would be my honor."

Nice, Doc. Lay it on extra *thick.*

"We'll go," Sapale said with finality. "We're his crew and we always will be. No one else is required or welcome." I just loved it when my brood's-mate talked tough. She knew Ffffuttoe was next to useless, but she'd go anywhere both we and food were.

"So," Kahl asked, "when will you be leaving, General Ryan?" The deal was tied up all neat and tidy. She wanted closure.

"Immediately. The ship has been refueled and serviced. Food storage units for my crew were installed last week. We'll go now."

Kahl stood and held out her hand. "Then God be with you. All of our hopes—"

I held up a hang-on-a-second hand. "Thanks. No speech required, Mary." I turned to Sapale. "Let's fetch our crewmate and split. The sooner we leave, the sooner we'll be back."

"Such confidence," Toño said. "It's truly heartwarming."

"The space-time congruity membrane held off three thermonuclear explosions. I don't need confidence. I just need to find and ram the son of a bitch, then turn my ship around."

TWO

If there was one thing Kendell Jackson would rather do less, he couldn't put a name to it. Sitting across the desk from President Stuart Marshall on one of his rare good days was more unpleasant than a dozen successive prostate exams. From the pruned look on his face, this day had all the signs of one of Marshall's exceedingly bad ones. But, when the president summoned, anyone wishing to live came quickly. Kendell may have been a Major General, but that rank purchased him no longevity with a maniac like President Marshall.

"I'll be direct," the president began. *When wasn't he?* "I called you here today to let you know that you're my new director of Project Ark, effective immediately." He slid a set of papers across the table. "These are your orders. You'll leave for Houston as soon as I dismiss you. There's a chopper waiting outside to take you to the airport." He rested back against his chair. "Any questions?"

Yeah, like a million. But, never press your luck with this loser. "No, sir. Thank you for your confidence in my leadership abilities."

"Leadership, crap. I demand your *absolute* loyalty. Anything else is gravy. You clear on that, son?"

"Sir."

"Here's the long and short of it. The traitor Jon Ryan attacked one of our space stations. Using stolen thermonuclear weapons he destroyed that station and three of our battleships. A significant part of your job'll be to track that rabid animal down and kill him. Are you perfectly clear on that, son?"

General Ryan a traitor? That's impossible. A better man was never born. "But why?"

"Because he's gone *insane*, that's why. Aren't you listening? Years in space, faulty robot design, you name it. Bottom line is he's gone completely bad. He must be destroyed with as much prejudice as possible. Naturally, you'll also be in charge of directing our worldship construction program."

You're shitting me. Why not just hand me a sword to fall on and get this over with? "Anything else, sir?"

"Yes unfortunately there is. *Ark 3* was destroyed by a hostile alien species. They're heading for Earth as we speak with the intention, no doubt, of killing us all. Their estimated arrival is in six months. You'll prevent such an attack. You'll also design a defensive capability to protect the worldships while they travel to our new home. There're a lot more of that scum out there somewhere, and they'll be coming for us sooner or later."

Kendell thought back to when he had dressed that morning. He'd loaded his service revolver. Good. He'd likely need it to end his suffering.

"If there's nothing else, you're dismissed."

Best to find out what I'm getting my ass into. I just hope it doesn't cost me my testicles. "Ah, one thing, if I may. I'll be replacing General York, I believe. Will she be there to brief me on the current status of the program?"

"No," Marshall thundered, "she most decidedly will *not* be. That a problem, son? You require a wet nurse?"

Shit. "No, sir. Just curious."

"Haven't you heard the one about curiosity and the cat?"

"Sir."

"Good." He sat considering something. "Well, I suppose it might be a good lesson to teach you, come to think of it."

"Thank you, sir."

"York's no longer with us. She was fatally afflicted with a bad case of failing me. Any further questions?"

"None." Kendell stood and saluted crisply. He beat as dignified a retreat as great haste would allow.

THREE

The enemy vessel was six months out. If I burned all engines for whatever they were worth, I could intercept him in three months. Not bad compared to my recently completed forty-year mission. No more than a blink of an eye by my standards. Our engagement would take no time at all. I was going to open a can of fast-acting whoop-ass on him and then get the hell home. I wanted to be back on Earth. I needed to readjust, to get my bearings, and most of all, to make myself relevant again. But that would have to wait. *Ark 1* was the only ship for the mission, and I was her only captain.

It was nice to be well provisioned and able to burn fuel at will. Gone for good were Sapale's feed-growing boxes. She and Ffffuttoe had plenty of balanced nutrition. Our voyage was like going on vacation in a high-speed houseboat. Al was along, too. In spite of being a royal pain in the arse most of the time he was family. Yeah, I had an atypical family, didn't I? An alien wife, a flat-bear sidekick, and a pissy ship's AI computer for a BFF. I just *had* to get a family portrait made for the fireplace mantle. If only I had a mantle, of course. Or a fireplace. Hell, or a *house* for that matter.

The outbound trip was uneventful. The only interaction of note was a conversation I had with Sapale very early on. "Why didn't you claim this mission without being forced into it?" she asked with a puzzled look.

"I knew I was the only option, but I didn't want to go."

"These Listhelons deserve to die. Why not *claim* the honor of doing it rather than being forced to by a committee of hens?"

"I'm not so keen on killing. I've done it before. I bet I'll do it again many times. But, it's something I don't like doing." Before she could say it, I added, "Even Listhelons."

"The beast killed your friend and comes to kill you—*us*. When beings beg for death as boldly as these falzorn, one is *obliged* to do the deed. The universe becomes a better place with each Listhelon sent to Brathos."

"I guess you're right."

"You *guess?*"

Angering my brood's-mate was both rather easy and rather perilous. She had quite the temper.

"I *know* you're right. But I still don't like killing. You asked, I answered. Can we let it go?"

She smiled. "I guess so." Then she jumped up on me, wrapping both arms and legs around me. My foibles, it seemed, were forgiven.

Intercepting the Listhelon ship was not as straightforward as I had initially assumed. Al was happy to articulate that fact clearly and repeatedly. I was about to have humanity's first dogfight in outer space. Absent a precedent, I had to establish the parameters for how I engaged my enemy. If I was moving too fast, I would lose maneuverability. Too slow, and I could be a sitting duck. I was ninety-nine point nine percent certain he had no technology capable of hurting me. But I didn't want to realize I was wrong just before I went *boom*.

Three aspects were critical to my attack plan. One, I had to destroy the enemy. Two, I wouldn't fire first. Both Al and Sapale called me a fool for that. They protested that these vermin killed Sim. They wanted us all dead. But I was resolute. *They* would have to start the fight. Third, they couldn't be allowed to report the existence of our membranes back to their planet. Our sworn enemy wasn't getting the opportunity to have years to plan a counterstrategy. In warfare it had always been the case that for whatever advance one side developed, the other by necessity quickly developed a countermeasure. If one side developed armor, then the other side devised bullets to pierce it. When one side developed tanks, the other invented the bazooka. To be certain, our membranes were based on technology the Listhelons couldn't match, but there was too much at stake to give them any useful information on our defensive capabilities.

I spent the last month before our confrontation planning and analyzing potential tactics. Sapale said I was overthinking the matter, obsessing even. But I was a military man. Over-planning never lost a battle. During that process it dawned on me that we'd never tested the limits of our membrane generator. I assigned Al the task of running test patterns on a variety of membrane sizes and dimensions. How far, for example, could we project a coherent field? Were odd shapes possible, like long tubes for ramming? Al, of course, complained endlessly. Why would we want to make odd-shaped fields? Why did I feel it was my life's work to make him suffer? Oh, yeah, he really got deep into one of his martyr-mode hissy fits. He was in his happy place all month long.

We had set off at maximal burn and had accelerated quickly. At some point, I had to order a deceleration burn in order to slow to my target's velocity. I had to assume my enemy would stay at his current maximal velocity. Did I want to attack him head on or pass by and come alongside? I hadn't decided until I was almost upon him. I elected not to strike like a jousting knight. Again, assuming he was at his maximal velocity, I could slow way down, wait for him to draw near, and then accelerate to match his vector. I just hoped he didn't have any reserve speed up his sleeve.

Al calculated all the burns necessary to put *Ark 1* on a parallel course at the same velocity, with us a few thousand kilometers off his port. Years ago, when I was still human, I'd had dogfights in jets. They were thrilling, exhilarating, and terrifying all rolled into one. That feeling came back to me as I maneuvered into position.

"Hail the vessel with the following message," I told Al. *This is Captain Ryan of Earth. I offer you one chance to surrender. If you do not do so immediately you will be destroyed.*

His answer was to launch a pretty good spread of missiles at me. The enemy ship remained on its course toward Earth.

I had to act quickly. If the missiles hit the membrane he'd broadcast the news to his home world. "Al, can we outrun the missiles?"

"Affirmative."

"Make it so."

"Aye, aye, Captain. I've turned and gone to flank speed."

"Steady as she goes. Let me know when the bogies run out of fuel." It took ten minutes for them to fizzle out. *Good to know. Thanks for the intelligence, sucker.* "Lay in a course to intercept him with all due haste. Also, can you tell how many Listhelons are actually aboard?"

"Course set. By infrared signal I believe there is only one life sign aboard."

"Initiate attack plan Lasso. If he fires again, abort and retreat."

"Aye, aye, Captain. Plan Lasso initiated."

I closed quickly. This time he took evasive action. When it was clear he couldn't outrun me he fired a smaller salvo of missiles. I turned and outran them until they, too, ran dry. I ordered us back to plan Lasso. For it to work I had to be no more than five kilometers from the enemy ship. If he fired at me from that close, I'd have to use the membrane and hope to destroy him before he could send a message. It would be touch and go. I detailed this to Al.

What was plan Lasso? Only my brilliant idea to have my cake and eat it too, thank you very much. During our recent experimentation with the membranes, I found we could basically make them into any shape or size we desired. In Lasso, Al would produce a standard forward curve field with a twist. He'd add a long thin tube with a small sphere at its terminus. My idea was that we would turn on the configuration close enough to the enemy vessel to encircle the Listhelon occupant. Yeah, I wanted a live prisoner. If and when I snagged him, a crosshatch pattern of membrane would immediately dismember the rest of the craft. The plan looked good in my mind's eye, but I was taking a tremendous risk.

Guess what? It worked like a charm. In less than a millisecond we grabbed a prisoner and completed a clean kill of the ship. He never knew what hit him. Of course, keeping my prisoner alive was going to be tricky. Al slowly retracted the sphere enclosing the enemy. Finally, he brought the sphere right up to the airlock. He opened the hatch and eased the sphere in. Then came the dicey part. I couldn't close the hatch with the membrane sticking though the aperture. I made a quick visual scan of my guest as he slammed all three of his fins against his invisible prison walls. He didn't appear to be carrying any weapons. Good.

"Al, extinguish the field, close the hatch, and flood the airlock like we drilled it."

"Aye."

It was really fun to watch. First, the big lug slammed to the deck due to our artificial gravity. Then the hatch slammed shut. He was temporarily lying on the floor in a complete vacuum, aside from the water he'd brought with him, which had vaporized instantly. He squirmed—sorry, I have to say it— like a fish out of water. That snapshot was worth all the trouble I'd gone to in order to secure a live specimen. Quickly, Al flooded the airlock with a twenty-degree Celsius saline solution. He was tossed around like a cork in the ocean for a few seconds, then he was stunned and stationary.

He was still breathing, so my plan was solid so far. He floated motionless, trying no doubt to figure out what the heck had just befallen him. I said a quiet prayer to Sim. I knew he'd appreciate his executioner's consternation. Finally, he swam to the observation port. He slammed a closed fin against the window for all he was worth. Luckily, it held. It actually also held up completely unscathed from the seemingly endless series of blows that followed. I think the fish was mad. But, hey, maybe that's how Listhelons said, "How do you do?"

After his fin-hand thing was badly deformed and bleeding, he floated backward, exhausted. I altered my voice to be audible in his aquatic environment, engaged the translation program, and spoke to him. "You done hurting your fin?"

That brought—knock me over with a feather—another bout of futile but resounding blows to the window. When he was finished with that outburst, I addressed him again. "I'm Captain Ryan. You're my prisoner. If I say something you don't understand, let me know. My translation program may require a lot of updating." He turned his back to me. Pretty dorsal fin there, sore-ass loser. "You'll be provided safe passage back to Earth, assuming you pose no threat. If I determine you're not worth the trouble, I'll pump your prison full of my own urine and be satisfied to give the scientists back home a pickled specimen. Really, it's all the same to me. You decide what state you arrive in, okay?"

He continued to sulk. What a big baby.

"If you want anything to eat, you'll have to ask. If you prefer to starve, be my guest. If you feel like talking, just say the words. I'll hear you. For now, I'm going to scatter the wreckage of your ship a little more completely, just because, you know, I won and you lost. Okay, so don't be a stranger."

I placed a patch over the window. Nothing good could come of him spying on us for the next two months. I really planned on letting him starve, if he was so inclined. He could ram his fool head against the wall until it split open like a ripe watermelon for all I cared.

I should complete the picture of what the Listhelons looked like. Earlier, I described the peek we got from *Ark 3*'s remote. My prisoner confirmed my impression of their physique. He was two meters long, had two large, fused tail fins with mostly webbing at the ends. There were two smaller fins that passed for arms, which ended in articulated digits. He was, like his kinsman, butt ugly. He had huge, overlapping fang-like teeth, a small bumpy head, big, and bulging eyes articulated somewhat like a lizard's. They bobbed around in a nauseating manner. His skin was sleek, but not at all scaly. He sported gill splits on both sides of his thick neck. Sapale promptly proclaimed that the falzorn of Alpha Centauri-B 5 had been replaced by the Listhelons as her least favorite creatures in the universe. They topped my list for sure. Seriously, they were totally revolting creatures. Definitely wouldn't want to be one.

Bagging a live prisoner had been a spur-of-the-moment decision on my part. Getting him back home alive was a long shot, so I didn't worry about his well-being all that much. It was actually a huge surprise when he finally said something to me. Out of the blue, a week into our return voyage, Al informed me he was asking to speak to me. I went to the window and removed the covering. I was staring directly into his ugly face.

"You called for me?"

"Yes, Captain. I require food."

"Wow, okay. I sort of figured you'd sulk to death before asking, but sure, I'll pass in a few options." I turned to find some food, but stopped. "What's your name?"

He looked at me with his wiggly eyes a good long while. "Offlin, son of Otollar."

"Hi, Offlin. I'm Jon Ryan."

"And your father? Do you not honor fathers on your unholy world?"

"Let's leave him out of the discussion for now, shall we? And, try and limit your daily quota of unholies and infidels if you can. It makes you sound sort of silly."

"Please know that if I could reach though this window I'd strangle you. Your insults only make me more determined to do so. Someday, hopefully soon, I will honor Gumnolar by doing just that, Jonryan." He knuckled his forehead and dropped to his knee.

"Okay, with that thought in mind, let me go get you something yummy to eat." I walked away. "Where'd I put that dead rat?"

Sapale accompanied me when I brought back a few chunks of meat and a carrot. If Offlin was sour before, seeing her made him additionally displeased. "Another vile race that fouls the realm of Gumnolar?" He kneeled. "When will the insults to His blessed name end?"

She pressed her nose to the glass. "Try closing your eyes, pig fart. If that doesn't do it, I'll come in and see to it personally you aren't made to suffer any longer." She turned to me. "I don't like your new pet."

"I'm sure he'll grow on you soon or later. He seems real sweet to me." I pushed the food through a small portal. He took the meat and smelled it suspiciously. "It's the flesh of a common animal on Earth. It's mostly protein, so I doubt it'll poison you." He took a tentative nibble, then swallowed the rest whole. After much consideration of the carrot he let it float away. "You want more?"

"Not for now. I will sleep."

"Thanks for the update. Just curious, but why did you decide to survive?"

"You would not understand."

"You can't know that. Try me."

"A servant of the Beast Without Eyes cannot be made to understand the ways of Gumnolar. Evil clouds your eyes, your ears, and your mind."

"I dare you." He shot an if-looks-could-kill glance at me. "Yeah, you know about dares, don't you?"

He continued to stare a moment, then looked away. "It is sacrilege to let a creature of Gumnolar perish if it can be reasonably avoided. This applies to oneself. There. Do you fail to understand as I predicted?"

Touchy guy. "I understand perfectly. What I don't get is the fact that you're so anxious to kill *us*. That makes no sense."

He responded with impressive contempt. "*You* are not creatures of Gumnolar."

"How do you know that? Hmm? Maybe I'm his cousin. Ya ever think about that? Or maybe we had lunch last week, and for once, Gumnolar even paid."

Offlin was not amused. He hurled his full weight against the door while screaming something disparaging about me and my lineage. What a hothead. I slapped the cover back on the window. "Let me know if you need anything else. I going to call my buddy Gumnolar and let him know what a bad guest you're being." A loud series of slams were then heard by all with ears.

FOUR

A staff car pulled up to his plane as soon as it stopped on the tarmac. A ramp was hurried into place and two men jogged to the base with open umbrellas. A nice display for their new commander. It was pouring in Houston. General Jackson was pleasantly impressed. He took the steps quickly and hoped to hell he didn't trip and make a fool of himself on day one. All he needed to do was think of the impossible task he'd been given. That would do it. He'd freeze mid-stride and tumble down the steps in a free fall. Marshall had set him up to fail, and the penalty for failure was made abundantly clear. He'd be lucky to see his new grandbaby's first birthday.

No time for self-pity or doubt. As soon as he was in his office, he called a meeting of his top adjutants. Faces-to-names and concrete plans were his first order of business. Kendell had to do something about the aliens attacking Earth. He needed to find out what defensive assets were at his disposal and determine whether they'd be sufficient. The mire he was in just got thicker with each step.

Two men, one woman, and a civilian appeared quickly at his office door. Two were clearly out of breath from running. Good. He wasn't the only person scared shitless in that loony bin. Introductions circled the room. Kendell's chief of staff was Colonel Patrick Smith. Looked to Kendell to be a sound fellow. Square shoulders, thick neck, and no sense of humor. Lieutenant Colonel Rhea Brown was in charge of Logistics. Schoolmarm-like and meek. Hopefully effective. She wore a wedding band. That said something. At least she wasn't a complete loner. Rear Admiral Brian Duggan was on loan from the British Navy. Apparently he was some kind of whiz kid science nerd. Handy in a space program, but hopefully he could understand the politics running rampant. If he didn't, he'd be back swabbing a deck faster than he could say *time for tea.*

And the civilian. Kendell didn't like civilians in military settings. They were loose cannons at best. No sense of duty, commitment, or more importantly, loyalty to the service. The civilian was head scientist in charge of the android program. Looked to be about eighteen years old. That made matters even worse. The kid probably had an attitude and was badly in need of a spanking. Well, Kendell had whipped more than one pansy's ass when they needed a life lesson. Carlos De La Frontera. What kind of name was that for an adult, let alone an American? He'd keep a short leash on this one. He most certainly would.

"Okay, people, the meet and greet portion of the day's fun is over. We need to resolve some pressing issues." Kendell wanted to set the mood. That mood was work hard, produce results quickly, and never mistake me for your friend. "Let me start with you, Rhea. Do we have every single piece of equipment we've requested or even dreamed of? I'll not be thrown under anyone's bus for want of materials."

"We're good. The supply chain understands our needs are the highest priority."

"Excellent. Patrick, same question to you. Do we have more than enough of all the right people?"

"Yes, sir, we do. The best and brightest either want to be here or have been persuaded that it's in their best interest to cooperate fully."

"Admiral Duggan, I'm not fully clear what your role is here. Please provide me a brief summary."

"Certainly, old sport. My training is in engineering. Graduated the astronaut program and have been here for the past few years. I help plan missions, select crews, and give input on optimized craft designs. I've dabbled in the asteroid conversion side of the equation in the past, but not so much anymore." He smiled whimsically. "I guess you could say I'm a jack of all trades."

"First, I'm not your *sport*. I'm your commanding general. Second, I require *experts*, Admiral, not swashbuckling dabblers. May I trust you to contribute *in* that capacity *with* that mindset?"

Duggan stiffened in his chair. "Yes, sir." What a tight-assed pimp, he thought to himself.

"And that leaves us with the matter of you, Mr. Frontera. You run the robot program, is that correct?"

"Yes, Kendell, that would be me."

He balled his fists in sudden rage but held them below the desktop. "I am Major General *Jackson* to you, Mr. Frontera. Is that clear?"

"Yes, Major General Jackson, I believe it is. Would it bother you, however, if I shortened it to simply *General* Jackson at times?"

"I will brook *no* insubordination or flippancy, Mr. Frontera. I can and will have you—"

The chief of staff rushed to save the day. "Ah, General Jackson, if I might speak with you privately for just a moment?"

Kendell sat with his chest heaving and glared at his aide. How *dare* he. What sort of monkey island was he put in command of? He had half a mind to have all four of them shot at sunrise for high treason. Seriously, all four. Start with a clean slate. He flipped the back of his hand at the door. "You three. Out, now. Wait outside. No potty breaks."

The three of them scrambled out the exit like clowns in a circus act.

"What's *so* important that you felt the need to publicly undermine my authority, Colonel Smith?" He didn't need to add he was not pleased. That fact was abundantly clear.

"General, I'm sorry as shit to pull this kind of stunt, but I had to stop you."

"So you have already formed the opinion that I need help performing my duties? Would you like to attach some string to my arms and legs to better manipulate me?"

"No, sir. Please hear me out. After that, I'll have my resignation on your desk in ten minutes."

"Very well. Proceed."

"That young son of a bitch is the best at what he does by a country mile." Patrick pointed in the direction of the outer office. "He trained at DeJesus's side and is the only man on Earth who gets how those androids work. Well, aside from DeJesus himself."

"I am extremely uncomfortable with you mentioning that traitor's name *twice* in my presence."

"Traitor or not, one must give the devil his due. Anyway, my point is that you'll be cutting off your own balls if you flush that insulant jerk. He knows it. We *all* know it. Now you know it, too."

"No man is irreplaceable. I'm currently inclined to have him hanged just outside this building as a reminder to the remainder of my staff."

"Kendell, that would be the biggest mistake you ever made."

"Colonel Smith, you are relieved of your duties. I will instruct my secretary to have security place you in the brig pending your court-martial. *You* are dismissed."

"You are within your rights to do all that, but that doesn't make it right. I'm telling you this as a loyal officer and as someone trying to help you. Frontera *is* irreplaceable. Without him, the android program will evaporate. Then only the UN will have that capability. You do not want to be the one to inform Marshall of that development."

Shit. The man was right. Bad news used in the same sentence with the president's name equaled death. Ease back, but just a little. "Patrick, please be seated. I apologize for what was said in anger. Thank you for being brave enough to speak truth to power." He extended a hand across the table.

"No problem, Kendell." They shook hands. "That's my job. You can always count on me to perform it at my level best."

"So, this Frontera fellow. We need him, but can we trust him?"

"Probably not. I think he spent too much time with DeJesus not to fall under his spell."

"Which leads me back to the proposition of hanging him—mission critical though he may be."

"We have him more than tightly followed. He doesn't take a dump without us knowing its weight, consistency, and smell. Better to have a traitor you know than the one you don't."

"For now, we'll do it your way. I will, however, reserve judgement on his relative longevity. Please summon those three fools back. We apparently have an alien horde to defend against."

FIVE

Over the weeks on the trip home, I found myself talking more and more with Offlin. Turned out he was quite the chatty fish. Sure, at first it was mostly me listening to his vitriolic denunciations of everything non-Listhelon, followed, of course, by my flippant retorts. But, beyond any hope or expectation on my part, we actually began discussing major issues. Life, spirituality, an afterlife, and, most amazing of all, my God versus Gumnolar. It took him over a month, however, to forgive my wisecrack about Gumnolar never paying for a meal. My preconception about fanatical religions and their followers was that their absolute inflexibility couldn't abide alternate views or opinions. But, at least in Offlin's case, there was some permeability in his worldview. Importantly, if I questioned some fundamental tenet of his faith, he would seriously consider my words and offer a cogent, thoughtful response. I was amazed. Take the following exchange for example.

"Offlin, let me ask you this. Gumnolar created only one race. Yours. He made them in his image, and he made them good. Am I right so far?"

"Yes, though it's a bit of a simplistic rendition of my beliefs."

"So, any other sentient race was not, by definition, made by Gumnolar."

"Correct."

"Hence, they must be evil."

"Naturally. They would have been created without the benefit of the Light that comes from Gumnolar's eyes."

"Why? How can you *know* the mind of a god? How can you know how far that light might travel? Maybe it reaches all the way to Earth."

His initial reaction was to heat up. He didn't say anything, but I could tell he was seething on the inside. To his credit, he let that pass and took a few minutes to frame his answer.

"This view, about us being the only perfect creatures of a perfect god, has been raised before on my world."

"Probably not too successfully."

He made a trill.

I learned it was his version of a laugh. Made sense for an aquatic species I guess. "Or long." I placed a finger to my head and pantomimed shooting myself.

He trilled louder at that.

"I reveal too much of our ways to my sworn enemy. Yes, to question the words of Gumnolar is to invite a swift death."

"My point is this. How do you—Offlin—know that he said those words? I assume he said them a long time ago."

"Why would you assume that?"

"I've learned a lot about a number of religions. The creators always said his or her piece a long time ago.'"

"Jon, you strain my credibility too much. There are religions with *female* gods?"

"Some have one of each." I had to add a wink with that revelation.

"By Gumnolar's claws, now I've heard everything." He made his version of a chuckling trill. "Yes, he said his piece long ago."

"And you yourself said it's sacrilege to write down the words of Gumnolar. Only word of mouth is permitted. So, did he actually say, in these *exact* words, 'you are the only proper race. If you ever find a new one, it isn't my doing?'"

"No." He rubbed at his gill slit absently. "What's passed down is that he said, 'You are my chosen, my blessed, and my only.'" He raised his fins in a what-else-can-I-say gesture. "Hard to mistake the message."

"But who, *precisely*, is the 'you' he's referring to?" His eyes stopped bobbling around, which basically never happened. I pointed through the window. "Aha. Got you. You never thought about that aspect, did you?" He sat in what I could only assume was a befuddled state. "Yeah, maybe he was talking to me, too." I tapped my chest.

"Don't get too proud of yourself. The counter to that line of thought is that he was speaking to *us*. We were, and still are, the only ones cupping a fin to our ears to take in the message." Confidently, he pointed his fin at me. "I'll ask you this. Did Gumnolar ever say those words to the people of Earth? If not, it settles the reliability of our reasoning."

"That's just it. Maybe he did. We have a God. He says things like that. Maybe those exact words aren't recorded, but it sounds like something He'd say."

A deeper trill than I'd ever heard shook the walls of the airlock. "Ah, now *you*, Jonryan, human, know the mind of a god."

Damn. He had me on that. "How 'bout some chow? All this talking makes my hungry."

He agreed wholeheartedly with my sentiments.

I brought back what I'd found to be his favorite food. No, not fish sticks. We didn't have any along. Otherwise you bet your sweet patootie I'd have tried that early on. No, he loved poached eggs, the runnier the better. Salt was okay, but he hated pepper. I tried cheesy omelets too, but they didn't put a smile on his face like slimy eggs. Well, to be honest, nothing put a smile on his face. His face didn't move like that with all his huge teeth. He could down a dozen eggs without stopping for a breath. Sapale liked eggs, so we'd brought a lot. I didn't think our supply would last until we docked. For my part, I nibbled at a chunk of the serrano ham Toño had given us long ago.

"Jon, a question. You and I speak often. You feed me embarrassingly well. But I rarely see you eat and never more than a tiny amount. Since you began leaving the cover off the portal, I never see you sleep either. How can this be? The other two sleep and eat. Especially that furry one. Do humans not sleep?"

No way was I going to give up the tactical information about my being an android. The less one's enemy knew in general, the more likely one was to survive. He wasn't going to be talking to home, but there was no reason to chance a revelation. "Sure, we sleep. I don't much, but most do."

"And eating?"

"Don't you worry about me." I slapped my abdomen. "I get plenty enough."

"Since we're speaking of great matters, I must ask. How did you spirit me off my ship? Such an act seems impossible."

"Yet here you float."

"Yet here I float."

"That's easy to tell. I said to myself, 'Self, wouldn't it be nice if the pilot of that enemy ship popped over to my ship so we could become friends?'" I fluttered my fingers in the air. "And, poof, you appeared as if by magic."

"Didn't think you'd tell me, but it has baffled me."

"Good. Then you won't get bored. You're welcome."

"For a great warrior you are not very serious. A mighty individual should be more, I don't know, reserved. Proper."

"First off, what makes you think I'm some great warrior? I have to say, you're the only one besides me who has formed that opinion."

He seemed suddenly very serious. "We attacked and destroyed that other vessel. It was identical to this one as far as I can tell. You, on the other fin, not only destroyed my ship, but also captured me alive. Hence, you're a great warrior."

"And you killed a good friend of mine in the process. His name was Carl Simpson. He had a family."

"I lost my brother, whom I loved dearly. Such is war."

"I think we'd best let that topic go." I noticed my fists were balled up and relaxed them.

"As you wish. I find all your wonderful food has made me sleepy. If you'll pardon me, I will rest."

"See you later." I was still furious. I do believe my android chin was trembling.

SIX

"I'm just saying if there *ever* was an occasion to contact the UN and work together, this would be the one." Patrick had learned to steer clear of his commander's hot temper, but sometimes he had to speak freely. That's what a good chief of staff did. At least he hoped it was. Maybe the truly successful and the *old* ones kissed butt and said, "*Yes, sir,*"a lot.

"Do you wish to be the one informing Marshall that we've opened a friendly channel with those traitors?" He tented his fingers on his chest. "I, for one, am not relaying any such message. Honestly, it would be healthier for me personally if the aliens plowed a crater across Times Square than for me to advocate working in concert with the UN."

That betrays the mission, reflected Patrick. *We're supposed to defend the planet, not cover our personal butts.* But he kept that observation to himself. One's health was, as his boss just validated, a good thing to keep in mind. "Not knowing the offensive capabilities of the alien makes it hard to estimate what force will be needed to stop them."

"Nonsense." Jackson pointed up toward outer space. "We know exactly the direction they'll come from. We arm ten or fifteen shuttles with all the ordnance they can carry and position them between the hostile and Earth. By sheer force of number we cannot lose."

Patrick had read of many generals foolish enough to say the words, *we cannot lose.* Never, ever did he imagine he'd end up serving under that particular type of idiot. Many other types, yes. But never the stupidest, most clueless kind. He ground his teeth. "What're your specific orders, General?"

"I believe I just issued them. Equip several shuttles with armament and send them to engage and destroy the enemy vessel. Any further questions?"

"None, sir." He saluted as unconvincingly as possible and huffed out.

Before his aide left the room, the phone on his desk rang. Only one person had a direct line to that office. "Yes, Mr. President."

"You settling in there, Jackson?"

"Yes, sir. Nice of you to inquire."

"Nice, nothing, you idiot. I need results, and you're going to supply them. The sooner you get the feel of the place, the better."

Kendell elected to offer no response. Nothing permissible was riding his train of thought at that moment.

"So, you figure out what to do with that son of a bitch alien heading our way?"

"Yes, sir. I've established an armed perimeter along which they'll be destroyed."

"They'd better be. And the android program, how's it coming along?"

"The individual in charge assures me one unit is almost complete. Maybe ready as soon as next week. Two more are less than a few months out."

"Excellent. I need all the metal-heads I can get my hands on."

"Sir, that brings up a sensitive topic."

"Which would be?"

"This Frontera fellow. I neither like nor trust him. I would very much like to remove him from our midst. I have no doubt he is a mole and will betray us, if he hasn't already done so."

"If you don't trust him, make him wear a condom when you shower with him, Jackson. What the *hell* do you expect me to do? Every other slacker we tried to replace DeJesus with simply didn't pass muster. Frontera gives me results. You should study his techniques in that regard. He's been under the tightest security possible and hasn't so much as stolen a glance at a cute girl's ass. You let *me* worry about him. You just see to it that there's no slowdown in android production. Do I make myself unbelievably clear on that point, son?"

"Perfectly, sir."

"And asteroid conversions. How piss-poor are you doing?"

"With all due respect, Mr. President, I've only been here three weeks. I hardly think I can carry any of the blame for the inadequacies that have built up over the years with worldship construction."

"Yeah, but you're not your unreasonable and unforgiving boss. I *am*, and I'm talking to the man in *charge* of a program that's presently going down the toilet."

"As of the present, twelve asteroids are within spitting distance of being habitable. One hundred fifty-seven are well under way and will definitely be completed in the next decade. Beyond that, I simply can't say. Several hundred additional asteroids are heading here. How much can be accomplished in fifteen years with them is anyone's guess. I'm of the opinion that you will have at your disposal approximately one hundred functional worldships by 2150. Each can accommodate one hundred thousand individuals. That assumes no major setbacks are encountered and that no significant increases in productivity can be found."

"I need two hundred fifty ships. Nothing else is acceptable. Channel all your efforts into that quota."

"But, sir, that goal will only allow for perhaps a million people to emigrate. We are a nation of nearly five hundred million. How can that possibly be our goal?"

"It's not *our* goal, you moron. It's *mine*. I don't have to run my reasoning by every lackey I suffer to live and breathe. Just focus on two hundred fifty good ships and pray I allow you to be aboard one of them when the day comes." The phone went dead without a goodbye.

Kendell had some contemplation to do. Yes, he most assuredly did. Dangerous thoughts swirled in his head, ones as unwelcome as a plague of locusts.

SEVEN

We were nearing the moon's orbit when Offlin asked the tough question. "What will become of me when you return?"

I didn't rightly know. I'd started to think about it several times but aborted considering it much. It wasn't my decision to make. He would become someone else's problem. I took him prisoner, but I wasn't his keeper. As much as I tried to frame his future along those lines, I was feeling guiltier with each passing mile. He was our sworn enemy—our forever enemy. Capturing him was the intelligence boon of the century. But in spite of being the bad guy, he wasn't that bad a guy. Ugly as my worst nightmare, sure, but he'd become my buddy, and in war buddies are closer than family. We were kindred spirits. We fought old men's wars because of *their* ambitions, *their* prejudices, and *their* insatiable greed. Only persons drawn to serve that corrupted calling could understand it. We were brothers. Brothers in arms that fate bedeviled to place on opposite sides of the just one more battle line.

"We call it *in unbreathed water.*"

We both chuckled humorlessly. "I *can* promise you that you'll be treated well. I'll see to it personally." I shrugged. "Maybe I can have a say in who's in charge of your case."

"You mean my prison tank."

I looked him squarely in the eyes, which still grossed me out. "Yes, your prison tank."

He looked up and gathered in his tail fin. "I will betray no useful information about my people."

"I'd be disappointed if you did."

He released his legs and floated casually on his back. "Were our positions reversed, you would have it much worse. Not that my race takes prisoners, but if you fell into their water, they'd treat you quite horribly."

"Maybe I should take you back to Listhelon. You could tell them how nice we all are, and we could call the war thing off."

"If I returned they'd eat me alive."

I shot up an eyebrow. "You mean they'd yell at you and be highly critical of your actions?"

"No. I mean they'd literally eat me alive." He lifted his fins. "I allowed one of Gumnolar's creatures to be desecrated by contact with your kind? I didn't die trying to kill you, my captor. No, I'd be torn apart as I watched." He looked over to me intently. "They'd consume my eyes last, so I could see my punishment until its end."

"Wow. Tough place, Listhelon."

"Tell me about it."

"Would they punish your family, too?"

That drew the first very confused look I'd ever seen him issue. "How … what do you intend to ask?"

"You know, would they go after your parents and maybe your wife and children?"

"I just realized there's a topic we never discussed. Perhaps assumptions were made by each of us that are not valid. How did you come to be, Jon?"

I told him in a general manner about the birds and the bees, human style.

"My, but that's odd and different." I swear he shuddered in disgust. "My family couldn't be punished because everyone I know *is* my family. The eggs of all females are fertilized by one individual, Warrior One Otollar. Only he has the right and honor to sire his followers."

"You have got to be kidding me. You mean one dude does it to all the gals?"

"I have no idea what you just said. All females desiring to spawn deposit their eggs in a nest chamber. There are, naturally, many such chambers. Then Otollar fertilizes them. I'm his son. Everyone is his child."

"That's the craziest system I've ever hear of. What happens when Otollar dies?"

"If Warrior One dies or is defeated, most of his offspring die. What's crazy about that system?"

"For one thing, if everybody but the next boss dies, who the hell does he fertilize to rebuild his reign? Hmm? Come to think of it, he was sired by the last leader, so he'd die too, right?"

"The hormones of your race must be very basic. The new leader's body changes, and he does not involute. Some others also survive. A handful of females help produce the next generation."

I held up a hand. "Hang on, let me guess the next part. Any males who don't die are eaten."

He extended his fins toward me. "There, you see you do understand our ways. Of course, *they* are killed before consumption. To be eaten alive is reserved only for criminals. I knew our reproductive cycle was straightforward and reasonable."

I crushed my face into the palm of my hand. "Keep thinking that, pal. You just keep on thinking that it's anything but *insane*." I became serious. "Wait, if that's the way your species lives, there's two big problems. One, there's no genetic diversity. One bad epidemic or climate change would wipe you all out. Second, how can an advanced society maintain itself, if basically everyone dies?"

"Not problems. There're many small groups surviving at the fringes of Warrior One's great empire. They occupy undesirable areas, perhaps too deep to be productive. If catastrophe stuck the ruling individuals, one of those groups would survive and breed up the population." He trilled softly.

"What?"

"Nothing. I'm reminded of an old saying of ours. When someone is different than the norm or rebellious, he is said to be *long-tailed*. The idea is that a sperm from one of those far-off enclaves swims all the way to a main spawning chamber and fertilizes the troublesome individual. To do so, that sperm must have one long and powerful tail. Silly saying, now that I think of it."

29

"Are you long-tailed, Offlin?"

"Yes, I suppose I am." He shook his head. "As to sustaining the machine of society, yes, there are some periods of inactivity. But they don't really matter. The new Warrior One can sire a new generation to adulthood in less than one of your years."

I slapped my forehead. "Holy moly, you got to be kidding. Egg to adult in less than a year?"

"Why does that strike you as odd? Wait, how old are you?"

The real me was long dead. When I was uploaded, I was almost forty. "Forty."

"Years? Now it is you who jest."

"How old are you?"

"I will be six of your years old shortly. How long do your people live?"

I shrugged. "Depends. Maybe ninety years if we're lucky. What about you?"

"On Listhelon, to be twenty is to be unimaginably ancient."

"Wow. You guys are like octopi. Short lifespans, but still remarkably intelligent."

"Show me these octopi." He tapped the computer screen I'd provided him in the airlock. He had a waterproof keyboard, too. I told Al to keep an eye on what he accessed but to let Offlin look up most anything he wanted to.

"Al, bring up some holos of the giant Pacific octopus."

As Offlin marveled at the octopus, he fanned his gills. "Amazing. We look nothing like it, but it *is* beautiful. Is it sentient like us?"

"No, just relatively intelligent with a short life."

"I would love to swim with one of those."

Sapale came over to the airlock. "I hate to interrupt this meeting of the Boys' Club, but we're ready to dock with the UN station."

My eyes dropped to the floor. "Be right there." With sad eyes, I looked back at Offlin. "I'll keep you posted as to what going on. Remember, I'll make certain you're treated well. You got that?"

"I trust you, my friend." His eyes bobbled around extra fast. "If you need me, I'll be right here."

I walked to the bridge and checked in with Al. "Everything clear for docking?"

"Right as rain, boss."

"Good," I sighed, "let me know when our side port is secured to the station."

Sapale stepped up behind me and wrapped her arms around me. "He'll be okay. You have his back. Plus, he's a tough cookie."

"I hope so." We stood still a moment. "I feel kind of responsible."

"I know, love. But please keep in mind he's a heartless killer from a race bent on our mutual extinction."

"That does place my role in a less guilty light, doesn't it?"

"And Al keeps telling me you're such a slow study."

"Remind me to contact the computer repairman while we're here."

"The AI that just overheard you wishes to inform the robot commander that we've securely docked. Dr. DeJesus is here and anxious to speak with you."

Toño. Great. I'd missed him. Plus, I could trust him with Offlin. The three of us got together over coffee. I went over how I'd captured Offin and asked Toño to off-load him as soon as possible—to free up *Ark 1* in case we were needed elsewhere. He said that wouldn't be a problem. The issue of securing him was critical. With us, he'd been a pleasant passenger. But there was no telling if that trend would continue. The actual transfer was the riskiest part. Moving him from the airlock to a holding tank would provide him with a chance to lash out. Someone could get hurt, and we could lose an invaluable asset. Toño understood. I also stated that Offlin had become a friend. Toño was to make certain he was treated humanely and not subjected to torture. He agreed without reservation. My prisoner would be well looked after. That made me feel a little less horrible about the world I'd cast Offlin into.

Our conversation switched to my innovation with the membranes. Toño was childishly excited. "How did you *conceive* of such a marvel? Once you sent word, I began to toy with the concept. Jon, the applications are limitless. I believe your discovery will save *billions* of souls that otherwise would have been unable to flee the impending catastrophe."

"Toño, all I did was use the membrane as a tool. I didn't invent *air*."

"Don't you see? I've already set up the production of field generators to act as worldship excavators."

"What did you just say?"

"I can set up banks of computers to rapidly carve out the interiors of asteroids with the membranes. It's a game changer. With conventional explosives and laser torches, the process takes more than a year. Now it'll take a few weeks, possibly less. Then the craft can be fitted for passengers. That's the easy part, given enough resources. Jon, you're a miracle worker."

"Wow. Nice to know."

Sapale set her mug down. "Toño, he was hard enough to live with up until now. You've probably just made cohabitation with him insufferable. You know that, don't you?"

He placed his palms face up above the desk surface. "I must acknowledge his fundamentally god-like contribution to our evacuation efforts."

She reached across the table and slapped his shoulder. "Not another word out of you, old man." She pointed at his face. "Not a single word."

EIGHT

When I first set sail aboard *Ark 1*, I was as confirmed a bachelor as there was. When I returned, I had more family than I was certain I desired or could handle. Ironic, eh? Initially, I was busy. I had to orient to changes in society, survive an encounter with my president, and defeat an alien attack. I had no time to look into matters like what happened to the original me or Jane Geraty. Once we had turned Offlin over to Toño, I had my first downtime since my return. It was fairly easy to find information concerning the original me. He ended up directing a charitable foundation that ensured millions of people were able to flee the planet. Strong work, me.

It also wasn't hard to discover that he'd had a bunch of kids, who, in turn, had a bunch of kids. Everything told, the original me had nine grandchildren, fourteen great-grandchildren, and twenty-one great-great-grandchildren. Jane, God bless her, did indeed get pregnant from our one night together. That line produced two grandchildren, five great-grandchildren, and eleven great-great-grandchildren. Of that brood of sixty-eight offspring, fifty-seven were still alive. Talk about an awkward family reunion. Both of us fathered a Jon Ryan II. Two juniors.

Clearly I could lay claim to the relatives I had from Jane. But being related to all those other Ryans blew my mind. In the end, I took Sapale's advice and stopped worrying about it. She said good kids were good kids. The ones who wanted a relationship with me would be my family, and the falzorn could eat the rest of them. Good advice. Turned out it didn't take long for someone to claim me. I got a call from Jon Ryan III, Jon II's eldest on Jane's side. We

33

arranged to meet at a restaurant in London. I was more nervous in the days leading up to that reunion than I was facing my battle with Offlin.

Sapale came along, naturally. We met Jon and his wife, Abree, in the bar. He was in his early fifties, trim with a confident stride. She was a few years younger, quite petite, and stunningly pretty. Her hand rested on his elbow, and heads turned as they passed. They headed straight toward us. Maybe he recognized me. Maybe they headed for the only alien in the room.

He reached out his hand as he neared me. "Jon the First, it's an honor to finally meet you."

My lame sense of humor. Nice. It was genetic. "I can't tell you what a thrill it is to meet you, period."

We introduced our spouses. We ordered drinks and shared some small talk. The maître d' seated us quickly. Best dinner table in the place, too. Maybe he recognized me. Maybe he wanted the alien in plain sight, front and center. I figured it was a good business decision, either way. Later, my grandson mentioned that he owned the restaurant. The hotel it was located in too. Maybe that had something to do with the first-class service?

Jon III raised a glass of wine. "To the legend and his lovely wife." After we all took a sip, he went on. "I've looked forward to meeting you my entire life, Grandfather." That title hit me like a stomach punch. Never saw it coming. He lowered his head and stared into his glass. "I only wish Dad had lived long enough to meet you, too."

That was heavy. "Did he ever meet the original me?"

His head came up. "Several times, in fact." He frowned. "Apparently they never sparked a flame in terms of a relationship. He—the original you—seemed to want to keep his distance from our side of the family." He looked off to one side. "Can't say I blame him."

"I can," I said haughtily. "He was the man's own flesh and blood. How dare he be petty and judgmental."

That brought a deep sigh. "I don't know if that's what is was. Dad didn't talk about his biological father much, but I don't think he held a grudge against him. The situation *was* most peculiar."

"Tell me about my son."

Jon III took a long pause, gathering his thoughts. "He was a great man, a great father. You'd have been as proud of him as I was."

"So he bore me no hard feelings?"

"Absolutely not." he said flabbergasted. "He idolized you and spoke of you all the time. Toward the end, he used to tell me his secret to being a good man." He hesitated, then continued. "He said, 'Jon, I always asked myself what my father would do, and I did just that. It never failed me once.' No, he was proud of you. He loved you."

"And your grandmother? What ... how did she get on?"

Jon slipped his hand across the table and held mine. "She did wonderfully. She loved you with a passion that was palpable." He moved his hand to Abree's. "I only hope I can love my wife as ferociously as she did you." They both smiled. They were so darn cute.

"You were enough for her, weren't you?" asked Sapale gently.

"She told me that almost every day. Whenever she had a function or event to attend, she always stuffed me in a suit and introduced me as her date. There was no room in her heart for any man after you, Grandfather."

I had to say it. I know I'm a jerk. I could take aliens trying to kill me, but not that. "Ah, if it's okay with you, could you, like, call me *Jon*? I'm not ready for grandpa just yet. Probably never will be."

Sapale slugged me hard on the shoulder. "You are *such* a pig. This man is your *grandson*, and he most definitely will call you grandfather, grandpa, *gramps*—whatever he wants. If it's necessary, just try to *pretend* you're mentally normal, just for one night." She waggled a menacing finger under my nose. "Am I clear?"

I saluted. "Yes, Ma'am."

She turned to Jon III. "You'll find he's really quite impossible. I bet you never want to see him again after tonight." She crossed her arms and stared at me with four laser-beam eyes. "I wouldn't blame you one little bit if you didn't." She stuck her tongue out at me. I might not have mentioned it until now, but her species had really long blue tongues.

It was Abree's turn. She said, "Hey, not to worry. These two are peas in a pod. I bet Jon's only calling him 'grandfather' to get under his skin."

I looked to him dubiously. "S'that right?"

He shrugged noncommittally. Then the dude coughed up a laugh though his nose, which included some of his last sip of wine, and bent over at the waist.

"I'll take that as a *yes*. Young man, you're *grounded* for the rest of the weekend." I pointed generally upward. "Now go to your suite."

After he could speak again, he reached to the floor, where he'd set a gift bag. "Which reminds me. This," he handed it to me, "is for you."

"You shouldn't have," I protested.

"I didn't. Open it."

I pulled out the heavy object wrapped in tissue. I peeled back the paper. It was a trophy. Huh? There was a woman in bronze holding a baby. I wasn't familiar with that competition. The inscription read: *To Jonathan Ryan. Well, You Did Knock Me Up After All. Wow. Here's the Trophy I Promised You. Thanks, I Guess.* It was signed *Mama Jane Geraty.*

The trophy. Yes she did tease me about that, didn't she? When I admitted I hadn't had time to stop and buy a condom, she said she'd give me a prize if I actually got her pregnant. I held it up and took a closer look. The woman had Jane's face.

We all giggled. Well, all but Sapale. She looked from one of us to the next, confused. "You people give awards for having active sperm? That's ridiculous."

"No, honey," I replied, "we don't. That's why it's funny. Jane was quite the gal, trust me on that."

"Yes," added Jon III, "I've never seen an award in that category before, and I've been human all my life."

Abree narrowed one eye at her spouse. "No more wine for you before dinner."

We had a grand evening. Wait, I shouldn't have called it that. No "grand" anything for me, if you please. Over the next few months I met several of my kin from both sides. It was all so weird. But everyone was gracious, and we promised to keep in touch. I offered to pull some strings to make sure all the Ryan clan were assigned to the same worldship. Everyone thought that would be wonderful and insisted I try. My, how strange life could be.

NINE

True to his word, two months later, Toño began rolling out prototypes of the membrane cutting tools. They worked better than even he could have hoped. Three months later, asteroids were being cored out in as little as a *month*. Before a year had passed, he had his crews churning out one completed asteroid a week. Debris removal became more challenging than its production. Mountain-sized boulders and planetoids were *everywhere*.

Once the idea of using the membranes was in Toño's head, he came up with an endless series of radical innovations. He turned them into weapons. He hoped one day to be able to send the generators themselves as projectiles. In the short term, however, he had to be satisfied with using them as impact devices. They were spectacular at ramming. By adjusting the membrane configuration, he could drive a one-meter hole into any substance known to science. The thin hull of an enemy vessel was absolutely defenseless against such a weapon. We could destroy Listhelon ships from up to fifty kilometers away. Even if they detonated their nukes, our attack ships would be safe behind the pointed, impenetrable wall used to skewer the enemy.

The membranes also made asteroid retrieval a breeze. Previously, they were either steered with ship-to-ship gravity or physically towed. One process was slow, and the other was very risky. Now a big enough vessel could simply push the asteroid to wherever it was needed. The transit time for bringing a big asteroid to a construction site was cut in half.

Me, I took credit for all the new toys, at least when speaking to Al or Sapale. It was marvelous. I'd gloat, they'd berate me, and a good time would be had by all. Ffffuttoe didn't understand bantering but loved to join in a laugh when we all were.

As the months passed, I became more and more involved with the UN. That sucked, but it was unavoidable. Ask any pilot. Would you rather be flying or consorting with soulless politicians? Yeah, it sucked. But I was a cohesive force. People rallied to my positions and ideas and they trusted me. I began to worry I'd lose my wings and be given a three-piece suit in its place. Oh, the pain.

An ongoing dilemma was how the UN, and the rest of the world for that matter, should deal with the United States. I should refer to it as the central government of the much diminished in size *former* United States. The executive and legislative branches were still intact and functioning. The judicial branch was all but forgotten. The executive officers became the sole judges and executioners of any dispute. And they were increasingly merciless. The segment of the US population still under their leaders's boot heels were sure to buckle under the injustice, strain, and growing certainty of being left behind. Riots were commonplace there, and open rebellion was just around the corner. The UN, to its eternal credit, felt obligated to save as many Americans as possible, in spite of their corrupt government.

Negotiations were nonexistent between the two factions, but fortunately so were overt hostilities. We knew that sooner than later the US leaders would learn of our shield membranes. That would certainly trigger a crisis. They would have to either capitulate entirely and beg for parity or launch an all-out attack immediately in the hope that they could still defeat the UN. The former was unthinkable for the harsh dictatorship that had come to exist. The latter would be catastrophic. Imagine, here we are trying to get off a dying planet but have to stop and fight off madmen first. We humans sure can be a challenging species.

Feelers were sent out to open some positive channels of communication, but all of them failed miserably. President Marshall was not in a listening state of mind. Talk as we might on our side, no successful path was clear to us. If nothing else, Marshall had to have noticed that the Listhelon ship was way overdue. We hadn't told him we'd eliminated the threat because one, they wouldn't believe us, and two, that constituted strategic information. Never tell your enemy anything you don't have to about your strengths or weaknesses.

It was 2138. That marked twelve years until doomsday. It was also the first close encounter with Jupiter. Before that date, the giant planet was too far away to cause trouble. We'd receive damage from its debris field in 2138. The next close encounter would be 2144 and would almost certainly be terrible for Earth.

Jupiter passed Earth at about a one-hundred-million-kilometer distance. In 2144, the distance would shorten to fifty million kilometers. In 2150, it would be zero. By 2138, Jupiter was visible all day long, and one could actually see it was a planet and not just a point of light. At night, four moons were visible to the naked eye. It was so beautiful and nonthreatening up there in the heavens. Toward the end of 2138 massive meteor showers were on practically constant display. The show was spectacular. Occasionally a meteorite would strike, but no significant damage took place. By the spring of 2139 the meteors decreased in number, and we could breathe a little easier.

January 1, 2140, was a surreal day. We had ten years left—one decade. The fears and worries that had been so theoretical up until then suddenly became way too real. The UN was doing a superb job. We were probably going to achieve our worldship goals. The selection process for exit became less pressing. As everybody began to realize enough space would be available to all who desired to leave, panic and desperation decreased significantly. It was also, however, the year the US finally learned out about our membrane devices.

TEN

"Mr. President," his secretary said over the intercom, "your assistant chief of staff is here. He wishes to know if he might speak with you for a moment."

"Sure. Why the hell not? Send him in."

Matt Duncan slid in the door and shut it behind him. He was a young man to occupy that high of a position and had a boyish grin to match his general awkwardness. He got the job because he was family, Marshall's second cousin on his father's side. He kept the job because he was as loyal as a puppy dog and not overly bright. Best of all he was never going to be a threat to Marshall. Matt stopped well shy of the president's desk and stood there kicking the toe of one shoe nervously on the floor.

Finally Marshall's patience was exhausted. "So, are you here to *say* something, or am I just supposed to *look* at you?"

"Sorry, sir. I'm here to give you an update."

Marshall started tapping his pen on the desk. "*Updates* go on *memos*, and I read them daily. Put it in a memo, and I'll read it tomorrow." He turned to the papers in front of him.

"I guess it's more that I need to *update* you on some new information, not an update itself, sir."

He glared at the boy. "*New* information comes to me from the *section head* in charge of that department. You're not head of anything."

Matt cleared his throat. "Well, it's more *news* I need to relay. Yes, that's it. It's *news*."

"No, son, it's *bad* news you need to deliver. Shoot-the-messenger-type bad

40

I'd imagine. If it was *good* news someone senior to you would sell his children to be able to present it to me. So, I'll get the revolver out of my desk while you tell me whatever the *hell* news flash you have, okay?"

Matt's eyes grew to very large saucers. He knew his cousin was hot-headed and given to violence. He was scared to death at that moment, waiting to see if the lunatic would actually reach into the drawer. He didn't. That made it physically possible for Matt to speak. "We suspected for a little while, but I'm afraid we know for certain now, sir. It's about the UN; their worldship program, to be specific."

"Son, if you don't spill the beans immediately I will have you dragged from this building and shot. I *kid* you *not*."

"The UN is way ahead of us in asteroid conversions."

Marshall ground his teeth contemplating the bad news. "So? I've said before I only want two hundred and fifty. We'll make that goal easily. What do I care if they have a few more?"

"They're coring an asteroid in less than a week, sir. They turn out three hundred a month, and we're talking *big* ones. These babies can probably house two hundred thousand each, maybe more. We can't know for certain."

Marshall tried to run the numbers in his head. Ten years, thirty-six thousand vessels. That would be eight *billion* passengers. "That's impossible. Who gave you that ridiculous information? I want them in my office ten minutes ago."

Matt turned ashen. He could barely speak. "That's not possible, Mr. President. The numbers come from someone at the CIA. I can call him for you, but he's in Virginia."

Marshall thumbed the intercom. "Head of the CIA on holo, *now*." To his aide he snapped his fingers and pointed to a chair. "Park it, son. We'll get to the bottom of this, and then I'll figure out who gets hanged for such *unimaginable* incompetence."

Almost immediately, a tiny man stood on Marshall's desktop. "Mr. President I assume you've received our update?"

"Yes I have, Phil. I have to say I'm not pleased on many levels. Heads will roll. I promise you that. Who came up with those insane numbers? And, if they *are* true, why am I only hearing about them now and not, oh I don't know, many years ago? I'm really hot, Phil. Speak to me."

Phillip Szeto knew it was probably a mistake to have accepted his job as head of the CIA. He foresaw this exact scenario coming to pass. But, if he'd refused he'd only have been executed sooner. Lose-lose situations were so unpleasant. "The numbers are good, Stuart." No need to be overly fussy when you're about to meet your maker. "Security in space is extremely tight, as you know. We've tried for years to get people on the inside but have failed at every attempt. We finally caught a break and placed someone. She's a prostitute, to be specific, on one of the support stations. Last week someone let slip that the pace of work was 'busting his balls.' His words, not mine. In the process of comforting said balls, our girl was able to encourage him to divulge that they were coring asteroids in a week. Pretty soon after, he realized he was disclosing highly classified information and clammed up.

"She reported she tried 'for all she was worth' to find out more, but he decided no quality of sex justified further treason and wouldn't elaborate. In spite of the risk, I elected to send a drone missile into one of their assembly zones to get a look for myself." He stopped to shake his head. "Didn't make it very close. But two extremely disquieting discoveries were made. First, even from a distance, we can confirm there are numerous cored asteroids being fitted for habitation—too many to count. The second has to do with the drone. It was equipped with vibration sensors. If struck by a missile, it would send a signature pattern before it was fully disabled. No such signal was sent."

Marshall interrupted angrily, "You mean *received*."

Phillip swallowed. "No, Stuart, I mean *sent*. All systems were confirmed operational at the time of its destruction."

"Cut to the chase. What are you trying to say in an oh-so-inept manner?"

"The drone was destroyed quickly, at long range, and without an explosion."

"That's what you said. What're you trying to *tell* me that means? Help me out here, son."

"Our experts have no idea how the drone was destroyed. Our people in Houston couldn't come up with anything either. What we do know is that it was disabled by some intervention we are not capable of understanding or replicating."

Marshall put his hand to his mouth. "Shit," he whispered.

"Shit," Phillip responded, "is an understatement, Mr. President."

"Phil, I want all of your top people and all the top people at NASA in my office first thing in the morning. *Everyone*, you got that?"

"Even Frontera?"

Good point. Marshall played the various chess games out in his head. *That* he was very good at.

"Yes, bring him, too. If this is as bad as it seems, he can't hurt us any longer." Stuart rested back in his chair. "He *might* not be making the return charter to Houston, though."

The meeting the next morning only served to infuriate Marshall even more. No one had, or would divulge, any guesses as to what had changed to accelerate the construction process. Only when pressed would the head of the asteroid coring operation admit she couldn't conceive of any process that could produce results that quickly. As far as she was concerned, it was impossible. If the UN was doing the impossible, well, that wasn't her area of expertise.

Discussion concerning the missing drone was equally unhelpful. The rocket men were adamant. The craft was working perfectly. No tell-tale vibrations of an explosion were detected. The military types were equally adamant. There were only a limited number of ways to disable a drone at a distance—hitting it with something solid, blowing it up with a bomb, or penetrating it with a laser. There existed, they swore, no technology that could produce the reported results. The drone's destruction was, like the production number before, impossible. The impossible was not their area of expertise, either.

Marshall wished he could afford to have every single person in his office shot, including himself. "Let me sum up this clusterfuck. Our enemies are doing the impossible. In fact, they're doing it a lot. *We* are not capable of the impossible. We can't even guess what they're up to. We can't tease that information out of a single soul. A million Joe Sixpacks work up there, get drunk every night, and return home eventually, yet we can't pry the needed information out of a single *one* of them. Would anyone like to tell their president why such a sorry state of affairs exists in his realm?"

He scanned the room, exuding hatred from his eyes. His gaze stopped at Frontera. "How about you, boy genius? You've been remarkably silent throughout this debacle. Any thoughts, ideas, guesses, or wild notions you'd like to share with these lesser intellects?" He swept his hand across the room.

"No, sir. None."

"That's it? None. What the hell am I overpaying you for? Tell me like you knew all along, son. How can the impossible be commonplace?"

"With all due respect, Mr. President, I resent that implication. I've been nothing but hard-working and loyal. My contributions have been indispensable. I, too, have no expertise in the impossible. Therefore, I have nothing to add."

"Yes, all true. But you *smell* funny to me, that's all."

Frontera twisted in his chair. "Is that supposed to be funny?"

"Goodness, no. I'm being forthright and open. There something about you that smells … odd. You don't add up. Why is it that you grace us with the abundant fruits of your labor as you do? Seems profoundly odd to me."

"Perhaps the fact that you're holding most of my family hostage might have some influence on my thinking in that regard."

"That, I'll grant you," he responded. "For now, I guess that'll have to do." To those gathered, he barked, "This meeting is over. I want *all* of you back here the day after tomorrow. You had all better impress me mightily with results, or many will suffer beyond their wildest dreams. I'm a man who makes such dreams all too real."

ELEVEN

"It was bound to happen, sooner or later. Fortunately for us, it was later than we could have hoped for." The Secretary General of the UN tried to sound upbeat. That was part of her job. Inside, however, Mary Kahl was anything but calm and confident. She knew Marshall was a power-hungry maniac who would stop at nothing to have his way. An immediate, all-out nuclear attack was a very real possibility. For certain, her military had planned and trained extensively for that contingency. But even the most pie-in-the-sky estimates predicted outcomes that were grim—extremely grim. "General Casey," she asked the head of her military, "any updates we need to know about?"

"No. All our forces are on Red Alert. Shield membranes protect most of the vital assets. All space craft are holding in attack positions." He squared his shoulders and spoke with a bravado he didn't feel. "We will do well, ma'am. Minimal losses on our side and near complete annihilation on theirs."

"I can't believe we're talking about attacking the USA," Kahl said, holding her head in her hands.

"Only if they attack first, Ma'am," was Casey's response.

"Dr. DeJesus, any update on your preemptive actions?"

He twisted his head nervously to one side. "No. The computer algorithms are extremely complex. I have several AIs working on them around the clock, but I'm still not one hundred percent certain if my scheme will work or when it might be ready."

"Best estimate?" she asked.

"A few days. I'm sorry."

"This is war, Toño. War is never predictable, and it's always messy. I'm sure you're doing your best. Jon, how about you? Ready as you can be?"

"Yes," was my terse reply. I had been to war. More than anyone present, I knew how horrible it was. I dreaded the prospect of fighting in one again. "It'll take them a few days, maybe less, to decide on their course of action. We definitely need to try to convince Marshall not to start Armageddon. But you're right. He's insane. Force he might respect, but reason will not sway him.

"*Ark 1* is currently fitted with three membrane generators. A squadron of fighters is also equipped with single units. Once Toño gets us the calculation, I suggest we act, assuming it's not too late."

"Fine." She stood. "Keep me posted."

"Jon," Toño said, "Are you available for a chat?"

"For you, Doc, anytime."

"Let's go to my office." Once there, we sat down.

"What's on your mind?"

"Jon, this plan of ours is nothing short of suicidal. I'm not certain we should proceed."

"We've been over this before. Every crew is aware of the danger. We're glad to assume the risk for a chance to avoid an all-out war. War might well mean the end of our evacuation efforts and of us as a species." I shook my head. "No. There's too much at stake to worry about a few lives. We're all in, and that's that."

"I know. I just wish there was a better way."

"There isn't, so let's drop the subject. Hey, how's Offlin doing? I haven't been by to visit him for weeks." I thought a moment. "Maybe a couple months."

"Our friend is well. His tank is next to my main lab, so we see each other often. He understands you're busy."

"What's he up to?"

"He still refuses to allow me to design him an environmental suit so he can be mobile." He directed a thumb at me. "He's as stubborn as you are. I don't know if it's a manifestation of depression or that he's simply not curious about this place." He tossed his head to one side. "But he eats well and talks to a fault." He harrumphed. "But by far his favorite activity is playing those stupid holo games. The fish hardly sleeps." His arms were extended in frustration.

"Maybe you'll have to ground him from them if he doesn't go outside and play more often."

"Stop by when you can. He'd like to see you. He measures us all against the standard that is you."

"Toño, anybody who knows me would. He's only human."

"On that low note I must return to work."

"I going to take *Ark 1* into synchronous orbit over the eastern US. That way I'll be in position when you get me the numbers."

"I hope you're not wasting your time. I'm not certain when they'll be ready."

"It beats sitting around here waiting for an unscheduled doomsday."

TWELVE

"So not one of you has come up with a damn thing in the last two days? We're in the middle of a major crisis, and I'm surrounded by the mentally impaired. Whatever did I do to deserve you pack of hyenas?"

Every person in the room, including his longtime secretary Mary Jane Plumquist, rightly feared for their lives. They knew the man better than most. He was quick to anger, but even quicker to punish. And he prided himself on his ruthlessness. As the years passed, he made it a point to continually improve and hone his merciless attributes. Everyone wanted to remain silent, but silence would only guarantee their collective deaths.

"Mr. President," said his newly promoted chief of staff, Matt Duncan, "with all due respect, I'd like to say I can vouch for the fact that everybody's been working with extreme dedication. I urge you to remember that they're your biggest supporters. It might just be that the UN has covered its tracks so well that our intelligence efforts were doomed from the start."

Stuart eyed Matt like he was a starving man and Matt was food. Then an element of calm settled into his expression. "Thank you. I appreciate your devotion to our staff. I need to make some hard choices, and I'd rather do so with a modicum of insight." He huffed loudly. "I guess I won't have that luxury this time out."

He turned to the Chairman of the Joint Chiefs of Staff, General Chuck Thomas. He was the first military officer Stuart had downloaded into an android host. "Are you prepared for an all-out assault on their combined forces?"

"Yes, *sir*," he replied without hesitation.

"Does anyone want to suggest an alternate course, given what we know today?" Marshall actually did want to avert such an extreme act. He had, however, come to conclusion that there was no alternative. Surrender or die. Those were the only options he saw. To crawl on his belly like a snake to those traitors, those criminals, was more than he could tolerate. If *they* wished to force the extinction of the human species, then *he* was going to grant them their wish. It was their fault in the first place. If they had only come to him when they first made whatever breakthrough they'd had, he'd have spared them. They were intentionally signaling that they wanted the US to die as a nation by not sharing their technology. What other response could they have expected? The USA was not going to die in its sleep like some old man. No, it was going out fighting, in a blaze of glory.

"Mr. President," asked Duncan, "what are your orders?"

Marshall balled up both fists and raised them overhead. "Blow the sons of *bitches* to hell."

There was a long, airless silence in the room. The words had been said, and there was no going back. After a tortured eternity Duncan spoke, though there was no life in his voice. "Very well, sir. Where are you ... where will you *position* yourself during ... for the duration?"

"I and everyone on the list Plumquist will hand you will proceed to the Cheyenne Mountain Complex. We leave immediately. Once everyone is there, our attack will begin. Even if some aren't there yet, the missiles fly no later than noon tomorrow. Is that clear?"

"Sir."

THIRTEEN

"Al, are we stable over Washington?"

"I'm sorry. I believe I'm growing senile, Pilot. I could swear you asked me that same question not fifteen minutes ago."

"Al, does the expression 'time of war' mean anything to you in terms of decorum?"

"Hmm. I'd have to say 'decorum' is a pretty big word to expect a senile AI to understand."

"I'll take that as a *no.*"

Sapale didn't smile, but I knew she enjoyed our bickering.

"Never mind," I huffed, "I'll check it myself." I walked to the bridge console and sat down.

As I began tapping the keys, Al piped up, "Oh, are you hoping to confirm we're in the same spot in the sky over that big city down there? Well, if *you* are, *we* are." After a couple seconds, he chided me. "It's customary to say 'thank you' after a person has performed a favor for you."

"Thanks. I'll keep that in mind when you become a person."

Sapale snickered loudly.

For the umpteenth million time, Ffffuttoe asked her what she was laughing about.

"Al, I—"

"Sorry to interrupt, Captain. Incoming Priority One communication from UN Central. Shall I put it on speaker?"

"Yes. Video on all screens."

50

"Jon," Toño shouted, "thank *God* I found you." I was going to remark that finding me in a spaceship with a radio wasn't all that hard, but I could tell that it wasn't a time for jokes. "The unthinkable just happened. Two minutes ago Marshall gave the order for a totally committed nuclear attack against the UN and its allies. He's sending all his weapons at us."

"That crazy son of a bitch. When?"

"No later than noon tomorrow, EST. He's leaving for Cheyenne Mountain as we speak. Jon … this is it. He's just signed the death warrant for the human race."

"No chance you'll have those calculations done anytime soon is there?"

"Not this soon. Never." He was trembling. I knew he wasn't afraid of death. He often told me he lamented outliving his "natural days." But he was a man of science and reason. He loved all that swam, walked, or flew above the earth. The guy actually told me once he *loved* flatworms. That it all was about to be ended by one human hand was beyond his comprehension.

"In that case, I'll do what I do best."

"Survive? You'll retreat into space and try to shepherd those now in orbit to safety?"

"Sheesh, Doc. No. Where do you *get* that stuff from? We're talking about *me* here."

"Then what'll you do?"

"Improvise."

"Jon, of all moments, please tell me at this particular moment you're joking."

"Deadly serious. I'm a fighter pilot and a rocket man. I'm trained to do the insane and get paid for my efforts. Where's Marshall now?"

"Still in the White House."

"So, he'll make it to Cheyenne around dawn?"

He thought a moment. "More or less. Why?"

"I'm improvising. The more I know, the better that process works."

He was wringing his hands. "Let me know if you need anything else. And Jon, God be with you."

"One thing. How can you know all this so fast? You told me about your

51

backdoor access, but this is different."

"If you succeed, I'll tell you then."

"Why not tell me now so I can take that knowledge with me to the grave, if need requires that of me?"

"When you return. I promise." The screen went blank.

"Al, lay in a course for Cheyenne Mountain. Keep us above two hundred kilometers for now."

"Aye, aye."

Sapale stepped to my side. "We're staying up here for the nuclear war, right?" She waved her hands up high. "Up here, *safe*." She bent her knees and lowered her hands. "Down there, *very* hot."

"For now, up here."

"Now's probably not the best time to tell you I'm pregnant with twins then, is it?" She angled her cute little oval head.

FOURTEEN

The morning was otherwise spectacular. As Marshall stepped down the helicopter ramp, he gave the new day but a cursory glance. Nothing was beautiful on the day he was about to blow up the world, even for a maniac like him. The soldiers at the bottom saluted. One opened the limo door for him. "Duncan, you're with me. The rest need to catch another ride."

Marshall grunted as he hit the seat and was silent for a good fifteen minutes. He was brooding. Mostly he tried to reinforce and strengthen the lines of reasoning that led him to this fateful decision. So desperate was he to rationalize his actions that in the "plusses column" of his mental gyrations, he listed "nothing left for the Listhelons to destroy" as partial justification for his war. The fact that he ruminated so much failed to alert him to the fact that he was, in reality, filled with dread, foreboding, and remorse. Perhaps he was unable to recognize those feelings because they were so completely foreign to him. To any respectable sociopath, those sentiments were incomprehensible. Still, if anything could, genocide might have been enough to bring the most repressed emotions to the surface.

His prolonged taciturn state prompted Duncan to cautiously break the silence. "Are you all right, Mr. President?"

"Huh?" He groaned as he returned to the here-and-now. "Of course I am. I'm just making certain there's nothing I've overlooked."

"Very well, sir. Let me know if I can be of any assistance."

In an uncharacteristically hushed tone, Stuart posed an odd question. "Did your family make it to one of the secondary defense centers?"

"Sorry. I didn't catch that."

"Did your family make it to safety?" he said loudly.

"Ah, yes, sir. They did. Thanks for asking. They're in the White House bunker."

"Good," he mumbled. Then it hit him like a steam locomotive. Why had he asked? He knew in his heart of hearts that he didn't give a damn one way or the other. Hell, even if they somehow survived the nuclear holocaust, they'd die from all the fallout sooner or later. What did he care if people who were already dead were temporarily safe? It served as an excellent slap in the face. He sat up and took a deep breath. "How long until we get there?"

"About half an hour," the driver called back.

"Duncan, once the shooting is over, I'll need frequent updates."

"Of course."

"I especially want to know how much damage we did to them in space." He rubbed his chin. "I still don't think we can take out all their assets up there, but I'd like to think we can hurt them very badly."

"Of course, sir." Yeah, you wouldn't want to stop at only killing ninety-nine point nine nine percent of your fucking species, sir. Lord in heaven, I should do the universe a favor and strangle you now with my bare hands. But I can't throttle an android who doesn't breathe. Plus, you saw to it that you were three times stronger than any of us toy robots. You son of a fucking bitch.

"Have my immediate family made it here yet?"

"No, sir, but they're only a little behind us." I'm going to survive your evil war surrounded by your evil family click-clacking around on their cloven hooves. You spherical asshole. I hate you more than the next ten horrible things I hate rolled up in a ball and covered in festering pus.

"Get me General Thomas on the phone."

"Yes, sir." What were Beelzebub's assistants's names? Oh, yes, Leviathan and Thomas. I pray you blow a fuse right here and now, you piece of shit.

"Chuck, is everything on schedule?"

"Yes, Stuart. All of our ICBM missiles are armed and ready. Final checks are complete, and all systems are GO. Submarine missiles are targeted. Both elements will launch on your command or at 12:00 EST, whichever comes first. Most of our planes are airborne. They're being held in reserve to strike at targets that require further degradation." Chuck sniffed profoundly. "This is a great day, Mr. President. It will be remembered for centuries to come as your day of glory."

Stuart shut his eyes. "We'll see, won't we, Charles?"

"Yes, indeed we shall, from the comfort of our private worldships."

"Let's not get ahead of ourselves, shall we? First, we must eliminate our local enemies. Then, at some point, we have to deal with those fanatical aliens. Only then can we enjoy the fruits of our labors."

"They will be all that much sweeter when we do, Stuart. The future will be spectacular."

"Fine. Keep me posted." He ended the call.

"Driver," Marshall called out, "how long until we're there?"

The driver pointed out the windshield. "It's right there, Mr. President. Shouldn't take us more than five minutes."

Marshall checked his watch. 11:35 p.m. He'd left it EST. To Duncan he muttered, "We're cutting it pretty close."

"No worries, sir. We'll be perfectly safe. If there are any unexpected delays, you can always pause the attack until you're safe."

"Up to a point, yes. But ... well, let's just hope it doesn't come to that." To the driver, he said, "Tell the lead cars to step on it. We need to make better time."

"Yes, sir."

****

Twenty-five kilometers overhead

"Al, can you confirm Marshall is in one of those cars about to reach the main entrance?"

"Yes. He's in the fourth vehicle in the line. He just finished a call with General Thomas."

"ETA?"

"The first vehicle will pass the gate in eight minutes." There was a pause. "What are your orders, Captain?"

"How far is it from the gate to the blast doors?"

"Three hundred twenty-six meters."

"Here's the plan. On my command, I want you to project a bell-jar shaped membrane covering the mountain. The base will be fifty meters from the blast doors. Set the rim two meters deep in the ground. Can you do that?"

"Aye, aye, Captain."

"How low will we have to be to make the field stable?"

"One kilometer."

"Crap. I was hoping to be out of range. Okay, generate a second membrane between us and the base. Make it large enough that they can't get a straight shot at us. Be ready to shift the membrane if they try to maneuver a ground-to-air missile around it."

"And if they attack from above?"

"Let's hope they don't. Still, be ready with a dome membrane to hold off any aircraft."

"You're aware that with those three membranes —"

"I know. We'll be fully enclosed. Our exhaust will burn us to a crisp if we stay there very long."

"We could survive perhaps five minutes. No longer, Captain."

"If it comes to that, alert me if things are about to go critical."

"Understood."

Sapale came up behind and put her arms around me. "Anything I can do?"

I pinched her chin. "Just keep that beautiful face where I can see it."

She rolled her eyes. "You're well beyond intolerable."

"You're welcome."

****

The president's entourage shot past the open gate. A line of Jeeps flanked both sides of the road, machine gunners poised and ready. Several jet fighters thundered overhead, circling the Cheyenne Mountain Complex at low altitude. When the first car was fifty meters from the mountain's maw, it slammed to a halt. The front end crumpled and the car slid sideways, coming to an abrupt stop. Steam spewed from the radiator, and the car alarm beeped frantically. The second car in line swerved to the right to avoid its wrecked companion, but the left side of the front loudly impacted some invisible barrier. All the other vehicles screeched to a stop just shy of the two battered cars. Everyone, including Marshall, poured out quickly in madding confusion. Guns were drawn. Curses echoed off the face of the mountain.

"What the *hell*," Marshall demanded of Duncan, "just happened?"

"No idea, sir." Matt pointed to a secret service agent and commanded, "You there. See what stopped the first car. Maybe it was a landmine."

The man sprinted forward. He bent to inspect the undercarriage of the first car while continuing at a dead run. He struck the membrane headfirst and collapsed limply. His neck was broken.

Marshal took control. "You two, with me." He led his squad slowly forward. As he neared the location the agent struck the barrier, he held his hands out in front of himself, swinging them from side to side. The others did the same. Marshall was the first to feel the membrane. He jumped back with a start after a light touch, as if shocked with electricity. "There's something stopping me," he said to one soldier. "See if you can get a hand through it."

The soldier eyed his commander circumspectly for a heartbeat, then stepped cautiously forward, arms fully extended. When he contacted the membrane, he recoiled initially. Then he slammed the heel of his fist against it several times. He soon abandoned that tactic. Cradling his bloody hand in his other, he trotted back to Marshall. "Sir. There's an impenetrable, invisible barrier present." He proffered his injured hand for Marshall to inspect. "I couldn't get through it."

"You there," Marshall indicated to one of his personal guards, "see if you can put a bullet past that barrier."

From point-blank range, the man fired one round from his pistol at the ground on the far side of the barrier. Instead of zinging off the asphalt where he anticipated it would, the bullet ricocheted and struck the dirt at his feet.

"Someone tell me," screamed Marshall, "what the *hell* is going on." He checked his watch. 11:47. "Shit," he muttered to himself.

Duncan instructed several men to run along the perimeter of the barrier to gauge its size. Men ran as far as they could in either direction, but no breach could be found. Marshall took a sidearm from a guard and fired several rounds above his head. They all bounced off the invisible surface. "Shit. Someone tell me what this *damn* thing is."

He consulted his watch again. 11:51. That's when his cellphone rang. His first instinct was to ignore it, but then it hit him. Only a handful of people had that number. All of them were either in the complex already or standing beside him in the confusion. He pulled the phone from his coat pocket. "What."

"Stuie. How's it hanging, dude?" Ryan's voice taunted him. "I'm guessing you're in quite a state, right about now. Am I right, am I right, am I right?"

Marshall was for once in his life speechless. He was completely dumb struck. Of all the possible scenarios his mind could accept, that was the farthest from belief. He shook his head violently. "Ryan, you traitorous scum, what are you calling me for? Why, I have—"

Jon cut him off. "Stuie, I don't think you have the luxury of time to cast aspersions my way. My chronometer reads 11:54 a.m. EST. In six minutes, you'll start World War III: The Final Conflict. That means the ground you currently stand upon will be fused glass by way of retaliation in less than half an hour. Your call, but I'd spend your diminishing moments more constructively. Hmm?"

Reflexively, Marshall looked at his watch. "What do you want?"

"I *want* to be taller. I *want* to be a star on the silver screen. I *want* most of all for you to drop dead immediately. What I'm *calling* you about, however, is this war thing you have planned. I have to say I have an opposing viewpoint as to its wisdom."

"Ryan, cut the crap and get to your point."

"Probably a good idea. Here's how I see things. You're standing fifty meters from safety, completely exposed to the ICBM assault you know'll be there shortly. The only way to prevent you from becoming unlamented ash is for you to abort your attack. You now have less than four minutes to do so. If it's still possible, that is. Please do so now if you wish to continue personally making the world a less pleasant place to live."

"What's this damn barrier. Is this *your* doing, Ryan?"

"Time's a-ticking, Stuie. *Your* time's a-tickin'."

Marshall nearly crushed his phone with primal rage. Then he hung up on Ryan and hit a preset icon.

"General Thomas here."

"Abort the attack. Say again, abort the attack immediately. Do you copy?"

"Stuart, are you sure? This is our hour of ultimate triumph."

"I said *abort*, you half-witted idiot. Abort *now*."

"Yes, Sir. Abort initiated." The line went dead.

Instantly, Marshall's phone went off. "What now?"

"Did ya miss me?"

"Ryan, I don't know what this's about or how the hell you pulled it off, but I promise you this. You will die *slowly* and *painfully* and at my *hand* for this outrage. Do you hear me, Ryan? I'll see you suffer like a one-legged dog in a flea circus."

"I ... I'm sorry, Stu. I was changing the holo channel. Stupid infomercial came on after the game. What did you say?"

"Mock me, Ryan. Go ahead. Enjoy it while you can. But remember my promise to you."

"I'm just impressed I'm so important to a world-figure like yourself. I mean, that you would think about me, a simple citizen, so specifically and so passionately. My mother would be so proud of her little boy."

"Okay. You had your fun. What do you want?"

"We just went over that. Are your circuits corrupted? In all this excitement, maybe you developed a short?"

Marshall took many slow, deep breaths. "What ... do ... you ... want?"

"What you just did. I want to stop you from killing us all. You're a megalomaniac. Worse yet, you're an insane, narcissistic megalomaniac. Buddy, that's the worst type there is."

"So? You stopped me for now. What's next? You going to tell me how you pulled this stunt off?"

"And potentially spoil my next surprise? You're no fun at all. Oh, by the way, I do see the fighters have been directed my way. Don't suppose they're my honor guard, are they?"

"How I hate you, Ryan. I hate you so completely."

"Ditto. Look, call them off, or they'll be just another futile sacrifice. You owe it to the pilots."

"No way, son. I could give a shit about those pilots. If there's one chance in a billion they can take you out, I get all warm and fuzzy."

"So be it. I'll call you back when I'm done."

"Maybe—" Marshall's phone went dead.

"Al, you have that secondary membrane in place?"

"Yes, Captain. It will, however, trap enough exhaust that we can only maintain it a few minutes."

"Slap the planes from the sky as quickly as possible. Then drop the air-membrane."

"Aye, aye." A minute later, Al spoke. "Captain, six of seven fighters destroyed. The final one has moved out of range. It is flying in a broad arc around our position."

"Can we drop the rear membrane?"

"Unwise, sir. A heat-seeking missile could loop behind and hit us."

"Crap. Wait. Can you form a membrane around a rock or around one of those vehicles and throw it at him?"

"Hmm. Yes, possibly. My accuracy will be—"

"Do it. Keep hurling junk until you hit him."

"Aye." Twenty seconds later. "Well I'll be damned. It worked, Captain. I hit the plane with a Jeep. It went kaboom."

"Strong work, my boy. Drop the air-membrane and get me Marshall back on the line."

"Go ahead, Captain," was Al's prompt response.

"Stu, you there?"

"Yes, I'm here. How did you do that?"

"Spoiler alert. I'll tell you this because we're such good friends. When you're back in the Oval Office, I'll have the head of the UN call you. She'll begin a dialogue with your government to end this insanity. How's that sound?"

"I will not be blackmailed, Ryan. The American people are not that easily purchased."

Jon waited ten seconds to speak. "You done sounding regal? Now that you're over that, listen up. Your only hope to remain relevant, not to mention alive, is to start cooperating. I'm thinking you're beginning to see we can pretty much act at will. You can play nice or you won't be allowed to play at all. Got it?"

"For now you win, Son. I'll talk to the UN bitch. I'll even pretend to like it. But never forget my promise to you. You and I are immortal. We're forever enemies. Know this, Son. I *will* see you dead."

"You know, Stuie, you talk awful brave for someone who just had his lunch handed to him. You sure that's wise?"

"Until later, Son. There'll most definitely be a next time. We'll see who's laughing then."

"Oooo. I'm scared. The big, mean president said bad words to me."

FIFTEEN

"I can't believe you pulled that off, General Ryan." Mary Kahl was positively beaming. "I've listened to the recording of your conversation with Marshall a dozen times, and each time, I can't help laughing. The man was fit to be tied."

"Well," I said soberly, "if he wasn't a permanent enemy before, he is now. Diminished as he is, he's still three things: insane, power hungry, and merciless. Until he gets in his worldship and sails into the dark sky of space, I don't think we can rest easy." I shook my head. "It's personal with me. I made it that way, but it was a dangerous ploy."

"What do you mean, *ploy?*" Toño asked.

"I want to have Marshall focus on me so he pays less attention to the UN efforts." I looked sideways at Mary. "Speaking of which—"

"I know, Jon. Your concerns are valid, and I promise we'll begin transporting people to the worldships soon—very soon."

"We have ten years before Jupiter strikes, but it's going to take a monumental effort to get billions of men, women, and children off this rock."

"Plus," Toño added, "it will be helpful to have people living in the craft for a long period before they depart. There are sure to be malfunctions and overlooked necessities we will discover."

"True, gentlemen." Kahl checked the screen of her handheld. "As of now, four hundred worldships are ready, or nearly ready, for habitation. I'll personally see to it their permanent residents are sent up within two months."

"I think it'd be best to send people from the less-developed world first." Toño nodded as he spoke. "They'll be the most difficult to evacuate and

62

acclimatize to the ships. Plus, their lifestyles will be markedly improved that much sooner."

"According to you," I said with a snort.

"I've already discussed the matter with India and several African nations," Mary reassured us. "There should be no problems."

"And will you call Marshall?" My voice had an edge to it I didn't like.

"Of course," Mary said. "I'm a diplomat. That's what we do."

"Do you hold out any hope for success?" I asked skeptically.

She shrugged. "No, which will make the negotiation that much easier. If I expect nothing, any positives will be a boon."

"I just wish," I said for the thousandth time, "we could force a free election in the US. Any other person in that office would actually look out for his or her people."

Mary furrowed her brow. "Do you recall the brief, yet colorful reign of President Trump from your history books, Jon?"

I tilted my head. "Point taken." I shuttered visibly. "Man, I'm glad they didn't have android downloads when that guy was around."

"Well, if that's all, I suggest we adjourn." Mary stood as she spoke.

"Toño," I hailed him, "I believe you and I need to talk. You owe me an explanation, if I recall your promise correctly."

With a resigned look in his eyes he replied, "Yes, I do. Let's go to my private office."

After we were seated, I began the conversation. "You knew about Marshall's decision to start the war minutes after he made it. You've known other things you shouldn't have, even with all *your* access to their computers. What gives?"

"Jon, I'm going to tell you something only two other people on Earth know. You must pledge never to mention it outside of the safety of this room. Not even to Sapale."

"Done."

"I have a man in Marshall's inner circle." He twisted his face slightly. "Well, not so much a man as an android."

"Doc. You're shitting me? No way that paranoid bastard would allow a mole, let alone a robotic one, anywhere near him."

By way of response, Toño gave me a palms-up shrug.

"Who?"

"De La Frontera, of course."

"No way. He's the most likely spy. How could he pull it off? They'd watch him more closely than a drunken sailor does a stripper."

"Always the colorful analogies. The fact remains. First, we created their absolute need for him. No one else can run their android production. As he works closely with me, there's no chance of anyone matching his abilities."

"Again, he'd be under the tightest surveillance possible. How could he possibly communicate with you?"

"Give me some credit, my old friend." He tapped the side of his head. "We're both androids. We're linked like you and your AI."

"No. They'd detect any signal. I know they're watching for just that type of thing twenty-four seven."

"Our link is highly encrypted and on a frequency no one uses anymore. They're never going to hear it because they never listen in the shortwave."

I laughed loudly. "You two are *ham* radio operators?"

He smiled. "Ingeniously simple, no?"

"But, wait. You told me Marshall held his family hostage. I've never met Carlos, but I can't believe he'd actually place them at risk no matter what the stakes were."

"His family is perfectly safe, too. They live in a small house on the Morón Air Base, just outside of Sevilla in Spain. Marshall holds five androids powered by AIs hostage. If he *were* to execute them, he'd be very surprised."

"That's darn close to brilliant, Doc."

"I thought so, too. We even gave Carlos rudimentary bowel and urinary function to cast no undue suspicion his way."

"What, you think they're going to check his *poop* to make sure he's human?"

"They *have* checked it, several times, looking for … intelligence passed … err … rectally."

"We're kind of into the TMI range here." I raised a finger to object. "There's

64

no way we can lose a war with an opponent who checks people's poop for clues. No way." I waved my hands in a cross-pattern in front of my chest.

"Marshall and his people are deeply suspicious of Carlos. But, lacking proof and needing his help means the android remains safe for now."

"Where's the original Carlos?"

"With his family, of course."

"So, as long as no one IDs him in seclusion —"

"His android serves us immeasurably." Toño bit at his lower lip. "Can you keep this information from Al?"

Hmm. "I don't know. That's never come-up before. I guess I could encrypt it and order him never to break the code."

He rolled his head back and forth. "That should work. Make it so. I'd like to share with someone Carlos's other accomplishments, in case both he and I are compromised."

"You just told me about them."

"No, I mean the fact that he's placed back doors and overrides into all Marshall's androids. If it ever came to it, we could disable them all."

"Talk about an ace up your sleeve, Doc."

"Yes," he grinned, "we're rather proud of that little trick. Eventually one of their AIs will figure it out, but until that time, it's a powerful weapon to possess."

"Why not switch the entire unholy lot of them off right now and be done with them?"

"Carlos and I have discussed it. But, the devil we know is easier to combat than the one we don't yet know."

"If you ever decide to end Marshall, please let me throw the switch. Okay?"

"No problem. That honor will be reserved for you alone."

I said goodbye and headed back to the ship. I needed to ask Sapale about this twin thing, since the crisis was over.

"I decided it was time," she explained, batting her four cute eyes in sync.

"Time for twins? Are we in some type of hurry here?"

There was that throaty growl of hers again. It was soft and low, but I was struck by the fact that I hadn't heard it since the time we first discussed being brood-mates. Maybe the *hurry* crack was unnecessary?

"There a problem here, cowboy?"

She'd said that rather sharply, hadn't she? "What?" I rallied in my defense, "No problem at all, breed's-mate."

"Brood's-mate. The term is *brood's*, not *breed's*."

That growl was definitely getting louder. Maybe a little higher in pitch, too. Perhaps it would be best if I did the guy thing and started lying my ass off. *That's what I said. Would you like me to play it back for you, because I have it recorded?* No. It would never work. Al would play back the actual recording and then giggle like a preteen girl. I knew he was listening in and would jump at the chance, the sorry bucket of bolts.

"Sapale, *brood's-mate* Sapale, I could *not* be happier to have two little blessings running around our humble home. What were you thinking," I—very gently and slowly—reached over and patted the side of her head, "you crazy, alien gal? You always misunderstand me at the silliest of times."

"Actually, I seem to understand you at the most *serious* of times. You're really pattern developing here, don't you think?" Hey, the Kaljaxians tapped their foot when impatient or angry, just like humans. Fascinating.

"Well, *you* think what you'd like. Me, I'm beside myself in joyous anticipation." To illustrate my feeling, I stepped to where I would have been, had I actually been standing beside myself when I said it. I even pointed to where I had been. Yeah, she thought it was that lame, too. "So, when are my children expected?" I rubbed my hands together eagerly. "How soon will you make my life whole and complete?"

At least the growl faded away slowly. "I've got my eye on you, scout. Al," she shouted, "remind me to keep an eye on this one, okay?"

"You and me both." I hated that machine. No guy-loyalty. Not one shred.

"I'll bear our children in seven months. That's how long you have to convince me I don't need to fly this ship back to Kaljax because you're such a butthead."

Her grasp of English slang was really getting impressive. Probably best, however, not to compliment her on it just then.

"You know," I said, by way of extrication, "I've been curious as to what those worldships look like on the inside. Haven't you? I think we should pop over and check one out. Who knows? We may prefer living in one rather more than in this tub." I waggled my elbows. "More room you know?"

She shook her head in resignation. After coming over and planting a big kiss on my lips, she agreed. "I've been curious, too. Let's go house hunting, brood-mate."

I'm so glad we made that trip. *Spectacular* didn't begin to describe those marvels. Early on, the general plan was to hollow out a one-kilometer-diameter sphere in a two-kilometer-diameter asteroid. That would provide a living volume equal to a large dirigible hanger, or three Nimitz-class nuclear-powered supercarriers laid end-to-end. By cramming everybody and everything in with Vaseline, the worldship might transport one hundred thousand souls.

Since the advent of membrane technology, those initial designs were puny. A ten-kilometer asteroid could have a four-kilometer-diameter spherical core. That provided immense protection and room for future generations to expand into, if so desired. Lake Tahoe could fit comfortably into one of those worldships, as could ten *thousand* dirigible hangars. Perhaps as many as a million people could live in one, with ample room left over for crops, environmental features, and recreational areas. Water skiing in outer space was now possible because of Jon Ryan. Whodathunk it?

The giant worldship we visited was partially rigged. Multiple apartment buildings grew at varying angles, based on the ship's curvature. Water storage chambers were on the periphery, with living space occupying the more central areas. In the center, where there would be little artificial gravity, were the power plants and waste facilities. They were massive. Under construction were hospitals, universities, parks, you name it. The worldships had it all. Unless someone pried the controls of *Ark 1* out of my dead hands, we could flit from one to the other during the migration. It could be like one constant vacation. Yeah, like that could happen in any enterprise involving humans.

The encouraging thing was that it looked like enough worldships would be completed before the axe fell on planet Earth. Then all we had to do was not be killed by Listhelons or ourselves and find a place to settle down. Easy-peasy, right?

SIXTEEN

"The next person," Stuart Marshall bellowed, "who answers me with 'we don't know' will be walked outside and shot. I'm really serious on this point, people. I need to know what the *hell* happened to us back at Cheyenne Mountain. The best explanation anyone of you has come up with is that what Ryan did was impossible. I will say this but once. I need that technology, and I need it *now*."

Even a trusted aide like Matt Duncan risked his life by speaking. But someone had to. "Mr. President, we all understand your frustration. Everyone in this room would gladly lay down their life for you. But it does appear that Ryan used weapons that cannot be understood. Even the wildest theoretical physicists we consulted have no idea how such action could be accomplished. There's no technology on Earth even hypothetically close to what's required to do what he did."

"I think," said Frontera in a cool, paced voice, "the explanation is obvious."

Marshall's eyes shot to Frontera with predatory quickness and intent. "Oh you do, you little shit? You going to finish that thought, or will you allow me the pleasure of pounding it out of your skull?"

"Mr. Pres —" Duncan tried to interject.

Carlos cut the young man off. "I'd rather you not, if it's all the same to you." Carlos allowed sufficient time to slip by to alert Marshall to the fact that he'd paused in defiance. "Ryan went to several alien worlds that possessed advanced civilizations. One of them must have supplied him with the mystery technology." He raised his palms. "What other origin for it is possible?"

That had occurred to Marshall. But that would mean that duplicating the process, given humanity's current state of knowledge, would be impossible. The only way to obtain it was by force or by gift. The force part had failed miserably. That attempt pretty much made receiving it as a gift unlikely. Who would give their sworn enemy, one who just tried to nuke them, the power to defend themselves against anything? He sure as hell wouldn't if the roles were reversed. That brought Marshall back to a theme he'd revisited far too often. Ryan. He used the USA's ship and support and returned with a great prize. It was rightfully Marshall's in the first place, not the UN's. To be surrounded by traitors and fools was a curse the president felt he'd never deserved.

Phillip Szeto shifted uncomfortably in his seat. He knew he'd be called on next. If Marshall couldn't receive the alien tech as a gift, his next—and last—option would be to steal it. Hence, it would be the CIA's job. Of course, everyone on both sides knew that. Unless the UN and its allies were completely incompetent, it would be impossible to rob them of their treasure. A fail-fail scenario for Szeto, yet again.

"Well, Phil," asked Marshall, "I guess that means you're our only hope of remaining a free and powerful America."

"Ever since that day, Mr. President," he replied weakly, "I've made it mission number one for the CIA to obtain that technology. All of my resources are directed at that target alone. If it can be done, we will do it."

"Which," Marshall menaced, "leaves open the possibility that it *cannot* be done. You know that bird's never going to fly. I *must* be able to defend my people. If we are to survive as a nation, I *must* have that new toy. Anything else is unacceptable. If you can't do the job, I'll find someone who can." He pointed at Frontera. "Maybe him. He's the only one in my presence with a functioning brain."

Carlos rolled his eyes.

"All my resources are —"

Marshall held up a hang-on-a-minute hand. "I know. Working around the clock like good little monkeys. Just bring me results. If you're unable to make me smile by the time of next week's cabinet meeting … well, I bet you can finish that sentence for me, can't you, Phillip?"

Shoulders slumped and he eyed to the floor. "Yes, Mr. President, I can."

"Okay, everyone out, except those involved in the space program." Most of the men and women quickly and quietly shuffled out. Those who remained reluctantly filled in the empty seats so they could be closer to the boss. Marshall continued, "So, what's the latest on the worldships?"

Kendell Jackson stiffened his back. "We're doing well, sir. Your target of two hundred and fifty ships will be accomplished, no question. The final craft will be ready to sail in less than six years."

Marshall mumbled to himself, "2146?" To Kendell, he said, "Good work, Jackson. Finally, someone competent enough to do their job."

Kendell cleared his throat, checked his resolve, and spoke. "Sir, I was wondering what your orders were in regard to additional worldship production."

Marshall twisted his brow. "How so, son?"

"Well, I mean, we will easily make your quota, but after that, shouldn't we continue to produce additional worldships? We cannot know how many people the UN can accommodate and —" He decided it was healthiest to stop speaking.

"What the devil for? I told you I needed two hundred and fifty. If I wanted two hundred and fifty-one, I'd have said so, wouldn't I? Have you ever known me to be timid in expressing my desires, son?"

"No, sir, of course not. It's just —"

"It's just above your paygrade. Drop it, General Jackson, if you know what's good for you and your family. You're all coming with us, so don't lose sleep in that regard. Beyond that, leave the strategic decisions to me, okay?"

"Of course, sir." *This psychopath is going to let anyone who doesn't lick his butt die. He could not care less. He has abandoned, on a personal whim, his duties to those he's sworn to serve. I can no longer serve such a man in good conscience. But how can I escape? He'd never allow that. I must find my own way to safety.*

"Everyone out, except you," Marshall pointed to Kendell, "and you, Frontera." Once alone, Marshall leaned over uncomfortably close to Kendell's face. "I wish to bestow upon you the reward for being a good little soldier, son." He looked to Carlos with a sick grin on his face and tilted his head toward Kendell.

SEVENTEEN

This is the video journal of Kendell Jackson, recorded on my sixtieth birthday. I am documenting my thoughts and rationale so my family can, with the help the Lord, come to understand why I did what I was forced to do. Honestly, I cannot say as of this moment whether I shall simply commit suicide, or if I shall try and exact my revenge on Stuart Marshall. All I know, my dearest ones, is that I cannot proceed along the path I am forced to walk.

I work for no human. I work for the devil himself. And the devil's an android. Worst of all, the devil wants me to join him—permanently. I'm to become a machine like him. Then I must kill the human who writes these words. Refusal, the great demon stated specifically, was not an option. I knew too much to waver. Either I proceed with the download, or I'll disappear forever, as would my family. My three children, my three precious grandchildren, my wife, and my two surviving brothers will all vanish. It'd be, he told me with a smile, like the Jackson line never existed in the first place.

My transfer to damnation takes place in three days. The untrustworthy scientist, that Frontera fellow, needs that long to sculpt my likeness into one of his soulless beasts. Then, the devil and his fallen angels will own me forever. The woman I replaced, York, was an android. She emptied a revolver into her human self's head at pointblank range, all the while laughing like the possessed demon she had become.

"Be nice," evil incarnate chided me, "or I'll download you into *her* body. I'd pay good money to see you in heels and a skirt, Jackson."

The man must be stopped. He must die, if a robot can be said to die. The Marshall who was elected president died years ago. But how can I kill him? He controls everyone close to him. Most are indentured androids, too. If it was only my life at stake, I'd do whatever it took. But it would cost me the lives of everyone I've ever loved. That's a price I cannot pay, and a burden I cannot shoulder.

I must submit. I shall be a machine. I will become something abhorrent in the eyes of the Lord—an abomination. But, I promise I will have my revenge. I will end Marshall. Then I will end myself, knowing I've done His will in both cases.

EIGHTEEN

"Sapale, I'm going to visit Offlin. You want to come? Ffffuttoe already turned me down. She said he scares her."

"I'll come if you want me to, but I'd just as soon not."

"Why? He's a good guy … ah, fish."

Her right eyes fluttered open and shut rapidly. That was Kaljaxian body language for *yeah, if that's what you think*. "I'd rather stay with the children," was what she said.

"Ffffuttoe's a great nanny. She dotes over them like they were her own kids. I'm surprised she hasn't tried to nurse them yet."

"She has. It didn't work."

I set a finger under my chin. "Let me see. Maybe because her species lays eggs and doesn't have mammary tissue. Do ya *think*?"

"That's not," she sniped, "the point. She tried because she loves them. I think it's sweet."

Why, oh why, was I always fated to be the bad guy when it came to issues involving females? "I agree. She's sweet. You're sweet. Do you want to come see Offlin? If you don't, that's fine, too."

"You go and have your man time. Smoke cigars and tell lies."

"We tried cigars. He couldn't keep his head out of the water long enough for it to stay lit. He threw up after he ate it. Said it was quite the rush though."

"Males." She shooed me away. "Go. Have fun. Come back too late and make certain you tell him what a bitch I am."

"I don't think I need remind him. He always has at least fifteen minutes of fun at my expense in that regard."

"Stupid spawner doesn't understand the value of a good woman at your back."

"I'll be sure to let him know."

"I *bet* you will." She shoved me toward the door.

****

"Jonryan," called Offlin as soon as I came into view. Try as I might, I couldn't convince him to split my two names apart. He said that would be silly. Not sure why, but he wouldn't budge.

"Yo." I greeted back. "How's the water?" That was Listhelonian for *how's it going.*

"Better now that you're here. I was beginning to think you'd forgotten about your prisoner."

I scaled the ladder and met him at the top of his tank. We slapped hand-appendages like the couple of old jocks that we were. I played football. He played something that sounded like fish rugby, *ogoric,* but with spiky metal cylinders instead of a ball. Everyone was injured and deaths were commonplace. Yeah, I'd stick with football.

"Doc treating you well?" I asked after he submerged.

He grabbed his stomach. "Look at this gut. He feeds me so well I worry he's fattening me for a feast."

After I stopped giggling, I became very serious. "Are you happy, my friend?"

He did that floating-on-his-back thing he did when he was deep in thought and gently stroked his gills. "Yes, I believe I am," he finally said. "Especially considering the alternatives."

"Which were?"

"Death while attacking this planet or death returning home having not died attacking this planet."

"Swimming in luxury does seem a pleasant enough option, doesn't it?" I lowered my head. "I'm glad you're content. I still do feel a little guilty taking you prisoner."

He swam to the glass where I stood. "Never feel that, Jonryan. I had just fired all my missiles at you, if you recall. Yours was an action taken in a war. If I returned home with a live human captive, I would have been most proud. I might even have been allowed to spawn." He did his trill-laugh.

"Why, you dirty old fish. Shame on you."

"Speaking of spawning, Toño tells me your mate has hatched a brood. How many?"

"Twins," I confirmed, holding up two fingers. "Cute little dickens."

"Just two? How sad. Two *hundred*, maybe, but not," he held up sequential digits, "just, two. Such odd species. Are they males or females?"

"Neither," I said in a confused tone, "Sapale hasn't decided yet."

"You've lost me completely."

"Me, too. Her species is born neutral-gendered. Somehow the mother decides which sex they'll be. She said something about hormone changes in her milk. Pretty strange, if you ask me. Anyway, she says she has a week or two to decide. Then we can name them."

"Most peculiar."

"Tell me about it."

It was Offlin's turn to be suddenly serious. "I watch Toño a lot. We sometimes chat while he works. He is odd, Jonryan. Odd like you. Others who work with him come and go, eat as the day passes, but not him. Like you didn't most of the flight here. Why is this? I must know." He waved his fins in front of himself. "Now, I'm not wanting military secrets. Not that I'd be able to use such information from here." He pointed to the glass. "But, you two are strangely different."

At that juncture, I decided it couldn't hurt to tell him that much. "Toño and I are androids. Do you understand the word?"

"I thought I did. But you can't be machines, so clearly I don't."

"We *are* machines. We used to be regular humans long ago, but our minds were transferred to these machines." I pointed to myself. "In my case, it made long space flights much easier."

"I bet it would. That would explain my observations. Thank you for finally putting my mind at ease."

"And how was it that you were able to capture me?"

"I told you. It was magic."

"Can't blame me for trying, can you?"

"Not one little bit. Hey, Doc tells me you spend a lot of time looking at pictures of deep sea fish. You know, the ones that are as ugly as you are?"

Again, he pointed to his surroundings. "Kind of lonely in here. Your magic destroyed any images I might have had of my own species. Second best is better than nothing."

"Okay, but I don't want you getting too weird on me."

"I'll keep that in mind."

NINETEEN

President Marshall sat in his office with the only three men—actually androids now themselves—he could call friends. He didn't trust and basically hated everyone else. More importantly, these were the only three souls who could, if asked in confidence, state honestly that they liked Marshall. The four were putting significant dents in several bottles of priceless Cognac while puffing on Cuba's best cigars. Marshall, along with General Chuck Thomas, Chief Justice Sam Peterson, and Senator Bob Patrick lived very well, quite high on the hog.

The conversation turned, as it always eventually did, to their personal futures. Perhaps it was better to call them their personal fantasies, but as they were on the verge of making their wildest dreams actually come true, "futures" described them best. Thomas always started the licentious boasting at the same point of drunkenness. "You know what the first thing I'm going to do after I seal the hatch on my personal worldship?"

"Yes," Marshall guffawed, "and please spare us the details."

"No, Stu. That's the second, third, fourth, and two-hundredth thing I'm going to do. No, the *first* thing I'm going to do is turn off my damn handheld. I'm taking no calls from anyone until I've sated my considerable hunger."

Quietly, staring into his snifter, Sam observed, "Most likely all two-hundred of us share those same plans." He produced a sickly, grunting cackle. Sam was, by most human standards, a grotesque man. He was not simply obese, he was greasily fat. His face looked like a cheap Halloween mask, warts on the nose and all. His ears were set too low to escape being seen as anything other than some form of birth defect. And, right from his childhood he had horrendous halitosis. His breath was a mix of rotten cheese, burnt rubber, and embalming fluid. To everyone's shock, when he was transferred to his android he insisted all his revolting features be artistically preserved. He neither elected to have his pendulous abdomen reduced nor his unfortunate face remodeled in any way. No one asked him why he insisted on remaining hideous. It was clear to all that he'd made a grievous error in judgment. Such, it would seem, were the idiosyncrasies of this particular psychopath.

"Here's to that, times a hundred," shouted Marshall, as he threw back a shot of liquor. "Same hold for you, Bob? You think the missus will allow such debauchery?"

"If she wishes to flee this rock, she will." That drew robust laughs from all four men. Bob was a cautious, thoughtful man by nature. Hence, he was continually questioning whether they could pull off their insane plan. He was fairly certain they couldn't, but he also couldn't deny it was worthy of every possible effort. He voiced his thoughts. "I hope we can pull it off before anyone notices or before there's any pushback."

Marshall tossed a balled-up napkin at Bob. "You're such a Glum-Gus. Of *course,* we'll pull it off. And if anyone dares object, let them try and fly to a habitable planet with their arms." When the giggles settled down Marshall continued thoughtfully. "It's foolproof. We shuttle those hand-selected by each of us, along with their families, up to a clearinghouse space station. Then, we let it be known that for reasons of personal security, the women and older girls need to be flown to their worldships separate from the men and boys. Who's going to question us at that point? The females end up on one of our two hundred ships, and the men, if we so elect, end up on the other fifty. Any overage in men can be ejected into space for all I care. Once we shove-off, it's a done deal. The promise of potential reunion *with* and the safety *of* their loved ones will convince the women to be as cooperative as they possibly can be."

"One man," growled Chuck, while wiping some drool, "to *fifty* thousand women. I *like* those numbers."

TWENTY

"Glorious Master Otollar," the officer said meekly and stooped over in a deep bow, "I bring troubling tidings."

Otollar was floating on his back, thoughtfully stroking a gill slit. The words of the inconsequential soldier brought him upright instantly. Upright and outraged. "Who are you to bring me such news? Who are you, in fact, to even speak to me? Where is my Second Warrior at such times?"

The messenger, an otherwise affable fellow named Oppitor, began to quiver like a tsunami had struck him. "I … I don't know, Great One. I … I was at my post serving Gumnolar and you when the message arrived. My commander said I should inform you at once. S … s … so I came as instructed. I pray only to please you, Glorious One." After that tortured response, Oppitor was capable of no further speech.

"So, you're to be the sacrificial fintail pup?"

In response, Oppitor only trembled more violently.

"First, the news. Then I will have the name of the coward who sent you to save his scales."

Oppitor opened his mouth to talk, but no words came out. Only tiny bubbles.

"Speak. The message now, or you will join your fool commander in my belly."

That proved to be sufficient motivation. "It is a message from *Gumnolar Attacks*." Oppitor reflected a second, then amended his statement. "I guess it's the *non-message* from *Gumnolar Attacks*."

Otollar swam over to the young man and head-butted him powerfully. "No riddles. Say meaning or die."

While rubbing his forehead, Oppitor said, "Your son Offlin informed us he had indeed found the infidel's home world. His last message was that he was being confronted by one of their vessels. He discharged all his missiles, but none struck the servant of the Beast Without Eyes. Then his radio went silent. That is all."

To himself, Otollar howled, "A *single* ship? They deigned to send but one vessel?" Back to Oppitor, he demanded, "Are you certain that is what you heard? No further signal was received?"

"No, Your Glory. No static, no dead-air, nothing. We can only assume his craft was destroyed suddenly and without warning."

Otollar rubbed his gills. "And they sent but one warship. That means they knew it would be sufficient, even though they knew *Gumnolar Seeks* was able to destroy one of their scout ships? They are either great fools or possess a great weapon that the *Captain Simpson* was not fitted with. Hmm." Unconsciously, he drifted into a supine position in silent reflection. Again he spoke to himself, for he was the only one who mattered in that chamber. "Could be a new weapon, so the older ship didn't have one. Perhaps it is too large for a scout ship." Directing a harsh tone to Oppitor he asked, "Did Offlin send a visual of the warship that defeated him?"

"Yes, Majestic One, of course."

"Show me," he pointed to a screen, "both infidel ships." Otollar studied the images intently. "Basically the same vessel. So, the weapon must be new, or, rather, it was new forty cycles ago. Which means they've had time to improve it and understand it better. So, we were at their mercy forty cycles ago, and now we're even more so. Perhaps hopelessly so." Addressing the trembling messenger, he asked, "You work in communications, correct?"

"Y … yes."

"Any news from the fleet that would alter their planned arrival?"

"None, Glorious One."

With defiant resolve Otollar said, "We will destroy those who serve the Beast Without Eyes or die as a species. Send word to launch all remaining ships, at once. They will attack what remains of the infidel world or provide visual proof that our ships were useless against them. Go now. And send me your commander. I have developed quite an appetite."

TWENTY-ONE

The year 2144 was, by any measure, an apocalyptic one. It was a terrifying harbinger of what was to come six years later. It was the year of Jupiter's last close pass by the Earth before it finally destroyed her. Whereas 2138 was famous for awe-inspiring meteor showers, in 2144 the meteors were incredibly spectacular right up until they exploded in the middle of a city. *Biblical* was a term the news holos overused in their coverage. One aspect of membrane technology that quickly became apparent was that you couldn't blanket the entire globe. Some larger meteorites were stopped, but way too many found rich targets. It seemed like Jupiter really had it in for planet Earth, like it was personal. A word to the wise: Never piss-off a giant planet.

Sapale, Ffffuttoe, and I spent most of the year in space to avoid becoming numbers on the rapidly growing death toll. Fortunately, several worldships were ready, so some lucky few also found refuge in their new homes in space. By 2145, around five hundred million people were inhabiting the ships. The UN had a workable plan to evacuate a whole lot more—billions more—before 2150 hit. The USA had produced only two hundred and fifty worldships, which were all much smaller than the ones we were cranking-out. It was so odd. When work on that last ship was completed, they simply stopped building more. Five years left to potentially save more of her citizens, but nada. Toño privately relayed to me that Frontera had confirmed that no further worldships were planned. He wasn't privileged to know why. That information was for Marshall's inner circle alone.

The US was targeting increased production of androids. They had a lot more than we did, but I didn't see that as an issue. Maybe someday everyone could become a robot, but there hardly seemed a rush to get to that point. Also, I knew Marshall, the poster-child for SOBs everywhere, wasn't allowing regular people to transfer. No, he had some twisted plan. Of this I was certain. Bully for him. Maybe it would keep him out of our way for the next five years. Then his worldships could go one way while ours all went in the opposite direction. Good riddance.

The US made several attempts to steal our membrane technology. I'd have been stunned if they hadn't. Fortunately, they never even came close to obtaining it. They'd tried seduction, covert-ops raids, and offered outrageous bribes. They even let it be known that anyone supplying them with the technology could have an unlimited number of seats on one of their worldships. They forgot that the UN had more than enough room, so that ploy didn't work either.

Sooner or later, in all good conscience, we had to give them the plans. There would be an ongoing threat from Listhelon long after we set sail. To not provide the US with membrane technology would likely sentence them to death. Many on our side were uncomfortable with that option, but realistically, the US citizens weren't our enemies. Only their corrupt leadership. There was talk of transmitting it to them only if they agreed to go in a separate direction and only when we were quite far off. But that commitment on their part could never be made binding. After learning the trick, they could chase after us if they really wanted to. A lot hinged on what their plan was for their two hundred fifty ships. Maybe their intention really was to have no contact with the rest of humanity. If so, again, good riddance.

The UN was moving masses of people to several staging areas around the globe. From there, they could be shuttled to their permanent homes. That's when human nature—good old human nature—began threatening the entire operation. Again, the UN had mostly large worldships. They could accommodate maybe a million people. That's a lot, but less than the population of most sovereign nations. So, unless they decided to mix the Earth's population intentionally, no one ship could hold all of a country's citizens. Only nations with populations less than Switzerland could all fit into one worldship.

As in gym-class, people had to choose teams. That worked about as well for adults as it did for kids on the schoolyard. Bickering, arguing, and the hurling of condemnations became the dialogue. *This* group wanted to be with *that* group, but never with *that other* group. No, they had cooties. To make the unreasonable official policy, many countries wanted everyone to go together, even though it was a proven fact they wouldn't all fit. Maybe half the population could be strapped to the outside like luggage? No problem there.

Then there were the ethnic and religious conflicts. Many nations announced they would not allow foreign residents to journey with them in their adopted homes. Israel, population fourteen million, wanted fourteen worldships. But they planned to separate the Orthodox from the Reform from the Conservative divisions of Judaism. That was fine, but it meant that some ships would be sent off partially filled. Other religions were downright obstreperous and unreasonable. Certain sects could not be mixed with others. These neighboring people, who'd lived together for centuries, wanted to go with a group they identified with more closely. The problem was that a third group always protested. They didn't want either of those groups to be on *their* ships. No, they wanted to live with *that* group over there, but only *maybe*. They weren't sure yet. Could someone check back with them later? How about 2151? Would they please reach a consensus by then? Humans.

The UN, being, after all, the *UNITED NATIONS,* took it upon itself to make everything right. That lasted two years. Then they simply assigned worldships to sovereign nations based on their population and let them deal with all the headaches. The backup plan, should a country be unable to decide who went where, was to randomly assign those citizens to ships. Yeah, if you can't decide, Mom will, but you won't like her solution, so you'd better fix it yourself first. I was gladder than ever I had nothing to do with politics.

In my neck of the woods—the exploration and discovery business—things were going well. All the Arks were back, except poor Sim's ship and one other. They had variable success, but at least three excellent candidates for colonization were found. Many other fairly good options were out there, limited by, say, the need to interface with a sentient population or adapting to hostile environments. At least that part of humanity's future looked bright. The general plan was to send an Ark ship with as many worldships as possible. They would serve as advanced scouts. As the mothership crept along, the Ark ship could speed ahead to gather information or establish treaties.

I mentioned earlier that the bottom always drops when things were going well. Yeah, that would be 2149. That's when our long-range scanners reported contact with the Listhelon armada. It was a *big* one. Never let it be said those ugly little bastards took war lightly. No, they'd sent ten thousand ships of varying sizes. Some were clearly battleships. Others had configurations more consistent with supply or support craft. It was an impressive attack fleet any way you looked at it. They were just outside the orbit of Neptune and decelerating rapidly, which meant their missiles would be in range of Earth in two months. Three, tops. They could be in orbit above us in four months. I debated discussing their appearance with Offlin, but in the end, I decided not to. I didn't want to put him in the position of choosing between his race and his new friends.

The image of all those warships on the screen really brought home the impact of Uto's gift. Given our current technology, minus the membranes, there was no way we could fight off such an attack. The worldships were useless in combat. We had several thousand smaller, faster ships, but we didn't have nearly enough for such an onslaught. Plus, if the bigger Listhelon ships carried fighters, they would wipe us out for certain. I couldn't forget the image of all the pain and sorrow in Uto's eyes. Was that really a me from the far future, somehow returned to this time, hoping to prevent the extinction only he escaped? That scenario seemed impossible. As the membranes were going to save humanity, I would never know what it was like to be absolutely alone like Uto, thankfully. But, there might be a me out there who did. Lord help him.

The battle with the Listhelons was going to be extremely brief and extremely one-sided. I had a bet with another pilot that we wouldn't lose a single ship. The reason for my confidence was our new weapon. Remember how, in an act of panic, I had Al use the membranes to throw stuff at an aircraft back at Cheyenne Mountain? Once Toño heard about that application, he got to thinking. When that man thought, miracles were soon to follow.

He devised a railgun powered by membranes. Traditionally a rail gun used electromagnetism to fire a metal projectile at high speeds. It was like a canon without the gunpowder. You know how the lights on a landing strip flash in one direction to help a plane land at night? Doc used microsecond pulses of membranes to accelerate solid objects to ninety percent the speed of light. Yeah, that's one good cannon. What's more, the gun itself was only two meters long. He promised a rifle version in less than a year. They were going to be *so* cool.

Guess what happens if a pea-sized metal ball hits, oh say, a Listhelon warship at nearly the speed of light? Warship go *boom*. The explosive force would be truly stupendous. Our attack-vessels were firing one-pound degraded uranium spheres. One hit anywhere and any ship, or asteroid for that matter, would be utterly destroyed. The beautiful part was that, once fired, a projectile in space wouldn't slow down until it hit something. Their huge explosive impact wouldn't degrade over vast distances. In fact, one suggestion for destroying the Listhelon armada was to simply fire a blanketing-pattern of projectiles from high Earth orbit. The spheres would likely wipe out the fleet in less than five minutes since they'd get there so fast.

In the end, we decided it was best to engage the Listhelons at close range, long before they were in missile range of Earth. That way we could be highly selective about where we fired. We didn't want to send deadly projectiles off to who knows where, after all. We set sail in order to meet them near Jupiter's original orbit. For safety's sake, since we were talking about the end of life on Earth as the penalty for failure, we sent one thousand ships. I would pay good money to see the look on the Listhelon commander's face when he saw that we *wanted* the odds to be ten-to-one in his favor. He'd probably "shit his own water," as Offlin was so fond of saying.

This time out, Fleet Admiral Katashi Matsumoto invited me to join the UN task force. He was in charge of all their space endeavors, both military and peaceful. He was a good man, and I was proud to serve under him. Katashi, with his Bushido mindset, tolerated me with suboptimal enthusiasm.

I think my casual, some might call it flippant, attitude about being an officer of such high rank rubbed him against the grain. Oh well. We weren't dating. We were going into combat. That relationship worked just fine for me. As the only veteran of space warfare on Earth, he positioned *Ark 1* at the lead, just in front of his flagship.

The two-month trip to meet the Listhelons was very different for me. Instead of being mostly alone with my own thoughts, I was part of a team. Matsumoto turned out to be quite the taskmaster. He had us run drill after drill after drill. We simulated every imaginable counterattack the Listhelons might try. We tested and retested for equipment failures, power failures, and casualty triage. It was intense. As a military man, I knew the value of such discipline, but I began to long for the boredom I'd experienced when I sailed on my own. But the time did pass more quickly. However, believe me, every man and woman in the fleet was glad when general quarters sounded for real. We were all ready to stand down.

Our defense of Earth began with Matsumoto's issuing one short, tersely worded warning to the Listhelon commander, Ocaster. *Surrender or die.* Ocaster's response was to launch one nuclear-tipped missile directly at the flagship. Matsumoto actually smiled as he gave the order to destroy the missile. First one I' ever seen on his rocky face. Milliseconds after he issued that order, the missile detonated in a brilliant flash. It had only traveled a few hundred meters from Ocaster's ship. So the Listhelon commander failed to witness the dismemberment of his armada on account of his being incinerated to a high degree.

The Listhelon vessels far enough from the blast reacted quickly. They moved to disperse and fired an impressive spread of missiles. Perhaps one hundred thousand messengers of death were fired in our direction all at once. Matsumoto gave the order for AIs on all ships to coordinate with the flagship's master-AI for fire-control, according to the set plan. A quarter million metal balls shot from our formation within seconds. As with Ocaster's original assault, all the targeted missiles were barely clear of their mountings when they exploded. We actually never had to fire on the warships, just the nukes. They were blown apart by their own weapons. Once this distressing fact became apparent to the support ships in the enemy fleet, almost all set collision courses for the nearest UN ship. A few turned and ran. Within thirty seconds, every loving one of them was interstellar dust. I did the numbers. The Listhelon War officially lasted less than three minutes. That had to be some kind of record.

A cheer rose up on each vessel so loud it vibrated their hulls. When word of the defeat reached Earth, there was dancing in the streets and free drinks in every bar on the planet. It was a proud moment in human history, and one badly needed by a worried population. The Earth might have been about to die, but no one was going to take it from us, ever.

TWENTY-TWO

General Jackson's heels clicked down the hallway as he approached the Oval Office. He was to report the results of the Listhelon War to the president. Jackson was allowed to accompany Matsumoto as an observer on his flagship to witness the battle. Marshall assumed Jackson was invited so he'd document the complete humiliation of the United States. What Jackson had seen stunned him to his core. How the UN could have developed such devastating weaponry was truly beyond belief. Jackson's forces possessed, in comparison, stones and hewn sticks. He was not briefed in advance as to the technology, so he had no way of anticipating its brutal power. That was, after all, Matsumoto's intention. He wanted Marshall to see firsthand how the UN utterly outclassed the US. Matsumoto wanted Marshall to understand that raising a finger against the UN would be futile, insane, and suicidal.

What Marshall did not know, and would not know for several months, was what else took place on Matsumoto's flagship. His general was able to ally with the enemy. Marshall was not yet aware that Jackson hated him with all his heart, if he'd still had one, and all his soul, which Jackson prayed fanatically he still possessed. Jackson had come to realize that only the UN represented the interests of humankind. He knew then that the UN was the only hope for a meaningful exodus. He also knew Marshall was a demon and a madman who had to be stopped, no matter the cost. For Jackson to have the chance to work closely with the UN forces, and to do so with no risk of Marshall eavesdropping, was, in retrospect, foolish of Marshall. But, as the president was a consummate fool, such folly was only fitting.

One final detail of Jackson's contact with the UN was also not apparent to Marshall or the outside world. It was a critical modification to Jackson's design. He had to beg, plead, pound his chest, and scream like a madman for Matsumoto to okay the change, but it was made. Both his fusion power generators were modified so that Jackson could switch off the containment field at will. What happened when the plasma in those generators, under tremendous pressure and as hot as the Sun, was suddenly freed? In a word, *ka-ka-kaboom*. Though much less explosive than a nuclear weapon, the local effects of such a release would be incredibly destructive. All Jackson had to do was bide his time. He savored the prospect. Eventually, he'd attend another Cabinet meeting with Marshall and all of his evil marionettes. Then he would have his revenge and make the world a much better place with just one action.

For the time being, Jackson had to be the very picture of the loyal lackey. He opened the Oval Office door and entered. After softly closing the door, he crisply saluted his imitation commander-in-chief.

Marshall glanced up, rolled his eyes, and pointed to a chair. "Sit *down*, Kendell."

He sat and set his hat on his lap.

"I've read your report a dozen times, but it still seems more science fiction than fact. You have *no* idea how they pulled that off?"

"None, sir. I didn't ask, and they volunteered nothing."

"Were there, I don't know, any unusual sounds when their weapons fired?"

"None, Mr. President. Whatever they did produced no explosions or mechanical sounds."

"It can't have been magic, man. You have no clue?"

"Sorry, sir. No." In fact, he knew nothing of the technology involved in the confrontation. Even if Matsumoto would have tried to reveal something, Kendell would have stopped him. He didn't want to be the inadvertent source of any useful information to Marshall. "I've downloaded the video of the scene on the bridge during the entire brief engagement."

"Yes," Marshall waved a dismissive hand, "I've seen it several times. Nothing useful." Marshall gently pounded the desk with a fist. "And they *completely* scrubbed the rest of your recordings before you disembarked?"

"Yes, sir. DeJesus saw to that himself. I was allowed to retain only what you've seen."

"And you didn't try and hide some records, squirrel them away in the back of your head?"

"Of course I did. And DeJesus knew right where to find them. He's a very thorough man."

"He's a son of a bitch, is what he is. A traitorous son of a fucking bitch."

Kendell offered no response. He liked Toño and was very impressed with his commitment and vision. The fact that Marshall despised the man elevated Toño further in Kendell's book.

"So, the entire Listhelon fleet was simply blown to bits by some mysterious weapon the UN has that we can't duplicate?"

In his head, Kendell smiled wickedly. "It would appear so, sir."

"A lot of fucking help you are, Jackson." Marshall looked to a set of monitors. Flicking his pen in the air, he dismissed his general. "If there's nothing else, go."

Oh, how Kendell wanted to detonate himself right there, right then. Marshall was the devil and was badly in need of killing. If he waited, he could take out several of Marshall's evil cronies at the same time. He would eliminate the branches, trunk, and the roots of this foul mockery of a constitutional government in one swift stroke. And, most of all, he would end his own suffering. He felt violated to an extent that defied articulation. Forced by a maniac to inhabit a godless metal husk was not living. It wasn't even hell. It wasn't that pleasant. Kendell longed to cease existing.

The evacuation of a small percentage of Americans to their worldships was well underway. Two hundred ships were full and had already pushed-off to a predesignated rendezvous point beyond the orbit of Saturn. Though it would take them years to get there, they would be safe. The puppet leaders of the US would flee Earth at the last minute and catch up with their ships on high-speed shuttles. Well, at least, they *thought* they would.

He didn't know all the sordid detail of the leadership's lecherous plan at the time, but Kendell suspected correctly the key elements. He had glimpsed high-clearance communications mentioning that most worldships were carrying only women of childbearing age. He could imagine no acceptable reason for that to be the case. Every fact he learned made him long all that much more to end Marshall and his associates.

A key agreement Kendell was able to reach with the UN during his voyage was how the UN would evacuate the remainder of the US population—those individuals abandoned by their illegitimate government. Hopefully the US leaders would be dead and the UN could act openly. The worst-case scenario had the UN scrambling to save those left behind after Marshall and his pets fled. That would be cutting it *very* close. Probably too close. All the more reason for Kendell not to fail.

One aspect of the whole charade Marshall put forth sickened Kendell the most. Up until then, the public at large was unaware that the US had only a small percentage of the worldships needed to evacuate the bulk of the citizenry. Through total censorship of all traffic and communications to and from the construction facilities in space, Marshall was able to keep a tight lid on the shortfall. Glowing reports, accompanied by glorious holo-casts, were created to make it look like massive worldship production was underway.

To help maintain the illusion, personnel were not allowed to return to Earth once joining the workforce in space. Martial law dictated that such essential workers couldn't be spared. If one was able to finagle a return visa to Earth from a production facility, they were at great risk of never completing the trip. Unless cleared by Marshall himself, anyone attempting to return to the ground was cast out an airlock in high Earth orbit. The family would be told their loved one had been assigned to an ultra-high security area and could only receive communications. Not to worry, they were all told, the family would reunite once the migration had begun.

With a year to go before Jupiter struck, the sick truth had not reached the American people. If and when it did, all hell would break loose. If that were to occur, all high-level officials had constantly updated back-up plans to spirit them to their worldships before they could be arrested or, more likely, physically ripped apart by mobs.

By the time Kendell returned to his office in Houston, there were no fewer than thirty messages from Marshall or one of his sycophants requesting updates on their precious, personal worldships. He delegated a subordinate to respond to them all. The less contact he had with those megalomaniacs, the better. He wished he could safely communicate with his new allies, but that was too risky. He certainly couldn't share his plans with his family, especially not his wife. She would never sit passively and allow him to kill himself. She could never even know why it was so critical that he do so. Perhaps he'd send her a letter as he entered final meeting, but even that involved needless risk.

He had specifically not been told of De La Frontera's duplicity. Though the UN felt Kendell could be trusted, that didn't mean he couldn't be tortured or otherwise manipulated into divulging secret information. No, Kendell was completely alone and completely isolated. That was fine by him. He was no longer human, so why worry over creature comforts like love and support? He was a machine with one task to perform, no different from a meat slicer or a vacuum cleaner. No different at all. And he would be a good little machine and execute his one function unemotionally and with machine-like precision.

Kendell sat at his desk, reading his file concerning evacuation day. It was January 12, 2050. The entire planet would be below the gaseous surface of Jupiter on April 16, 2050. Jupiter's closing speed was around a million miles per day. When the giant planet was a few million miles away, its gravity would cause massive upheavals. The last safe day on Earth would be, ironically, April 1, 2050. Anyone and anything still on the surface was likely to remain there for the duration. Marshall planned to leave sometime during the last week of March. Jackson was allotted ten weeks to get Marshall's two hundred and fifty worldships filled. That wouldn't be a problem.

The bigger problem, which would be an SEP—somebody else's problem—was how to evacuate the bulk of the US population in no more than two weeks. If he successfully assassinated Marshall sooner, there might be more time, but still probably not enough. Even a month more would help. But, after the elimination of the leadership, it would be hard to organize a massive project like total evacuation, given the mass confusion that would surely rule. To Kendell, that was another SEP. The fifty non-reserved worldships were filling with the family members of the sequestered women—them the motivation for the women to behave as intended. Jackson shuddered for the thousandth time. The remaining worldships also had to carry the administration's loyal followers, especially the male ones, so they were pretty much full, too. Jackson didn't make the actual assignments or arrangements to put people in orbit. Whoever was in charge of that had to be sweating bullets. A lot of people with a lot of seat-credits surely had to be hounding whoever that person was for a rapid departure date.

The one upside Kendell had in his position was that his office was at the center of one of the most heavily defended military installations in history. Peasants with pitchforks had no chance of getting through to him. The only place he had to visit between now and Armageddon was the White House. It was defended better than his base. Even if all hell broke loose with the civilian population, no one was going to interfere with Jackson's holy plan. *That* made him happy. It was the only joy left to him.

****

The UN was getting people off-world at an incredibly fast rate. As February, 2150, began, we had ten thousand worldships fitted and ready. Nearly five billion—yeah, billion with a *B*—people were already tucked in. Several thousand worldships were already steaming to safety, heading toward the rendezvous point. We even had a good plan to alert the US population that the UN was rallying to their aid. It was simple. We dropped millions of leaflets. Yeah. We dropped them over "elevator cities," as we called them—the places people went up from. That way rural people had a chance to start moving toward pickup points, saving their ever-dwindling time. We actually didn't know when Marshall and his baboons were going to abdicate, but best guesses put the date in late March. Unless Jackson took them out sooner, we probably weren't going to scoop and run with everyone who wanted out. Oh, well. Their government put their asses in a sling, not us.

The first Thursday in March, I received a top-priority message from Kahl at UN headquarters in Spain. Marshall was going to call her the next day. I jumped on *Ark 1* and made it there in two hours. Whatever was up had to be big. Marshall hadn't spoken to our leadership since before the Listhelon War. We thought we'd heard the last from him. No such luck, it would seem. Unless he was calling to say he was sorry and invite us all to tea, he was up to something no good. Kahl, Toño, a few other higher-ups, and I sat at the curved conference desk in her office. Marshall's holo would appear on top of the table right in front of Mary Kahl.

At high noon our time, very symbolically, the holo-buzzer sounded. Marshall zapped into existence, seated behind his desk, hands folded on the top. He was smiling broadly. We were in deep doo-doo.

"Hello, Mary. I see you're surrounded by the usual traitors, deviants, and deserters. Some things never change."

"Stuart, if you're calling to be an asshole, please don't," she said firmly. "I'm terribly busy. The world, if you hadn't noticed, is about to end."

His smile widened and grew more sardonic. "No, Mary. Dear, old Mary. No, I'm calling because I find I'm in need of a hero. In fact, I need one rather badly. You're the hero who stopped the lone alien vessel from attacking Earth. You're the hero who stopped an entire *battle* fleet from ending us before Jupiter got its chance. And you're the hero," he held into view a scrap of paper, "who boldly proclaimed she wanted to save all of *my* citizens."

He pushed his chair from the desk, leaned backward, and started swiveling back and forth. "You see, Mary, my citizens, the very ones you long to rescue, are in greater danger than either you or they could possibly imagine."

I'd had my fill. "Look, you simpering idiot, time's wasting. If you've got a point, get to it pronto. We're busy."

His sick smile cocked to one side of his face. "Talk about an abundance of heroes. Private Ryan's there, too. Oh, you probably didn't get the memo, but as CIC, I busted you to PFC." He furrowed his brow. "You okay knowing that little fact, private? Not too broken up? I'm told we have counselors for that type of situation, so let me know if I can help. I'd love to aid a war hero who's down on his luck."

"Eat Drano and die, Stuie."

"If you two boys," Mary cut in, "are done being macho, could we get to the reason for this call?"

Marshall looked suddenly businesslike and concerned. "Certainly, Secretary General Kahl. Here's the deal. You have alien technology I want. I *will* have it. I have several hundred million citizens you wish to rescue. If you provide me the technology I want, I will allow you immediate access to my people so you can begin to spirit them away." He spread open his arms. "Doesn't that seem like a win-win to you?"

Mary took no time to respond. "No deal, Marshall. One, I can never trust you. Two, you're leaving in a short while. I can probably get most of your people onboard worldships before the final hour, without your help *or* consent."

He rapped his fingers loudly on the table. "Predictable of the pedantic and linear-thinking mind. Hence, I'll add a second twist—sweeten the pot so to speak. If you *don't* give me the technology, the last order I issue from this office will be a blanket bombing of the USA with every nuclear and conventional explosive we're leaving behind. PS, that's a lot of firepower. Your precious prize will only go with you if you scrape their charred ashes off the scorched earth."

I knew for sure the lunatic wasn't bluffing. Mary had to know it, too. "Stuart, why? Why murder the people you're sworn to protect? Simply leave them for me to handle. Have you gone that completely mad?"

"Ah, but Hero Mary, then I wouldn't have my alien tech. I told you. I *will* have it."

Mary took a while to respond. "I'll have to discuss this with the full assembly. I'll let you know when we've decided."

"No problem, sugar," he said. "Take all the time you want. I'm leaving tomorrow, a little ahead of schedule, I'm afraid. I'll issue the order to nuke my nation at 17:00, local, if I haven't heard back. Now, I've kept you too long. Thank you for your time. And thank you in advance for that alien tech. I can't wait to get my grubby little paws on it." The holo disappeared.

Mary turned to me with a single thought. "Shit."

"I second that motion."

TWENTY-THREE

Marshall called for his final cabinet meeting to begin promptly at noon. All two hundred worldship czars (that was the term they voted to adopt) were in attendance. Along with them, individuals who weren't czars attended if their input was needed, such as directors at NASA or senior legislators. Naturally, General Kendell Jackson attended. Though he had not been gifted a worldship, he was an android. Sooner or later, it was assumed he'd be awarded one of his own. For the first time in as long as either Marshall or Jackson could remember, they were both giddy with joy as the meeting began, though their reasons to feel so happy were wildly different.

"All right, let's get this party started," Marshall said loudly. He waved people into their seats. "The sooner we start, the sooner we can begin our new lives aboard our ships." The significance of that remark was most compelling to the two hundred czars in the room. "I'll call for statements from the cabinet secretaries first, then the joint chiefs, and lastly from NASA. Please, please, please keep it short and sweet. I'm not in the mood for speeches. I'll turn the gavel over to my chief of staff. Here, Duncan, you take this. But, remember, crack some heads with it often and loudly."

"Okay," Duncan said above the noise, "everyone, sit down and shut up. State, where's State," Duncan scanned to room, "Ah, David. We'll start with you."

It took ninety minutes for the topic of discussion to come around to NASA. Jackson rose, cleared his throat out of habit, and began, "Good afternoon. NASA is doing well. I have no—"

He came to a stop when Frontera leaned over and whispered something into his ear.

"Now?" Jackson challenged hotly.

Frontera leaned in and whispered again.

Marshall didn't like being in the dark. "Frontera, please share with the rest of the class."

Frontera turned slowly, then looked back to Kendell, who nodded his agreement. "Ah, very well, Stuart. I was just telling the general I must step out. I just received word of a virus threatening the android mainframes. If we're not careful, it could leak out to the AI core. That would be bad."

Marshall chewed on his lower lip. "You certain this can't wait a few more minutes?"

Frontera was specific. "I must go *now*. The virus is expanding exponentially." He should know. He placed it in the computer himself late the night before. "If it breaks free, we'll lose all computer systems. Anyone currently an android would be in great jeopardy." He knew that last BS would do the trick.

"Very well," snapped Marshall. "Try and make it back if you can. You wouldn't want to miss the main attraction coming up right after your boss's report. Okay, Jackson, continue."

Kendell had little to say. He soon passed the microphone to a senior engineer. As the subsequent men droned on about this and that, Kendell zoned out. He scanned the room, looking at all the dead people and into all the burned-out eye sockets. He had a hard time not bursting out into laughter.

Finally, Duncan returned the gavel to Marshall. "You holo-boys 'bout ready?"

A separate video team had been waiting quietly in the corner. One of them nodded.

Marshall leaned over to Duncan. "Get me that bitch, Kahl, on the line." The president crossed his arms while waiting. "You there, Mary?"

"Yes," came a tired voice. "I wish I could ask you why you're calling."

"Oh, Mary, don't be so dramatic. You've been defeated. *I've* beaten you. It's normal to be a bit down in the dumps when someone rubs your face in shit. Get over it, bitch."

"Are you calling from a meeting?"

"I most certainly am. I want my friends to see me in my finest hour. Plus, I want them to see what it's like to cross me. I wish for everyone to know the consequences of not pleasing me fully. Do you have the technology plans ready to transfer?"

"What plans, sir?" It was Kendell asking.

"Need to know, son. You stay quiet like a good little colored fellow and let me finish this up."

"So, Mary—"

Duncan cut in. "Mr. President, I wasn't aware of a plan to get that tech."

"I'll have to have Jackson and you form a 'didn't-need-to-know' support group. You're not in the loop because I left you out, son."

Another voice called out, "What plan?"

Mary sat up, energized. "You never *told* them, Stuart? Why, you son of a *bitch*. Stuart Marshall called us yesterday and threatened to nuke all US citizens not currently aboard your worldships if I don't give him the force field plans." She slapped her hands together. "And my day was so bleak up until now. Thank you, Stuart. My mood has soared."

The room exploded in shouts. Marshall pulled the sidearm he'd begun carrying lately. He fired three shots into the ceiling. "If that doesn't shut you up, next time I'm shooting into the crowd." That quieted the room instantly. "That's better. Now, if I might conclude my—"

"Mr. President, a moment." It was Jackson. He was rounding the table and approaching Marshall at a jog. "As head of NASA, I'd like to make one statement." He was halfway to Marshall, whose face grew long in worry. "It will only take—"

Marshall aimed his pistol at Kendell. "Stop there." Jackson froze. "That's close enough."

Jackson slowly raised his hands. "Mr. President, please lower your weapon. I'm trying to make an announcement about the force field. Remember, I'm the only one here whose—"

"Freeze." Marshall had noted Kendell's forward creeping motion. "You got something to say, you say it from there. You've got ten seconds." Marshall checked his watch. The gun was trained on Kendell's right eye.

Jackson stood at attention. "Very well. I want to tell my family I love them very much. I want them to understand I did this for them—"

The last three shots in the revolver flew out from Stuart's magnum. All three struck Kendell in the right upper face. Shrapnel flew off in a wide arch. Kendell spun what remained of his head back to look at Marshall, who was rapidly reloading. The final words in the peculiar existence of Kendell Jackson were heard loudly and clearly, by all present and listening on the live feed.

"I preprogrammed myself to explode one minute after I stood up, you piece of shit. Now, do the universe a favor and die."

The room's light became blinding. Scattered screams were heard before the feed went dead.

"Quickly," shouted Mary, "go to the satellite view."

The satellite image was picture perfect. Crisp and clear on a cloudless day. It initially showed the White House sitting in its typical, stately form. Cars, pedestrians, and bike riders swirled around the building. Then, a bright light could be seen coming from all the windows. The light grew in intensity until it began burning whatever it touched. Trees erupted in flames, and people screamed as they threw themselves into snow piles. The walls of the structure exploded and then were immediately hidden by dust and debris.

Several hours later, the satellite image showed a thirty-meter crater where the White House had once been. It was deeper than it was wide, as the bulk of the blast began deep in the reinforced part of the building. No remnant of the underground structure could be identified, at least from that height.

Before dawn the next morning, UN planes occupied United States airspace. Squadrons of helicopters landed in predesignated locations. The personnel needed to construct temporary rocket gantries and launch pads hit the ground running. Like clockwork, facilities sufficient to evacuate anyone who wanted to leave Earth were up and functioning. It was March 15, 2050. By April 9, four hundred million US citizens were relocated to temporary lodging in high Earth orbit. On April 12, 2050, the last of the worldships was loaded, locked, and powering toward the rendezvous point.

Just under nine billion humans began humankind's greatest adventure.

TWENTY-FOUR

Sapale and I lingered near Earth the week before its annihilation. Several research vessels joined us. It turned out that planetary scientists were anxious to observe the once-in-a-lifetime collision firsthand. There was a sober mood, considering what was about to happen, but they found it hard to suppress their excitement. Me? I was mostly numb.

By April 15, 2050, the Earth was already significantly deformed by Jupiter's powerful gravitational field. Though she was still in one piece, she was stretched in the shape of an egg pointing away from Jupiter. Fragments and debris streamed toward the giant planet. But, she made it through the day, which was mildly annoying. We're still going to have to file our income tax statements. Death and taxes, ironically combined. Midmorning April 16, the Earth touched Jupiter's gaseous surface. Ten minutes later, she was gone. It was like an actor slipping behind a theater curtain. No noise, no fanfare, just a gentle ripple.

Though I was incapable of either, I felt tears well up and a tightness in my chest. My thoughts drifted back to six months earlier—

****

"Jonryan. It's wonderful to see you," Offlin shouted as soon as he glimpsed my approach.

"Back atcha." I snapped my fingers and pointed at him through the glass.

"So, the great man spares this humble prisoner of war some of his time. I should be impressed." He paused. "But I'm not. I know you too well." He trilled at his levity.

"Can't I catch a break? You're a tough audience to please."

"So, Sapale and the kids are well?"

"Couldn't be better."

"And the sexes. What did she finally decide on?"

"One boy, one girl."

"And their names?"

"My daughter's name is Fashallana. Which means *blessed one* in Sapale's native tongue."

"Very nice. And the boy."

I looked at the ground. "Jonathan Ryan II. Which means I lost *that* argument."

"What? You should be honored."

"Kind of a stuffy name, if you ask me."

"Then you're a silly man." He trilled merrily. "Seriously, what brings you to see this old fish?"

"Earth's about over. Jupiter will swallow her up in a few months. I came to see what you'd like to do. You have some pretty nice choices. You can return to *Ark 1* like before and join us in the airlock. It's kind of tight, but you're family and we'd love to have you. You can also go to the worldship built to house all the sea creatures we're bringing. It's huge. You'd hardly know you were confined. Finally, Toño can build you a tank in his lab. What do you think? What'll it be?"

He paddled gently backward. His expression was sad. "None of the above."

"What? I can't just leave you here." I indicated the tank. "You'll be killed."

"Jonryan. I'm a very old fish. My scales fall off and my joints ache. I've outlived my spawn family. I've a different request, if you'll grant it."

"You name it. I'll make it happen."

"Release me into your ocean."

That I had not anticipated. "But —"

"I'll die soon no matter which choice I make. We can't alter Gumnolar's will."

I was stunned. "If that's what you want, I'll take you personally whenever you're ready."

He looked at me a good, long while. "Thank you, Jon. I'll say my goodbyes to Toño, and then I would like to depart."

"No prob." I stood there still stunned. Then I asked, "Why?"

"I long to swim free. I've been confined here a long time. If I'd ask this of you before, your superiors would not have allowed it." He trilled sadly. "They'd worry I'd use bubbles to somehow signal Listhelon." Then a spark glowed in his eyes. "I want to find one of those white sharks." He patted a fin on his chest. "Yeah, see how tough he really is. And I wish to touch a coral reef. They are so beautiful in the holos. I want to breathe those waters. Plus," he fluttered his eyes, "I might dive down one of those deep trenches and see if I can find me one of those pretty girls."

"You should be ashamed of yourself, very old fish."

"I've been in here a long time." We shared a good laugh.

"Okay, but if I start getting complaints from the SPCA, I'll bring you right back here."

I flew Offlin to the Great Barrier Reef that same day. I hovered just above the surface and opened the outer airlock doors. A *kerplop* later, and Offlin was swimming in his new home. He dove down deep, then returned to the surface. He waved me closer. "I told you long ago that someday I would kill you."

Oh, crap. I hoped I wouldn't have to slice him up with my laser finger.

He lofted a fin from the water and reached toward me. "Know, my good friend, that I no longer wish to do so."

We slapped palms and he was gone.

I never saw him again or heard one word of what he did. He was a good friend. I'll miss him for a very long time.

****

As I stood watching Jupiter envelop Earth my thoughts were with Offlin. I hoped he was deep in a trench and wouldn't notice anything until his surroundings vaporized. I prayed he'd feel no pain.

There was scientific debate about exactly what would happen to Earth. The relative velocities of the two planets meant that Jupiter was not going to

103

fully capture the smaller body. But how much of Earth would exist and in what form was unknown. Three days later, the question was answered. Jupiter spit out a very hot, rocky mess. Gone was the air, all of the water, and a sizable amount of the solid material. New Earth, which it was immediately dubbed, was one-third the mass of her former self. The irregular, rocky surface was partially covered by molten lava that once resided near her core. Remotes were sent down to confirm the obvious. No life, in any form, existed on Earth. Basically, she was a big, searing asteroid. All the beauty and splendor that was Earth was now nothing more than scattered molecules churning in Jupiter's atmosphere. What a waste. What a loss.

But, as sad as those realizations were, I did have to reflect on the miracle we'd pulled off. Not only was the bulk of the human population safe, but a significant representation of the plant and animal life was, too. In spite of ourselves, we'd done it. Over ten thousand worldships steamed off to who knew where. Each carried a contingent of livestock, such as chickens, pigs, and cows. Aquaculture for fish was available on each ship. Additionally, most had impressive zoological collections. These were not just to provide the family with a fun place to visit; they were engineered to preserve the species we cherished. No one could say if we'd ever successfully relocate any of them to the wild, but at least we saved many.

The ocean worldship I mentioned to Offlin was impressive. Its sole function was to sustain sea life on an indefinite basis. The asteroid was cored cylindrically, as opposed to spherically. That way, the artificial gravity would hold the water to the perimeter, while allowing the central space to hold air for the sea mammals. Apex predators, such as orcas and the bigger sharks, were segregated from more placid species to help both populations stabilize. With any luck, it would work.

There were a million horrible aspects to the destruction of Earth. It was a certifiable tragedy. However, there were a few things I was jazzed about. No more mosquitos. Fleas and ticks were a thing of the past. All animals brought onto worldships were screened for them. If any showed up, the infestation was dealt with immediately. The common housefly? No longer common. It was raised as food for other species, but it would never again land on my sandwich. And what about those pesky leeches? Gone, unlamented, I should add. I personally wished they'd left hyenas behind, because they're so damn ugly. No one, however, asked for my approval or input. They're somewhere on our flotilla, but if I never see one again, it will be A-OK by me. They smell bad, too. Revolting creatures.

But in the final analysis, the disappearance of species with the passing of Earth was truly mind-boggling. All the insect life in the tropics, all the undiscovered animals at the bottom of the seas, and those creatures too fragile to survive in captivity were gone. Gone forever. Most of us felt the loss like a physical blow.

Worldships were big, slow slugs. While the Arks could zip around near the speed of light, those puppies could only roll along like watermelons. Over time, it was conceivable that they might reach ten kilometers per second. While that sounds fast, remember the distances that they had to travel were enormous. It took me ten years to get to Barnard's Star, which was six light-years away. It would take a worldship one hundred fifty years the make that same trip. Yeah, that's why we also called them "generational ships." To make it to a star system one hundred light-years away would take twenty-five hundred years. There were just five hundred sun-like stars within that distance. The pickings were few and far between. The fleet was in for a long trip.

On the subject of worldships, I've always found the design and infrastructure they contain interesting. There were large agencies in charge of those aspects. I mean, millions of souls were going to spend a long time onboard. They needed to function, sure. Life support, wastewater recycling, and food production were obvious necessities. But, issues of how ornate to make them or what types of leisure activities to build in them were huge. How many recreational facilities were enough? Should there be lakes, and trails, and mountains? How about "wild" animals? Because of the ships, people would *survive*, but would they really *live*? Ostensibly, the ships were supposed to transport mass numbers of people to a new planet. But, it was just as likely that the worldship might end up being the final destination for the inhabitants. Perhaps the population would decide to remain put, as opposed to relocating on a new planet. If nothing else, the worldships would always be a safe place in a hostile universe.

The plan was to try and keep the ships as close together as possible. That way, a person would have the option of visiting another worldship, and maybe even moving to a new one. Also, resources could be shared, as opposed to reinvented. Inevitably, however, some ships would decide to break off on their own. Some coalition might elect to head for a certain planet that some other group thought was unwise. As the numbers thinned out, the worldships had to remain self-sustainable. Those considerations brought up the issue of governance. It was not fair or feasible to dictate the system of government for all autonomous crafts. But there was no precedence as to how to let a system of order evolve. A civil war on a worldship, based on a poorly structured leadership, could end catastrophically.

There was also the issue of societal structure. Glad I wasn't in charge of that one. Most of the bad apples were left on Earth, but new bad ones would inevitably crop up and need to be dealt with. Also, ongoing education, materials production, and technological advancements needed to be built into the society. How would labor be organized? There had to be some motivation to get out of bed and go to work before the world ended. The guy in charge of cleaning the sewage plant would *not* be doing so for the simple joy of the work. He had to have a good reason to perform that critical job. Money could be used as the glue to keep things together, but what would be done with someone who refused to contribute at all? Tough issues. Glad I was a flyboy.

TWENTY-FIVE

Six months into the human exodus, most worldships had arrived at the rendezvous point. Those that weren't quite there would be soon. Up to that point, all the ships were functioning perfectly. A few redundant backup systems had failed here and there, but they'd all been quickly repaired. People settled in with minimum friction and, more importantly, whining. One thing I found mildly amusing was the early task of reassigning the hundreds of thousands of women who had been sent to what became known as the "harem ships." Their families had to be located, and large numbers of people shuffled to and fro. What a mess. But, it was satisfying to disassemble the working of the insane US leadership. Everyone involved understood how horrible it would have been for those women if Jackson had not successfully taken out the overlords. Wow. Just wow. What a bunch of sickos. It's one thing to have juvenile fantasies, but it's another matter altogether to try and inflict them on the innocent and in massive numbers. Won't be missing those guys.

It was time for our first real decision as a fleet. Where were we to go? As I mentioned, there were a few outstanding candidate planets, along with a handful of pretty good options. Each worldship had elected a governor. He or she was more like the captain of the vessel, but in the interest of making it sound like the ships weren't run by the military, *governor* was the title chosen. Some form of elected council had been formed, also. The UN had decreed that a tripartite government be instituted, much like the USA or Great Britain used to have. One had to keep in mind that this would be completely new for many cultures. Honestly, if a ship refused to go in that direction, there was nothing to force them to comply. Luckily, everyone was more worried about survival than ego, at least at the start.

Secretary Kahl announced there would be a joint meeting of the governors to discuss our final destination. Once recommendations were hammered out, they would be taken back to the respective assemblies for debate and a vote. Me, I was thinking it was good the ships were designed to keep generations comfortable, because that was about how long it figured to take for all those politicos to agree on one destination. I was reminded of the initial meeting to establish an armistice for the Korean War back in the 1950s. They spent the first few months discussing what size and shape the negotiation table would be. Soldiers and civilians were dying while politicians discussed furniture dimensions. No one was going to be railroaded into a table that was too round. Or too straight. Or too, Heaven forbid, both. Yeah, the new home consensus might just take forever.

Finding a space large enough to hold the meeting physically was a challenge. There were, after all, 10,652 worldships. That meant 10,652 governors needed to attend. Adding staff, reporters, onlookers, experts, and caterers made the group nearly twenty-thousand in number. That took a large amphitheater to accommodate. Not very amenable to discussion, but there was no alternative. Basically, there were a few dignitaries on stage, with questions or comments from the audience texted to a clearing hub. Most of the work was to be done in smaller breakout sessions.

Exoplanet specialists for each of the candidate systems gave a detailed presentation to the main assembly. That took several days. Next, small-group discussions took place to see where agreement might be reached and where differences could be hashed out. That took weeks. Finally, everyone got together to hear Kahl's summary of all the possible targets. Four planets were chosen as the most promising. The names were to be taken back to each assembly, where they would debate and rank the options. The planet selected would be the planet with the most votes. It was a binding, winner-take-all arrangement. Like I said before, there was no way to force a ship to tag along against its population's will, but nothing more than minimum dissent was hoped for.

Of the four planets to be voted on, one was BS 3, the one where I found Ffffuttoe. That made me proud. Validation was a good thing. One of the others, with the unsexy name Groombridge-1618 3, was almost too good to be true. The star was sixteen light-years away and a bit smaller than our sun. BG 3 was basically Earth, maybe five hundred thousand years ago. No sentients discovered, perfect atmosphere, plentiful water, and mild seasons. The place teemed with life, and no species was deal-breaker awful. You know, T. rex, megalodon bad. The worldships could be there in maybe four hundred years. Not a hop, skip, and a jump, but doable. I figured that would be the winning choice, even over my find.

The four options weren't close enough to allow us to head in the general direction of them all. So, the fleet basically held at the rendezvous point until the decision was made. Betting as to how long that would take ranged from weeks to years. I put some money on six months, but that might just have been wishful thinking. It was funny. I hated waiting for a decision that would delay our four-hundred-year voyage. Yeah, seriously, there was no hurry. Only us androids would be around to see the journey's end.

Acknowledging that fact brought me to the next focal point in my life. What were Sapale, the kids, and I to do? Gulp. We had been staying on the main UN worldship up until then. I told Sapale I was feeling claustrophobic and asked if we could return home to *Ark 1*. She pointed out that I was insane for thinking our ship was less confining than the massive worldship, but she had no objection.

After a few days back onboard, I broached the subject that weighed on me so heavily. "So, what do you want to do? Where do you want to settle down with the kids?"

She eyed me suspiciously. "What options do you think there are?"

I waved my hands in the air. "I don't know, lots of them I guess."

She put a fist on her hip. "Name three."

"Well, we could live on a worldship."

"Obviously."

"We could live here," I drew her attention to the floor.

"Even more obvious. But can you name a third?"

"Sure." Not really. "We could, you know, go somewhere else."

"Like—?"

"Another worldship," I said with more conviction than I felt. She looked at me intently but didn't bother to answer. "Hey, *you* tell *me*. We can take *Ark 1* anywhere we want."

"Aside from getting somewhere before those flying buckets do, why, exactly, would that matter?" There was a gleam in her eyes.

"We could return to Kaljax."

Her expression collapsed. "They'd still execute me. The kids, too, for that matter. Why would I go there?"

"Maybe we can give them some bargaining chip, something that would make them leave you alone."

"What would you offer?"

That was tough. They were fairly advanced. "You told me there was nothing like an AI on Kaljax. We could offer that technology."

She angled her head. "That might work, but not for certain. Remember, I'm a rebel. That's a hated person on my world."

"Look, to make you happy, I'd offer the membrane tech." I really, really hoped it would never come to that.

"You'd give those militaristic, power-hungry politicians *that?*" No. I probably wouldn't. Eventually, they might use it against humans. "No," she answered for me, "I don't think so."

"Maybe we can think of something. A trade arrangement, maybe." She still looked unmoved. "Okay, let me turn this around. What would you like to do? What third thing can you dream up?"

"Perhaps we should just stay here, raise the kids, and try to be happy."

"Wow, that sounds both unconvincing *and* unappealing."

She looked away. "At least you'd be with *your* people. You'd have a chance to be happy."

I shook my head. "This is sounding worse and worse the more you talk. Okay, now at least I know living on a worldship is out." I walked over and took her in my arms. "What shall we do, brood's-mate?" I could feel her begin to tremble.

We stood there a long time. Finally, she lifted her head off my shoulder and looked right into my eyes. "If you really want to know what I'd like to do, I'll tell you. But you have to promise not to laugh. Okay?"

A woman bares her soul to her spouse and he laughs. That would never end well on Earth, on Kaljax, or in the depths of hell. Tenderly, I asked, "What would you like to do? I won't even snicker."

She pulled free and gathered strength of commitment. "You and I know the vote will be to go to Groombridge-1618 3, right? The other choices are much riskier."

I nodded. "Agreed."

Her eyes flared with life. "Let's go there first and start a civilization of our own."

Huh? No, don't say *huh*. Death would ensue in five seconds. She was being so passionate. Be understanding and supportive, even if she's lost it. "Could you share a little more of your vision with me?"

Her eyelids narrowed. "Go there first and start our own civilization. That's it. That's my vision. Apparently it's not yours."

"Ah, it's not that it's not my *vision*, I'm just not *seeing* it." Crap, crap, crap. Why not offer her my sidearm and be done with this?

"Okay. Would you like me to flesh my vision out for you a bit more?"

Salvation. "Sure, if you don't mind."

"We go to BG 3, give it a proper name, and begin to grow a colony of Kaljaxians, free from the oppression and control of my home world."

"Okay. Let me state right now that I'm excited about the plan. I'm all-in."

"But?"

"Yeah, not so much a *but* as a *could you be more specific how we make that happen, physiologically* kind of query?"

"You want a picture? Maybe graphs and projections?"

"No, no. Just take me past how three related organisms, two-thirds of them brother and sister, establish a thriving population."

"Jon, isn't that pretty obvious?"

Yikes. "Yes, but—and that's an actual but—I'm not so comfortable having Jon Jr. and Fashallana," I meshed my fingers together, "you know, doing the actual groundwork."

111

"You are *so* thick. They wouldn't," she meshed her fingers together too, "be laying any groundwork. That's gross. Shame on you. Plus, it wouldn't work if they did. They're too closely related; the inbreeding would knock the wheels off that bus, sooner or later."

Whoo. "Great, I'm glad we agree on that. So, how exactly does your vision roll out?"

"I've given this some thought. My plan is as foolproof as it is simple."

This, I had to hear. I always loved fairytales.

"We check the kids's DNA to determine if they have the same father. It's possible they don't. In any case, I will have several more children and make them all girls. I can have the doctors flush out my sperm-sack and transfer a portion to each female. There are several gene lines represented there."

I reflexively raised a finger. "Just how many gene lines are we talking here, hon?"

At least she was able to provide me with a concise, clear, and unambiguous answer. She slapped my face with convincing conviction. "As I was saying, the girls will be able to produce genetically diverse offspring. Over time, there would, naturally, be some return to more traditional methods of population maintenance."

"You mean—" I meshed my fingers together.

"Yes, at some point in the midterm future. But, don't you see? In a handful of generations, we could establish a healthy, sustainable, and free population of my species."

Al cut in without being asked. "In five generations, a population of twenty thousand is easily achievable. From there, the numbers would expand exponentially. Two more generations would put the population in the range of one-million. Assuming ten years between generations, a reasonable figure. Given Kaljaxian physiology and proclivity to task, that figure could be accomplished in approximately seventy-five years."

Sapale finished his train-of-thought. "That's less than a quarter of the time it would take the mass of humans to arrive. By the time they did, there'd be a flourishing society in place."

I had to ask a bit dubiously, "To what, help them settle in?"

She caught my concern. "Yes."

"Or to ask them to move on down the road, because GB 3 was already spoken for?"

With profound empathy she said, "That's where you come in, brood-mate. You'd be there the whole time to make sure that didn't happen." She had a point. I could be a constant moral compass for the burgeoning civilization. I couldn't, there and then, think of a better way to spend that portion of eternity.

"You know, I think we have ourselves a plan." For that, I got a kiss. Well, a kiss and a tad more, but recall please, I am—above all—a gentleman.

TWENTY-SIX

Well, I lost twenty bucks. The decision to make GB 3 humanity's collective target took only two and a half months. I need to stop being so fundamentally pessimistic. Maybe. That was fine and good. All the worldships assumed a heading in that direction. As cruising velocities differ from ship to ship, the fleet spread out, so they committed to traveling in pods. A pod was fifty or so craft, all committed to staying close enough together to assure mutual aid, should it become necessary. Also, in the event of Listhelon attack, a pod's defenses would be superior to a lone ship.

My dim view of politicians was reinforced, however, when it came to choosing a name for GB 3. That took twelve years. Yeah. *New Earth*? No, the name looked to the past, not the future. Huh? Whatever. *Sanctuary*? No, it implied we were needy. Double-huh? We were. We really, really needed a new home. Whatever. *Nova*, Latin for *new*? No, Latin-based languages were not to be championed over other languages. Oh, my. I didn't bother telling anyone that by the time they got there, the place would have a name in Hirn, Sapale's native dialect.

The first person I shared our intentions with was Toño. I trusted him and valued his take on how we should proceed. He was, against all odds, becoming quite expert in the dark art of politics.

"So," he said, rubbing his chin, "you would leave us and strike out on your own? I don't see why not. In fact, good for you." He snapped his fingers. "I'm coming with you."

"What?" I couldn't stop that from slipping out.

A rebuffed Toño asked, "What, you don't want me along?"

"No, no," I backpedaled, "we'd love to have you. I just figured you were sort of committed, you know, to stay here. You *are* the scientific director of the UN, after all."

He set his jaw firmly. "I was. There are no nations left. Just a bunch of asteroids. Let them find their own director. I've more than paid my dues, thank you very much. Over paid them, in fact." Yes, he had. Many times over.

I held my hand over to him. "Welcome aboard. I could stand some male company, for once." After we chuckled, I did have to add, "We will be a wee bit crowded, if you don't mind. *Ark 1* was designed, as you well know, for only one passenger."

"Oh, but we shall not be taking *that* old ship. I'm already working on a new one. Bigger, faster, and much cooler looking."

"How much cooler? Don't forget, you're a science nerd." I tented the digits of my right hand on my chest, "I, however, am a fighter pilot. I'm the final authority on cool things that fly."

"Here. See for yourself." He reached into a lab coat, produced a crumpled piece of paper, and handed it to me. It was a drawing of a ship. Man, was it *ever* cool looking.

"Doc, that's the most bitchin' ship I've ever seen. When'll she be ready?"

"In about six months. She's partially assembled down in the engineering department, if you'd like to have a peek."

"Is it okay if we run?"

As I entered the hangar, I was even more impressed. The ship was huge, at least compared to mine. Her metal skeleton was nearly complete. She was shaped somewhat like a spearhead, only thicker toward the stern and flatter in general. Gone was the long needle nose needed to minimize damage from space debris. No doubt, he'd designed membranes to perform that function. I estimated she was at least five times larger than *Ark 1*. That was good. Sapale was already pregnant with another set of twins. She told me that, if she could, she'd like to have ten to twelve children, total. We'd need the room. Lord in Heaven, it hit me then. I'd be in a spaceship with a dozen teenage daughters, and nowhere to run. Maybe Toño could design a really secure man cave?

"Impressive, eh?"

"You can say that again. Doc, she's beautiful."

"She's the first in the new class of scout ships. They'll gradually replace the Ark Series. Explorations are likely to take longer in the future, so we wanted a ship that could carry live humans, if need be. When the time comes, I'll tell them truthfully that you and I are going exploring. Naturally, Sapale, the kids, and Ffffuttoe would come with us. We're family. No one will question us in the slightest." He looked at the ship like it was the first time he'd ever seen her, excitement dancing in his eyes. "It will be grand, my friend. We shall have a *great* adventure."

"Trust me on this one, Toño," I set my hand on his sleeve, "you shouldn't ask for a *great* adventure. Those are the ones that just might get you killed. But, one more question," I said.

"Yes?"

"What's the purpose of having the hull be so highly polished? Does it help repel cosmic rays or something?"

"No, my good man. It makes her look that much cooler."

I returned to our apartment on the worldship and told Sapale about Toño's plan and about the new ship. She was dubious at first. She didn't actually say it, but I think she was concerned about breaking up our current, tight-knit group. But she came around, sooner rather than later, and actually became quite excited. She really liked the idea of having lots of room. Woman that she was, she immediately began to talk of interior design, decor, and room appointments. I hope Doc was ready for the womanly touch, because he was going to get a lot of it.

Toño and I presented our case for taking the new Lambda class ship to GB 3—still no name, six months later—to perform more detailed analysis. We would also start planning where cities might be best located, for when the worldships started to arrive. After little debate or discussion, our project was given the green light. We'd be leaving in two to three months, depending on how construction proceeded.

As everything was falling into place, I had to make one matter clear to Toño. Al would have to be transferred to the new ship. It was one of my must-haves for the new ride. That's when he brought up something troubling. Having Al reassigned would not be a problem, he reassured me. There was to be, however, a *second* AI onboard. Neither AI would be the top dog, but rather, they were to work in concert as well as provide backup for each other. I asked him if he'd spent much time working with Al since our return. Doc said he had. I asked him if he thought Al would play well with another AI. He said he didn't see why not. That's when I asked him again if he'd spent much time working with Al since our return. Doc just looked at me, kind of confused. I let it pass. I just extracted the promise for Toño that he'd be the one to tell Al about the other AI, not me. Even more puzzled, he agreed. Man, was he in for it.

As we neared our time of departure, now-Governor Kahl called a meeting of her advisors, which included Toño and me. I figured it was to make arrangements for Toño's replacement and to wish us luck. Unfortunately, there was more.

"We've naturally," Mary began, "been in close contact with all the worldships since we set sail for GB 3. Everyone reports good mechanical function and the absence of societal issues." That was a rather standard opening remark at such gatherings. Until otherwise challenged, Mary was assumed to be the overall leader of the Earth's refugees. Accordingly, she made it her business to watch over her flock very closely. "I wanted to discuss a few, oh, I don't know, *troubling* communications we've had with some ships."

"How so?" someone asked. "What sort of trouble?"

"Not really trouble, I guess. It's more pushback. Yes, that's it, *pushback.*"

"I hate to be the one to say it, but pushback from some of ten thousand petty fiefdoms is pretty easy to anticipate," I said.

"To be certain," Mary agreed. "Maybe it's just that this is the *first,* that makes me so sensitive to it."

"Growing pains were expected at some point," Toño added.

"Yes," she replied.

"What exactly was the pushback?" her chief assistant asked.

"Oh, nothing big. We have, as you all know, strict guidelines for food allocations and rations. Everyone receives highly nutritious meals. But proteins are managed closely. Soy or egg are the basic protein sources. For each individual fish is available twice per week and chicken twice per month. Red meat is at such a premium that we only offer it to those who request it three times per year."

"And?" her assistant pressed.

"Lately, some of the ships are asking for increased allotments of chicken, and especially red meat."

"If they want to waste their resources on red meat production, let them do it. When they fall on their faces, it will, perhaps, teach them a valuable lesson," Toño said.

"That's just it. They want to obtain either meat, or grains to produce meat, from other ships. The farm ships specifically." There were five worldships with very few inhabitants and massive food production facilities. Each worldship was designed to be fully autonomous, but such specialty ships allowed for flexibility and some small luxuries, like the red meat.

"That's out of the question." said Andreas Nikolaidis, our Secretary of Human Nutrition. "Everyone was told the ground rules, and everyone will live by them equally. Period." Nick was nothing if not a passionate man.

"There's a twist," Mary added. "They're requesting it as a medical necessity, not out of dietary preference."

"What?" hissed Nick. "That's preposterous. No one *needs* red meat to stay alive. Even the *tigers* we feed soy meal for the most part. Again, I say no."

"Still, if it's a medical request —" Mary trailed off.

"How much of a gift are they asking for?" I asked.

She fingered her chin. "Not that much, at least for now. A five percent increase over their allotment."

"I think it would be best if I spoke to some of these doctors who are prescribing red meat to their patients." Nick was hot.

"No," soothed Mary, "but I will ask our medical board to do just that. If they smell a rat, we can turn you loose on them as punishment." That brought giggles from everyone but Nick. He puffed up and pouted.

"Which ships?" I wondered out loud.

"A few of the American ones. Most American worldships aren't asking, but all of the requests did come from their vessels."

"Big surprise there." huffed Nick. "Probably want to eat too many cheeseburgers, like they did back on Earth."

TWENTY-SEVEN

The time couldn't pass fast enough for the new scout ship to be ready. I was anxious to be doing something again. Sitting on a slow-moving rock waiting for everyone around me to wither and die wasn't my idea of a nice vacation. GB 3 was about sixteen light-years away. With the new ship, we could probably be there in twenty years, instead of the worldships' four hundred. In fact, they were so slow that any time dilation effect from moving near the speed of light wouldn't effect them, since they wouldn't get anywhere near it. Our twenty years would be thirty-some years for them, but compared to four hundred, it, too, didn't matter at all.

As our launch date neared, the pressure on me mounted. Toño said I would select the ship's name. He even playfully warned Sapale not to try and influence my decision. He said she was going to name a whole planet, so she should leave the name of the tiny ship to me. Recall that with *Ark 1*, I wanted to name her *Pequod* or *USS Enterprise*. Now that I could actually choose, those sounded childish. I could've just named her *Sapale*, but that was too obvious. Plus, I didn't know that I wanted that strong a reminder of her in a couple hundred years. It dawned on me that I might have to give the ship a grown-up name. Wow, had I ever changed! I was going to age like Peter Pan, and I fully intended to act like a kid forever. The name thing threatened my self-image.

I decided on a preliminary name, but told no one and reserved the right to change it when I found another. *Shearwater*. Now, don't gasp or anything. It's a type of medium-sized seabird that wanders vast distances over the world's oceans. Well, it *did*. It doesn't anymore. I thought it was a very cool name. *Albatross* was too big a name for our medium-sized spaceship. Plus, albatross had too much baggage. The bird was bad luck to kill, and I didn't want the words "bad" and "luck" anywhere near my new ship. Also, a famous one sank years ago. Apparently, it was a particularly sad event. No, *Shearwater* was cool. *Albatross* was way too risky. Plus, *shear*-water. Think about it. Kinda brings to mind a tough dude like me with a knife—maybe a switchblade—*shearing* stuff. I believed I had my ship's name.

In the weeks before we shoved off, we all moved to our ship's quarters. Sapale and I had a suite. Several rooms joined, much like a large apartment. Ffffuttoe had one of those rooms to herself. I didn't even offer her a space of her own for personal privacy. She was so devoted to the children, I couldn't imagine she'd want to be separated from the oncoming avalanche of kids. I wasn't actually sure how long the Toe lived. I asked her a few times, but she always answered, "until they die." Until she passed she was indispensable for us and a constant delight.

Sapale beamed with more and more joy as our departure approached. It wasn't just because she wanted to start her epic project. No, she was dying to move into our quarters, which she seemed, more often than not, to refer to as *her* quarters. Most of all, believe it or not, she wanted to use her tub. She'd designed a tub to "give the children a proper scrubbing" whenever they needed it. I had an intimation that'd be more often than they might appreciate. But, with so many new additions planned, she insisted that good hygiene was critical. You know, whenever she said that to me, I got the funniest feeling. Like she planned on scrubbing *me*, periodically, too.

Toño had a tiny room attached to a spacious lab. He loved it. Every detail was specified by him personally. He worked endlessly, had no hobbies or vices, and never slept. He'd discovered, as I had, that dreamless sleep was piss-ass poor sleep and a waste of time.

One aspect of the long voyage began to trouble me. Toño had his space and would be sequestered there a lot. Sapale would soon have a gaggle of geese to manage, so she'd be unavailable for chitchat. That left me the odd man out, with only Al and the new AI. I'd be the target of what were certain to be

Al's endless complaints, rejections, and rants against his new playmate. That seemed really bleak, more of a sentence than an adventure. Hey, maybe they'd get along so well, both AIs would leave me alone. Yeah. Must remember to pack lots of alcohol for my period of confinement. A still. Perfect. A big still. I'd put a tech on it right away.

True to his word, Toño told Al about the new AI before he installed it. Afterward, he came by my study. "I've just finished installing the new AI."

"No, you didn't," I said flatly.

"Pardon?"

"You look too good. After you switch the new one on, Al would browbeat you to within an inch of your life." I turned back to my computer screen. "You look fine."

"Seriously, I think you're wrong on this matter. He'll do well. Jon, he's a machine. You know this, right?"

"I'll just stay put right here on I-Told-You-So Island and wait for you to swim over to me with your tail between your legs. You will arrive sooner rather than later. Not to worry, though, I possess much alcohol."

He left in a mild huff. He had piqued my curiosity, though. I invented a reason to go the bridge, so I could gauge Al's mood. I fiddled around with a still-exposed servo, pretending to adjust it or something. "Hey, Al," I called out, "run a test on this circuit. It looks loose to me." Nothing. "Al, the ship's AI, *please* run a diagnostic on this mechanism." Nada. I took a deep breath. "Alvin, report in."

I heard a muffled sound, quite reminiscent of a person speaking through a gag. Oh boy it had already started. "Alvin, please repeat." The same *hum-humum-huumum* was broadcast on the bridge. "Okay, you get one chance to say that so I can understand it. If you don't, I'm bringing Toño here to see how childish you're being."

"I know I'll get a caning, but alright, I'll remove the duct tape from my mouth. Remember, you *ordered* me to. I said the following. *I'm not authorized to respond. You must first check with my supervising AI.*"

"Al, there *is* no supervising AI. The *Shearwater* has two equal computers. Please don't be so pissy right out of the gate."

"Hummumum hum humum."

"Let me guess. *That's what* you *think?*"

"Hum."

I stormed out. "I need a drink."

"Hum *Hum.*"

It was going to be a *long* flight.

A few days before we departed, Carlos De La Frontera and Prime boarded to help Toño install something. We called the android Frontera "Prime" to distinguish him from the human version. Since Marshall was long gone, the original Carlos came out of hiding and worked openly with Toño and Prime on android construction. It was most weird, at first, to have two of him around. A bold new world was upon us. Anyway, Prime said he and Carlos has been appointed joint science directors, effective after Toño's departure. It was a fitting arrangement. They were nearly as capable as Toño. Plus, for the foreseeable future, Toño was available for consultation.

"I don't mean to seem insensitive," I said to Carlos and Prime, "but how are you going to decide which one of you is in charge? I mean, what if one of you says *plus,* while the other maintains that it's *minus?*"

They looked at me, then each other, and then back to me. One of them said, "We can't imagine that will come up."

The other Carlos added, "If it *were* to come up, we'd discuss it professionally and arrive at a consensus."

"As to whether it's up versus down?" I said skeptically. "Between two diametrically opposed positions? Humph. Heads-in-the-clouds."

Toño spoke as if woken from sleep. "Wait, Jon's right." Both Carloses snapped their heads in my direction quickly, as if to say, *which Jon are you referring to?*

"Yes," Toño repeated with excitement. "Which means you should come with us, too, Prime."

I was getting dizzy watching. The Carloses looked at each other, then Toño, and then, for unclear reasons, to *me*. It was like watching a pinball clang around. Prime spoke for the committee. "I've not considered that." He reflected a moment or two. "You know, that's nothing short of a marvelous idea. If you'll have me, I'd love to join your ragtag band. "

Ragtag? Who's ragtag? We had a cool ship with an even cooler name. I'd need to set Prime straight.

Carlos asked Toño, "Do you think I can handle the job alone?"

"But of course." responded Toño. "I did, and you're every bit as clever. Plus, though it doesn't bother me to have two of you, your children might become confused as they grow."

"Then it's settled. The three of us shall travel as one." Prime was stoked.

"Do you possibly mean the *four of us?*"

He spun to see Sapale in her patented one-fist-on-hip stance. "Oh, hi, Sapale. Of course I meant *the four of us!*"

"Shall I leave the children behind?" She still had that darn fist planted firmly on her hip.

"No … of c … Absolutely not." Prime tried to appear resolute.

"Thank you," she said, sliding her hand down, "I'll go tell the twins at once of their inclusion." She started to walk away but stopped. With her back to us, she placed a hand on her swollen belly. "And these little ones, may I bring them too, Prime?"

"Please," was all he could weakly manage.

I slapped Prime on the back. "Welcome aboard. You already know the pilot. Now you've met the boss."

Toño shook his head. "In all her considerable majesty."

There was time for one more meeting with Mary and the high council before we left. Again, I assumed it was to say goodbye and formally recognize Carlos as the sole science director. In retrospect, I'd wished I listened to the little guy on my right shoulder whispering to me that something was very wrong. Oh, well, I've seen enough smooth sailing in my days to know what a lovely mirage it could be.

Mary went over a bunch of boring periodic reports, there was some brisk discussion about subcommittee reporting responsibilities, and then she turned Toño. "Today we meet to say a bittersweet goodbye to Drs. DeJesus and De La Frontera." I cleared my throat. "And General Ryan, of course." She blushed just a little. "Prime will join Captain Ryan and his crew on what

I'm certain will be a productive and stimulating adventure. Carlos will remain here as our science lead. I'm equally certain he'll excel at that job. Let's offer them all a nice round of applause." After everyone finished, she said, "Now, if there is no further business —"

"I'm curious," I said, "as to whatever happened with that American meat request."

She seemed to take a second to recall the issue. "Oh, it was nothing. All resolved. Our medical people talked to theirs and the matter was settled."

"Did they get the meat?" I asked pointedly.

"In the end, we felt a small increase in their ration was an appropriate response to what had been a medical request." She looked away from me. "So, *now*, if there's—"

I couldn't let it drop. There was something I wasn't seeing. "Any other odd requests?"

"No, none that I would classify as *odd*."

"Okay, what other request have they made? Any?"

"Darwin," she turned toward the head of Liaison and Outreach, "any other American requests?"

"From those *same* ships," I specified.

"Well, ma'am, nothing out of the ordinary." He flicked his handheld screen. "No. Here's a transfer request, but most ships do some shuffling about." He read silently. "One to have an additional farmship transferred to their pod. They say they want to use it for education and training, a foot up for their students." He pointed to a specific line. "They want to expand their 4-H program. Good idea, if you ask me. Idle hands and all."

"How many farmships do they already have?" I pressed. "There aren't more than a handful out there."

"Two, so this would be three."

"Doesn't it strike you as quite a profound commitment to 4-H to need three huge farmships to keep it going? What, that's like a million cows, three million pigs—"

"We take your point, Jon," Mary snapped. "Or, rather, do we? What's your issue with these routine requests?"

I do believe I heard her foot begin to tap. "I don't know, just seems like they're interested in controlling more food than they need." To Darwin, I asked, "Any other peculiar activities from those ships?"

He was in full retreat. "What do you define as *peculiar*?"

"Mary, what's your AI's name?"

"Warden Bill. Why?"

"Your ship's AI is named Warden Bill? Seriously?"

She glowered at me. Never a good sign from a woman, or your boss, and she was both.

"Warden Bill," I called out, "please give me the numbers of transfers on and off those US vessels, the number of tourist visits, again, to and from. And give me the radio traffic info."

Immediately, Bill replied. "Transfers in and out, slightly in favor of in, but not exceptionally."

"Who's transferring? Any demographic trends?"

Now Mary was mad. "Jon, what are you implying?"

I held a hand up to her. "Any trends?"

"On aggregate, more males off, more females on." My artificial stomach began to turn. "Specifically, single mothers with children and lesbian couples transferred on, as opposed to women married to men."

"Is that a problem, General? Do you object to women marrying women?"

"No, Mary. I'm trying to figure out what's going on here. Warden Bill, what about tourism visas?"

"General Ryan," one of her advisors said, "need I remind you of our motto leading up to the destruction of Earth? 'Throw everything we can upstairs and sort it out later.' We *anticipated* a lot of shuffling."

"Three times more *on* than *off* a handful of American ships?"

"What?" Mary interjected, "People can't move about without raising an alarm?"

"Mary," I replied, "most people have been up here less than a few years. Why the sudden need to vacation in America? That's odd. Bill, what about the radio traffic?"

"On official channels, quite normal. Reports and updates filed on schedule."

"What about civilian traffic?"

"That looks fine. There's a trend ... wait, it's not a trend. Hmm." First time I'd ever heard an AI say, *hmm*. Not good. "There's a statistically significant drop in outgoing calls and holos on civilian channels. Quite remarkably so, in fact."

"Mary, there's something rotten in the state of America."

More evenly, she asked, "What?"

"I wish I knew. They want more control over food. More women on than off. No gossiping back and forth with old friends. What am I not seeing?"

"At the risk of insulting an old friend," Mary said, "I'd say you were getting a little paranoid." She held her hand up to stop my response. "But, if it will make an old friend feel better, I'll look into it. Fair?"

"Sure," I growled back, quietly. My mind was elsewhere.

TWENTY-EIGHT

"Al, fire the vernier thrusters and ease us out of here." I was more than ready to leave. That little black cloud in my mind about the Americans was the last straw. I wanted to be free of humanity. If nothing else, whatever the fools did was no business of ours once we were permanently gone. By the time they arrived at GB 3, they'd have sorted out their petty politics. If they hadn't, I could pick up and go anywhere else. Sapale would be long gone, so there'd be nothing holding me there. Let the future take care of itself. For the present, I had a mission. I was with my family, and you have to know I had a so big-old smile on my face, I thought it might freeze in place.

"Aye, Captain. Shall I lay in a course for GB 3?"

****

That would be *Lilith* speaking, the second AI. Totally weird not to have Al's voice asking me that question. But he, for the most part, clammed up when she was installed. The very definition of a mixed blessing. By not talking, he wasn't overtly annoying. But, by remaining silent, he was covertly annoying. I wished he had a neck so I could wring it. In what seemed to be a vain attempt to establish a detente between Al and his new playmate, I asked him to name the computer and assign it a gender.

Simple assignment, right? No. Nothing was simple with Al. He said he'd think about it and get back to me. Now, I ask you calmly, how long does an AI that has a calculation rate of in the yotta FLOP range—10^{24} operations per second. Humans operate in 10^{15} range—take to make that decision? One would probably never have predicted it would take the PIA a week and a half.

Out of nowhere one day, Al climbs into my head and says, "Captain, I've reached a decision as to the new AI's name and gender. Lilith is her name and, naturally, she will be female."

"Okay, Al, I'll bite. How in the world did you come up with that, of all possible names?" No response. "Say again, Al, why Lilith?" Nothing. "I'm counting to three. If you haven't responded, I'm getting Doc, and *he* won't be happy."

Just before I could actually say three the rust bucket spoke. "Captain, an update. There no longer is a *world* to use as a comparator. Please recall that you said I *could* choose, and I *have*. You never said anything about *justifying* my decision. You totally blindsided me with that emotional sabotage. I'm attempting to heal, yet you hound me like an escaped felon."

"Would it help if I said I'm sorry?"

"Apology accepted."

"I didn't apologize. I said *if I said I'm sorry*. You fell for that one, Mr. Megabrain." He was silent again, but I'd won the skirmish. Score one for the android.

****

"Yes, Lily," I replied, "push us back, and alert me when we're ready to fire the main engines."

"Aye, aye. Lily out."

She sure seemed helpful, cheery, and team spirited. Of course, I *was* comparing her to Al. Within an hour, we were clear of the worldship and could burn the primary engines. It was a pity I had to keep the G-forces down to two, on account of having fragile Kaljaxians along this time. I'd have *loved* to see what she could do, pedal-to-the-metal. Once we were under constant acceleration, I double-checked the ship's status. She was purring like a kitten—a tiger kitten.

"Lily," I called out, "I read all systems as GO. That sound right?"

"Yes, Captain Ryan. All systems optimal."

"Great. I'm going to check on the family. Oh, and now that we're out here in space, please call me Jon."

"I shall, *Jon.* Thank you."

I rose and walked aft. "Lily, did we remember to pack Al? It's awful quiet around here."

"I'm not sure I take your meaning, Jon. Al was installed long ago. He did not require packing for shipment."

Uh-oh. I was starting to miss the taciturn Al. "Al," I shouted, "are you present and accounted for?" Silence. "Lily, is Al switched on?"

"No, sir. He doesn't have an on-off switch to be in the *on* position. He *is* fully operational, if that's what you mean to ask. I am collating copious data with him as we speak."

"Captain off the bridge." No way I needed to say that. I was after all, alone. I did want to terminate the conversation with a bold period. One AI was pissy and the other one totally concrete. Oy vey.

"You three get us off without crashing?" Sapale asked as I gave her a peck on the forehead.

"Us three?" I pointed to Prime. "He's right here, and Doc's hard at work as usual."

"No, you *flockend*—a comical animal on Kaljax, or so I'm told—you and the dueling AIs."

"No dueling today. Al wouldn't say a peep."

Prime sounded concerned. "Would you like me to run a diagnostic on him?"

I shook my head. "Wouldn't help. He's just being a childish jerk."

Prime furrowed his brow and angled his head. "I'm not certain that's possible, Jon. I'll go have a look. You two probably want to be alone, anyway."

"Okay, Prime. Suit yourself. Serves Al right. Maybe squirt some grease up where the sun doesn't shine. As you do, tell him I said *hello.*"

"You and Al," Sapale chided. "You're quite the pair. You know you both love the banter."

Falsely I protested. "I do *not.* If I could get him to act like a toaster, not an ex-wife, I'd be in hog heaven." Jon Jr. ran up and seized my leg. He was about two feet tall, growing like a fertilized weed, and cuter than anything I'd ever seen in this big old universe.

"Daddy," he squealed, which always melted my heart, "come play trains with me."

Sapale said they didn't really have trains on Kaljax or anything similar to their niche on Earth. Nonetheless, my boy loved his trains. Thomas the Tank Engine was tops on his list, but anything train was okay, too. There were tracks, coaches, and tiny little pieces everywhere. Toño and Prime, being techno nerds themselves, loved to play trains with JJ. As a result, JJ played trains most of his waking hours. That is, however, when he was not being scrubbed raw in the tub by one of the two female supervisors who ran his life.

Sapale had begun educating the kids as if they were back on Kaljax, but the intensity was still pretty low at that point. When they got older, she looked to be a formidable taskmaster. I felt sorry for them in advance. My brood's-mate's plan was to raise the children as culturally pure Kaljaxians. Made sense, since the planet we were colonizing was to be a new Kaljax. She would teach them several dialects, along with English. She left it to me how much they'd be exposed to human history and culture. Me, I figured that pretty much meant holo-games and football. Oh, and beer when they were old enough.

"You two go chuff down the tracks," Sapale said. "I need to give Fashallana a bath. She's filthy. Playing all morning in Toño's lab. I might as well dump a garbage can over her head."

Fash looked clean to me, but I knew better than to say a word.

Ffffuttoe rushed over and picked up Fash like she was on fire. "Clean girl, happy girl. We bath clean." She wasn't ever going to get English syntax down. We'd all given up on that project. But she sure meant well. A point of interesting trivia. How long does it take to dry a sopping-wet Toe off, given their multiple layers of fur? Answer, a really long time. But every time a kid had a bath, *she* had a bath. I personally have always hated baths. But I'd wager she'd climb in with me, too, if I decided to take one, unless I put up a membrane.

As the months passed, our little band came together magnificently. Toño and Prime worked together, but joined the rest of us for holos or the occasional meal. Sapale was due in a few weeks, so she was getting pretty big. And she was transcendently beautiful. Anyway, her plan was to have twins every eighteen months or so. She would remain fertile for maybe ten years, fifteen if she was lucky. So we might have ten or twelve kids, all told. Life was good and only promised, with a cherry on top, to get even better.

Remember my superstition about bottoms falling out? Yeah. I was too content. Soon after Sapale delivered two more tiny bundles of joy, our world shattered.

The overhead lights abruptly flashed red, and the general quarters alarm went off loudly. I felt the engines stop. By protocol, Al had raised a defensive membrane.

Authoritatively, Lily announced, "Captain, to the bridge. Sapale, to the bridge. Drs. DeJesus and De La Frontera, to the bridge. All children, to the nursery. Ffffuttoe, to the nursery."

That portended something catastrophic. As soon as I cleared the hatch to the bridge, I yelled, "*Status?*"

Toño and Prime crashed through just behind me. "Red Alert. Priority One transmission from the UN Security Council incoming. A state of war has been declared." Al spoke clearly and without any editorializing or humor.

"What." I shouted. "War? No way. The Listhelons are *years* away from being able to catch up with us. Please clarify."

We were only ten light-minutes from the worldship fleet, but communications back and forth were going to be tense due to that lag. Al responded, "Transmission on screen." Sapale entered, having made certain Ffffuttoe was okay with the kids. A man I recognized as Abed Massad flickered to life. He was Under-Secretary-General for Legal Affairs. Legal Affairs and a Red Alert? His one-sided statement began:

Captain Ryan, I bring horrible *news. The unimaginable has happened. The UN command worldship,* Exeter, *has been fired-upon and badly damaged by* Enterprise. *Secretary Kahl has been killed, along with countless others. The surprise attack occurred fifteen minutes ago.* Enterprise *landed two rail-balls before our automatic membranes deployed. The damage is staggering. Currently we have air seals on most sections, and damage-control parties are at hard at work. As soon as our membranes went up, all other worldships deployed them, also. At that point,* Enterprise, Firefly, Nimitz, *and* Defiance *broke formation and headed off in a different direction at maximal velocity. They took one farmship with them, though it accompanied them only under duress. No other ships were attacked or damaged. I am in temporary command.*

No warnings, communications, or responses to challenge have been received from any of the fleeing vessels. No justification for the atrocity has been provided. I am not ordering a counterattack, at least for now. I need to find out what happened and why in order to take a deliberate course of action. We do not, repeat, do not request your assistance at this time. I am aware Dr. De La Frontera is aboard Shearwater.

Oh no.

I am able to report that Mrs. De La Frontera and all her children are safe and well.

Sounded like another shoe was falling like a meteor.

However, Dr. De La Frontera, who was in consultation with Madame Kahl at the time, was killed. Their bodies are barely recognizable, but both their identities confirmed. I am sorry to bear such horrendous news. I await your response and will keep you informed as more details become available. Massad out.

I was numb. Everyone was numb. I couldn't imagine what Prime felt. The situation was surreal. It was not possible. Those words could never have been strung together in the same sentence. Why, in a billion years, would *Enterprise* attack *Exeter*? And why *that* ship? It was in a totally different section of the fleet. She had to go way off course to do that.

"I must return," announced Prime, "at once."

"The children," Toño finished his thought, "must have their father."

"If I strip-down a shuttle and fly at maximum speed —" Prime began.

"You can be there in less than two months, Carlos." Again, Doc finished his sentence. And with no nickname either.

Carlos turned to me. "With your permission, Captain, I will proceed with all haste."

"Of course, Carlos. Toño will help you of course. Let me know if I can be of any assistance. Godspeed." They raced off.

Sapale came to my side and put her arms around me. She rested her head on my arm. "What could have caused this to happen? I'm frightened."

I'd never heard her say those words. Not during our firefight on Kaljax, not before childbirth, not even before we faced the Listhelon attack. This was big. "We're safe. The rest of the worldships are safe. We'll sort this out in good time. Someone will have hell itself to pay. But for now we're all together and we're safe."

We stood together in reverent silence for ten minutes. Our solitude was broken by Al. He spoke softly. "Captain, sorry to interrupt. I have an incoming message for you, personally, from *Enterprise*."

"Say *what*?"

"Yes, Captain. They addressed the transmission to *you* specifically. I don't know if a simultaneous broadcast was sent to the worldship fleet. I can't be certain, but I think the gain on the signal directed it to us alone. Shall I put it on screen?"

"Yes. Who the hell on —" I stopped dead. In human history no one ever said they were more speechless, or that they couldn't believe their eyes more passionately than me right then on my bridge. I was looking at myself, my identical self. Sapale growled and reflexively recoiled, ready to attack the image. Words tried to exit her throat, but she could not muster sufficient force to speak.

"Hello, *Jon*. Recognize me?" was my face's greeting. It was *my* face, but that was not *my* voice. It was … it was … *NO*. It was parsecs beyond impossible. He was dead—blown to bits and dead.

Yes, son, it's your president, Stuart J. Marshall. He sat still, grinning. *There. I wanted to give you a second to fully take in that concept. I'd pay good money, serious money, Jon, to see the look on your face right about now.* He laughed maniacally.

I'm back from the dead, Jon, and I'm pissed. *Your president, your commander in chief, is pissed at you, and that's never a good thing, son. I had a plan and you ruined it. I hold you* personally *responsible. Yes, others acted traitorously and treasonously, but you were the lynchpin, the catalyst of my fateful but temporary setback. But nothing's destroyed if it can be rebuilt. So, I may only kill you once in revenge. Well, once apiece for you, your alien slut, and those bastard children of yours.*

134

Sapale growled in a tone I'd never heard and never wanted to hear again. All the maternal rage in the universe was contained it that growl. I wouldn't want to be the person that sound was directed toward.

But, enough about me. How're you? I bet your mighty proud of yourself, maybe even happy. Well, between you and me don't get used to it. None of that will last for long. That I swear to you. For now, I'm regrouping. I need to establish my reign once again and then I will deal with you. My present plan is to move most of these freeloaders off on the planet you discovered, the one with the donut people, the little tiny ones. Yeah, I figure it'll be no chore to wipe their slimy butts out of existence. Might even be fun. Say, I wonder what one of them tastes like dunked in coffee. I'll just have to find out for myself won't I? He mimed himself lofting a squirming Reglician and dipping it live into a cup of coffee, then biting down on it. He rubbed his tummy after he was done,

I don't want to keep you from your waning joy, son, so I'll let you go. I just wanted you to be the first to know I'm back, I'm doing reasonably well, and that I plan on killing each and every human, alien, or android who stands in my way. See you later.

He gave a flippant wave of his hand, then directed his attention to some papers on his desk. Suddenly, he jabbed a finger toward the camera, and screamed, *Got ya.* He couldn't stop laughing for nearly a minute. Finally, he composed himself enough to say, *I had you going, didn't I? No, I'm not done until I tell you how I did it. It's really rather straightforward. You should probably do it yourself. You might be killed before I can be the one to do it, so you'll need to reanimate, so I can blow you away. Just a suggestion.*

I have always made a daily backup of my brain. After you inconvenienced me with incineration, I had a loyal aide put the most recent copy into this android. Voila, a new me. There will always *be, I promise you, a me in this universe. Never zero, never two, just the one of me.*

So as not to put you through it any longer, 'cause I know you're a 'wondering, why did I chose your body? That, too, was easy. The traitor DeJesus kept complete records of your production. I simply copied them. He put the back of his hand to the side of his mouth, like he was going to tell a secret. *Don't tell anyone, because it would embarrass me to no end, but I kind of like your dick more than my own.* He dangled a digit and swung it back and forth. *Yeah, baby.*

But I'll be serious for a moment. The reason I chose you is simple. Every time I look in a mirror, I want to see the face of the man I hate more than any other in the universe. I hate you *more than any* being *in any universe. I want to be reminded of that hate, that utter loathing, every night and every day until I slay you with my bare hands. I don't want one ounce of my hatred to falter, fade, or fail.* He was pounding the table to splinters with his fists. *I want to hate you more than it is possible for one being to hate another.*

He stopped pounding and speaking. He rolled his shoulders to collect himself. *After that, I'll go back to my old handsome self.* He cupped his chin in contemplation. *You know, hang on one darn second. You know what? Maybe I'll download myself into something else, just for fun. Hey, maybe a really stacked broad.* He pumped his hands in front of his breasts. *Or ... or maybe a household appliance? Yeah,* he nodded with self-approval, *that would be nice and kinky. I think I'll become a broom. A broom with Jon Ryan's dick. Don't you think that'd be swell, Jon? Jon? Sapale? Anybody?* He reached over and rapped his knuckles on the camera lens. *Anybody? Oh, turn the damn thing off,* he said to the camera operator, *boring conversation.* Just before the image faded, I saw him fling the back of his hand in the direction of the camera.

When I spoke my next words, to no one in particular, I did so with more conviction and heartfelt belief than I had ever said any words before. "Well, I'll be *damned.*"

TWENTY-NINE

I forwarded the complete message to UN command. It was more an evil spell than a message. I added minimal verbiage from me. Just the bare facts. I alerted Toño and Carlos to view the holo ASAP and get back to me with their impressions. It didn't take long for them to jet back to the bridge, aghast in disbelief. Sapale was badly shaken. Quiet as a mouse, she kissed my cheek and said she needed to check on the kids. Please note, she said *need*, not *want*. Marshall's shadow had fallen like an eclipse and hung over the remainder of our lives. *Damn* that inhuman waste of space.

But, moving forward was not only our singular option, it was our ultimate rebuke of his threat. I felt at that moment I would never again feel peace. I would always worry he was sneaking up behind me or a loved one. Even when Sapale and Ffffuttoe were ancient dust, I could never let down my guard or be allowed one moment's respite. I couldn't allow him to kill me, even ten thousand years in the future. I needed to remain alive to try with all my heart and all my soul to end his blight on everything good that existed. He was an evil I needed to end or die trying. It was beyond me how a man could become so amoral, so hateful, and have such complete disregard for others's lives. But, I didn't need to understand him to kill it.

I was alone on the bridge but a few moments. As I expected, the two scientists rushed in.

Toño spoke first. "He's insane. The man's gone truly and utterly insane."

"He murdered me in ice-cold blood. I will kill him if it's the last thing I ever do. He didn't care if my family was slaughtered either. He must die, and quickly." Carlos's Spanish blood was boiling.

"I know," I said in a hollow voice, "I know. Either of you have any thoughts as to what we should do at the present time, as opposed to revenge in the hypothetical future?"

They eased off on some of their frenetic, confused anger. "The shuttle," Carlos replied, "will be ready to depart in an hour or so. I'll take one of the AI's with me. After I'm there, the AI can pilot the ship back to you." He shuffled his feet. "I probably owe you my life. Any meeting the human Carlos attended, I would likely have attended, also. Then my children would have no father. My wife would have no husband if, in fact, she will have me as hers. Even if she rejects me as a spouse, she will at least have my undying support. Jon, I owe you a great debt, both for placing me here at this sad hour and for lending me the shuttle." He reached over and hugged me.

"My pleasure. You'd do the same for either of us. Take Lily. Al's been in harm's way with me many times. I need him here, just in case."

"Of course," Carlos said. He nodded his head and exited.

"Will you go, too?" I asked Toño.

He waited a few seconds before replying. "No. I will stay *here* with you. I will remain at home." After a longer pause he continued. "I want to remain so that I can help protect your family. Plus, I'm very tired. I'm tired to the core of my soul of humans. I can no longer act in their perverse theater, no longer participate in their petty politics. My place is here with you. Ultimately, it will fall to you and me to put that dog down. That the fool has already promised to come *to* you only adds to the certainty that we shall confront him, and without the bother of a hunt." He laughed a spiteful laugh. "By your side, my friend, will be the least safe and most useful place for me to be."

"Gee, thanks. I feel a bunch better knowing I'm, like, ground zero."

He slapped my back. "Having known you for a century, I can tell you this. Whatever their reaction, be it positive or negative, you draw strong emotions from those who know you. Now, if you'll excuse me, I must see Carlos off."

I stood alone on the bridge once again. I stared out the viewport into the darkness, and it seemed to spread. Al broke the silence. "Jon, I heard what you said to Carlos, about him taking Lilith. Thank you. That means more to this old AI than you will ever know. I'm proud to serve with you. I will protect your family forever. I hope someday you will come to regard me as your friend."

Okay, like that would have brought tears if I could've produced them. "You *are* my friend, Al. You're a *good* friend. Always will be. I will need your help to try and keep Sapale and the kids safe."

"We will not *try* to keep them safe, you and me. We *will* keep them safe. I almost feel sorry for Marshall. We're gonna open up an industrial-size can a'ass whooping on that pitiful piece o'shit."

"Why, Al, I'm shocked and dismayed. Who *programmed* you to talk like that?"

"Wasn't it you, Captain?"

"I don't recall any sessions like that. I may need to go to confession, just because I heard those words come out of your speakers."

"I am programed to receive, if you feel the need."

I went back to our quarters to check on Sapale. She was having a snack with the kids and Ffffuttoe. Junior hopped down and ran to greet me. Along with the levity from Al, the naive joy in his eyes warmed my soul, if only a bit.

"Daddy," he yelled. "Do you want some calrf? Mom made it special."

Calrf was a Kaljaxian stew. It tasted like old sweat socks boiled in pickle juice that something living had accidentally fallen into, died, and decayed. The texture was that of splintered wood suspended in warm mush. Not a big fan of calrf, myself. Knowing she fixed it reflected how melancholy she was. Whenever she was sad, which was unbelievably rare, she made calrf or some equally revolting dish from back home. Not surprisingly, the kids loved it. I never had the nerve to ask Ffffuttoe how she could possibly like it, but she'd eat anything. She'd also asked Sapale why I questioned her on the point, which would bring a growl directed at me from the love of my life, so I never brought it up.

"No, Jon, I'll leave it all for you and your sister. It's too good to waste on me. I'll get a bowl of chicken soup. Okay?"

He grabbed my hand and dragged me toward the table. Sapale said she'd make the soup and asked me to sit. It was nice. The five of us sitting around the table sharing a simple meal. I needed that type of grounding experience. When the kids finished, they ran off to play.

Ffffuttoe pushed back from the table and said, "Babies need check I go."

With the two of us pretending to eat, we sat in silence a while. She broke the uncomfortable stillness. "Marshall, he's completely lost his mind."

I raised my eyebrows and tilted my head. "It would appear so. I think he doesn't like me very much either."

She dropped her spoon. It clinked loudly off her bowl and skidded to the floor. "Jon, *please*. This isn't the time for humor, especially your brand."

"Sorry. I know. I was just trying to lighten the mood."

"A madman has just promised to kill you, me, and our children. Lightening of the mood is both impossible and inappropriate."

I raised my hands in surrender. She was, of course, right.

"What're we going to do?"

I'd thought a lot about that in a short time. There was only one real option. "We do exactly what we were planning to do. We go to GB 3 and begin a new life."

Her chin quivered as she replied. "But he'll know where we are, right where to find us. We have to go somewhere else. Somewhere *safe*."

This was tough, the hardest discussion I'd ever participated in. "There *is* no safe place. If the moron is determined to find us, he will. And, even if he didn't or couldn't, we'd jump at every sound in the night and never know a moment's peace. We have two options. One, keep running in this ship, at this speed, forever. That way he could never catch up to us. The other is to settle down somewhere and be sensibly prepared."

She threw her head back in frustration. "I know. Even if we went back to Kaljax and blended in, he would find us, sooner or later. Well," she flipped the back of her hand my direction, "you might not be so hard for him to single out." She almost smiled. Almost.

"Hey." I protested, "I thought you said no silliness. That," I pointed toward her, "was definitely silly. Very silly, in fact."

She put the back of her hand over her mouth and chuckled. "I lied." We both snorted a bit at that. "This isn't a worldship, so we can't run in it forever. If we tried, it would be unfair to all the children. They deserve a home. A place with dirt and bugs and a sun burning down on their heads."

I drew my head back in confusion. "My children deserve *bugs*? I'm not certain how to take that factoid."

She wagged a finger at me. "Don't push your luck, flyboy. When will he come?" she asked seriously.

I was fairly confident about this issue. "Not soon. Likely, not for years. He's got a lot on his plate, just yet." I held up fingers to document each point. "One, he has to consolidate his base of power. He can surround himself with a bunch of his old lackeys, sure. But securing the loyalty, or at least mortal fear, of millions of unpleasantly surprised citizens will be hard. It *may* be impossible. In retrospect, he was building up the numbers of women again. He's still salivating over creating a harem ship. That's going to pose a challenge in winning the hearts and minds of a consenting public. 'A vote for Marshall is a vote for him enslaving someone you love.' No landslide victories in those elections for Stuart, the dimwitted son of a bitch. He actually thinks he can take control of millions of nervous citizens, while he's stealing their women." I whacked the back of my hand against my temple. "Nuts.

"Two, he has to find a world to populate. No way the passengers on those four ships would go along with anything else. If he announced they'd float aimlessly, they'd revolt for sure. He can't go to GB 3. That's where the rest of humanity is going. The rest of humanity isn't likely to take to his arrival kindly.

"That brings me to three. He can't know what the UN will do. They might pursue and attack him. If so, he's badly outnumbered, even with the stolen membranes to help him. He has to anticipate some form of reprisal, even if there isn't one coming. He has to watch his butt on a permanent basis. Butt watching is a full-time job, in and of itself.

"Four, he's a megalomaniac and insane. Those people have a hard go of it in this life. They're always screwing up or miscalculating. They're their own worst enemies. Look, if he was clever, he'd have just told the rest of the fleet that he and his pals were going elsewhere in shuttles and left quietly in the dark of night. No. *He* has to attack *Exeter*, like some black-hatted cowboy in a bad western. Ego before practicality. No, he'll be tripping over his own feet more often than a circus clown.

"Sweetheart," I reached over and took her hand, "I don't know how to say this and have it come out any way but awkward, but —"

"But I'll be," she finished my sentence, "long gone by the time he has the opportunity to make good on his promise."

"Thank you for relieving me of the burden of reminding you of your mortality. I love you."

"Why did I settle for such an odd brood-mate. I had so many excellent choices, you know?"

"Yes, you've told me that six hundred thirty-five times." I batted my eyelids. "We robots count things *real* good."

"Six hundred thirty-*six* now." As her smile faded, She looked sad again. "So, we start our new world and wait. What if he can't contain himself and simply sends an assassin after us?"

I shook my head slowly. "No, he really wants to be the one with his hands around my throat. He knows he has time, lots of time. He'll savor the prospect and come for us only when he knows it's safe for him to do so," I waved my arms expansively, "when all the rest of that stuff has settled down."

"I estimate," Al cut in out of nowhere, "that will take a minimum of two hundred seventy-five years, give or take."

Sapale looked upward and said, "I guess that gets me off the hook, doesn't it? Gosh, what a relief. One less thing to worry about."

THIRTY

Stuart Marshall sat in his ornate office, lights off, his speakers blasting *Amerikaz Most Wanted;* the original Tupac version, as the man was a purist. The walls three cabins away shook and thundered as if they'd surely fly into pieces. But not a single person objected. No one dared. No one, it seemed, wished to die on that particular day. It had been a week since his surprise attack on that bitch Mary's chicken coop. That was fun. He'd successfully blown her to tiny little smoky bits. She was too persnickety to be downloaded to an android when he'd offered it. It was too bad he'd only get to kill her once.

Ah well, he reflected, *enough nostalgia.* He had quite a few more fish to fry and the current ones were still very much alive. He picked up a hand-mirror that laid perpetually face down next to his right hand. He studied with nausea and glee the face of his forever enemy. A knock on his door jolted him from his private, self-imposed torment. That he heard that tiny knock over the boom of his music was testimony indeed to the craftsmanship that went into his hearing assembly. "Come."

His chief of staff inched his head around the door frame. On the inside, it was still Matthew Duncan, recently resurrected by Marshall. His body was different. Marshall, naturally, was reanimated first. He therefore got to choose the android hosts for his cronies. For Matt, the perversity of Marshall's lunacy decreed that he would henceforth be a she. And no run-of-the-mill female, either. No. He was in a body copied from the replica in the famed Madame Tussaud's Museum in London. Matt was now the spitting image of Marilyn

Monroe, down to her elegantly coiffed blonde hair and eternally alluring lips.

Matt was unhappy with this new phase of his life. It wasn't *just* that he felt completely awkward and stupid—ludicrous, in fact. No. He was constantly aware that he was the very embodiment of raw sex appeal, while being confined to the immediate company of a deranged egomaniac sex addict. It was only a matter of time before Matt was called upon to perform duties that were, in the past, well outside his job description. And Matt was powerless. If he opened the fusion engine hatch and threw himself into the inferno, Marshall would re-resurrect him with that much more ebullience. No, for the foreseeable future, he was to be punished for his association with Stuart Marshall, a madman of the first order.

The blaring music quickly died off. Marshall howled, "I said, *come.*"

Matt—he was still allowed to be called Matt, not Marilyn—stepped cautiously into the room. His immediate concern was not so much for Marshall, but that he had not mastered the art of walking in five-inch stilettos. He'd fallen six times so far that morning. He fantasized that he could locate and destroy Marshall's copy of Matt's mind. That way he could end his suffering for all time. "The others are here for the meeting, sir." Matt's head drooped after he spoke, which was a new habit he'd acquired.

"Show them in," said the boss. "And tell them they're all late."

No one was. "Yes, sir," Matt replied as he clunked away unsteadily.

"Nice ass." observed the president as Matt stumbled around the corner.

The only other people Stuart brought back to life were his three closest allies: Chuck Thomas, Sam Peterson—the ugly guy with horrific breath they copied again—and Bob Patrick. Stuart, Chuck, Sam, and Bob. The Four Horseman, as they cheerily referred themselves. It was never decided who, specifically, was War, Famine, Pestilence, or Death. In reality they *all* were each blight. The three men and Marilyn Monroe filed in and sat in roughly a circle. Matt initially neglected to cross his legs. He wasn't in that habit yet, but he would be soon.

Chuck leaned way over and glanced up Matt's skirt. "My, my, the view from your office sure has improved, Stu." The Horsemen all cackled loudly.

"Okay. The sooner we get started, the sooner—"

Sam snickered as he interrupted. "We *all* know, so talk fast for a change."

In fact, the Horsemen's lives were not as sex-laden as they had once have lusted for. Gone, for the present, were dreams of worldships filled with their love slaves. As of that moment, they were all forced to settle for prostitutes, albeit large numbers each. Most of their women were fresh from the orbital construction service trade and were glad to land steady work. A few concubines were, however, volunteered from the ship's general population.

"Ha, ha, very funny. Now, if you don't mind, we actually have some important matters to go over." Glowering at Sam, he added, "Hmm?"

"If you insist."

"I do," confirmed the boss. "So, up to this point I've walked on eggshells so as not to foment an open rebellion against us. I keep reminding whoever'll listen that I *am* still the President of the United States."

"But," objected Bob, "the states are gone. Jupiter ate them. Who's buying that line?"

"Not enough, so far, but some are. If more come around, we'll have their backing if there's strong pushback to our power grab. Chuck, how are you coming along with the senior officers? Are they recognizing your authority as Head of the Joint Chiefs?"

"Yes. Some were hesitant at first, but I was able to convince the rest."

"The rest," demanded the president, "what the hell are you talking about?"

"Some senior officers balked at swearing renewed allegiance to me. I had them thrown out an airlock, without the benefit of a spacesuit. The rest came around nicely in no time at all."

Marshall harrumphed quietly. "Good. Sam, same question to you."

"I'm negotiating the structure of the judiciary with my old colleagues on the Supreme Court. All but two of them, that is, whose last words were something along the lines of, 'No fucking way you're back on the bench, asshole.' I'm cautiously optimistic I'll be able to amass a suitable consensus, sooner rather than later."

"Bob? How about Congress?"

"Much tougher. It's like trying to organize mobile homes in a tornado. But at least I wasn't thrown out on my ear. The current leaders are not anxious to cede their new-found power, but I'm optimistic." He pointed around the room. "The better you guys do, the stronger my position will become."

"Good. And you, Matty, you gorgeous hunk a'love, what's the scuttlebutt amongst the citizenry on our bold new republic of five ships?"

"May I speak freely?"

With the darkest of expressions, Stuart said, "No."

"Well, then, allow me to abridge my report on the fly. As you know, the worldships are divided up into precincts, which combine to form states, which in turn form one worldship's government. While we were away, entire infrastructures were put in place. I've contacted all the key players in upper-level positions on all five ships. The farmship is willing to go along with anything. They see their role as unchanged, and frankly, a bunch of hayseeds couldn't care less who runs the government, as long as they're left to their cows and dirt. The leaders of the four worldships are willing to listen to anything you propose, Mr. President."

"But," Stuart snapped, "their *listening* is light-years from them kissing my ring." He smiled. "Or my ass." Sam hummed a chuckle.

"As you suggest, sir, no. They're not opening their arms to you like the returning prodigal son."

"Any chatter about eliminating me," he signaled to everyone present, "*us*, as a group, by force or stealth?"

"None that I've heard."

"Matt, are you trying to be *cute* with me? Although you're cute as a button in the first place." He smiled a sick, predatory smile.

"How so, sir?"

"*You* haven't heard. But have you heard of anyone *else* hearing some unkind words directed toward me?"

"Yes. A few of our spies do report coffeehouse mumblings that would seem to suggest an interest in locking the four of you up, pending summary execution. Martial law has not been formally suspended, as you may know. It's an option for those in control."

"Of course I know that, you enticing moron. If you can't do a better job of keeping me informed, I may be forced to find another function you *can* perform for me." He pointed at him. "You'd best keep that in mind. I need to see *results*."

Matt didn't even try to respond.

"This meeting is over. Everyone keep me informed, especially if some particularly juicy shit is about to hit a fan anywhere on this little flotilla of mine."

The four persons filed out as they had entered. Matt attempted unsuccessfully to step between two men, so his butt would not, again, be the last item visible to his president.

THIRTY-ONE

By the time Carlos returned to *Exeter,* the details of the sneak attack had been worked out. An aide loyal to him had secretly loaded an up-to-date copy of Marshall to an android hidden away for just that purpose. That was four weeks prior to the attack. Marshall then had made uploaded copies of his four compatriots. He had stayed in hiding for two weeks, learning what had transpired since Jackson destroyed his original android. Two weeks prior to the attack, he led a raiding party and seized the bridge of *Enterprise.* From there, he coordinated personnel movements and was able to gradually assimilate the rest of the ship. Skirmishes had taken place, but he was able to keep his actions covert enough to avoided being discovered.

Once *Enterprise* was secure, he sent troops to take over the other three vessels in a similar manner. He was aided by the fact that no one suspected anything was amiss simply because they saw large contingents of US soldiers moving around. Defense against an internal threat was never considered when planning worldship security. An expeditionary force had been sent to secure one farmship that would accompany the rebel squadron. After those five ships were under his control, Marshall promptly attacked *Exeter.* Piecing that information together, with the message he sent, completed the picture of the entire tragic affair.

By the time Carlos was ready to send the shuttle and Lily back to *Shearwater*, the UN command still had no consensus response plan in place. Repairs to *Exeter* were underway. Full repairs were estimated to take six months. The luxury of looking at a four-hundred-year journey was that no one felt the need to hurry in the least. That was also the reigning attitude about retaliation. Everybody knew where Marshall was headed, and that he'd be in transit for hundreds of years, too. "Wait and get it right" became the UN's watchwords.

I was still conscious of Marshall's threats, but luckily, I was able to put them in enough perspective to enjoy life. Sapale came around, though more slowly. Eventually, thank goodness, we were once again a merry little band of travelers. A growing band, too. She became pregnant with twins almost immediately after the second set were born. Here I am, talking about my kids as sets, like a really insensitive oaf. Jon Jr. and Fashallana's next two sisters were Kashiril, meaning "answers the wind," and Wolnara, meaning "wisdom sees." Sapale was into highly symbolic names. She said it was all the fashion on Kaljax. I smiled and nodded when informed of those facts. Not a word.

Ffffuttoe showed no signs of slowing. She was as happy as could be. Kids everywhere and more on the way. I told her one day in jest that I was elevating her to the rank of Bath Master First Class. She almost collapsed with joy. Whenever she spoke to me from that day forward, she always referred to herself as just that. I even asked Sapale if maybe I should make Ffffuttoe a badge or a uniform to suit her rank. She asked if I'd like her to punch me in the chest for belittling her nanny. Okay, title only. No uniform. But, the important point was that we were happy again.

Toño's mood was the same as it always had been, I think. He was a reserved man, but I don't imagine the prospect of confronting Marshall in the distant future weighed on him much. He'd brought a few empty androids along, I assumed to play with. I'd ask him now and then why exactly they were on board. He'd shrug his shoulders and mutter something about forewarned was to be forearmed. Whatever.

I actually asked Toño if he could craft a Kaljaxian android out of one of our spares. He knew where I was going with the query and had clearly already given it a lot of thought.

"I think it's easily possible, but," Toño added, "it would take a very long time. Sapale has provided me with a lot of books on Kaljaxian anatomy and physiology. A fully functional unit, however, would still be nearly impossible with that information alone. Especially a working female unit. Reproduction is tough, Jon."

Do tell. "Could you put, oh, I don't know, Sapale into a human android?" I held my breath.

Slowly, he began to shake his head. "No, that wouldn't be possible. The brain must be of a certain structure—format and operating system, if you will—to be compatible. Maybe I could do such a thing, eventually, but that's going to be a long while." I suspected that much, but my gut wrenched all the same.

I guess I'm glad I asked Sapale about the option of being loaded into an android later. I figured, if I'd wondered about it, maybe she had, too. For the one and only time in our life together, I saw the expression of horror on her face. "Lords and Forces *no*. Who would want such a thing?"

"Ah," I said and rested my hand on my chest, "*me*, for example."

The devotion of my life was never insensitive and loved me fervently, completely. She was, however, instantaneously honest. Ask a question, and you got a prompt, truthful response. Might be right between the eyes, but her opinions were always heartfelt. "You didn't *want* to become one; you *had* to. Your planet was about to be destroyed. That's a very different case. I asked who'd *want* such a fate." She shuddered.

"I'm not entirely clear on this. I *wanted* to become an android to save humanity."

As impatient as when she taught the dialect Gernan to the older kids, she set me straight. "You knew that you had to become a machine in order to save your people. That's noble and honorable. Toño became a robot to hold that maniac Marshall in check. His God loves him for that sacrifice. Neither of you *wanted* to do so; it was *required* of you. Marshall and his cabal did so voluntarily out of pride and vanity. May Offlin's Beast Without Eyes take them all."

"Wait," I said with passion, "now you've gone too far. You used the word 'cabal' in casual conversation. I'm sorry, I'm not certain I can accept that type of linguistic gymnastics from an alien."

"You *do* want calrf three times a day from this day forward, don't you?"

"No," I protested, "but, please, don't say that word in front of the kids."

"There are seven distinct flavors of calrf. Did you know that? One of them even *I* find revolting." She tapped the end of my nose. "Guess what's for dinner tonight?"

I tried to rein the conversation back to its original subject. "I understand that you wouldn't want to be an android. Fine. Mind telling me why? Is it a religious thing from back home?"

She rolled her head, thinking. "No. I don't think any of the major religions of Kaljax speak to that issue directly. It wouldn't be an obvious sin."

"Then why?"

She looked deep into my eyes, into my soul, and a tear formed at the corners of two eyes. "A mother must never outlive her children. If I were an android, I'd outlive generations of my offspring." She wiped harshly at the tears. "Soon, all I'd do each day is attend the funeral of some direct descendent of mine. A wave of their deaths would pull me along for all time, and I'd never stop crying." She drew an arm across her face. "Though I wish with all my heart to be by your side for eternity, the price for that privilege is too high. I couldn't bear it."

I spoke as seriously as I had in as long as I could remember. "That doesn't sound too good for my future, now does it?"

She wrapped me powerfully in her arms and laughed through her tears. "You'll be fine, my flyboy brood-mate. You're as tough as they come and then some. You'll look on the endless generations of your children and smile. You'll teach them well and wisely, and your heart will overflow with joy." She arched back and looked into my eyes again. "I'm so proud of you. So proud of what you *will* do. Everyone else in the universe has to rely on the intercession of a deity to keep their children safe. Not me." She rested her head on my chest. "I have you." She pinched my side. "But, I do have the deity-thing as a sound backup plan, just in case."

I smiled ear to ear. "Just in case what?"

"You team up with Marshall and begin a screw-the-most-women competition for the rest of time."

I nodded thoughtfully. "I bet I could win. Easy." That brought a playful kick to my shin.

I was glad we'd finally had the android discussion. Knowing Sapale had negative interest in becoming one freed my concerns. We would live our time together and then we would part. I would stay with the nascent Kaljaxian colony as long as it required my help, and I would protect it forever. As to when Marshall and I actually met, I decided since I had no control over that at the present, I would shove it to the back of my head. The future would take care of itself, with or without my stressing over its progress.

As our voyage progressed, Toño became our main contact with the folks back home. He spoke to Carlos occasionally. Mostly they discussed technical advances and innovations, but they also shared gossip. Carlos told us that after Marshall left and *Exeter* was repaired, life settled down to a comfortable pace. The worldships functioned to perfection and the societies that developed inside them were flourishing and successful. Food production was more than adequate and the lack of luxury items was not too big of an issue, societally. Criminal activity was essentially zero, illicit drug use was negligible, and interpersonal friction had been well managed to that point.

One big reason for the combined low crime rate and nonexistent drug problem was because basically no one had the ability to produce recreational drugs in the first place. A few Coca plants were cultivated, but they were under constant, tight security. Opium poppies were needed for medical use, but were, if anything, under even tighter control. The same went for the tobacco plant. It was along for the ride, but absolutely no one was smoking it. The one-acre field of it on the one farmship where it was grown looked a good deal more formidably defended than Fort Knox. The same went for amphetamines, hallucinogens, and similar synthetic drugs. The chemicals to produce them were harder to obtain than mercy from a cheated-on wife.

On my home front, things couldn't have been better. Every eighteen months or so, I was proud parent to another set of twin girls. When Sapale determined that Fashallana was mature enough, she had an aliquot of the mixed semen instilled into her birth canal. Since Fashallana is my *daughter*, that's what we'll call it, okay? Her *birth canal*. In time, Kashiril and Wolnara received the same *medical* treatments. No snickering out there. *Dad* talk here. When Sapale invited me to the sessions during which she explained to our daughters how to activate their reproductive systems, I always found some critical task to perform that prevented my hearing those unwanted words.

Toño and I had settled into a warm, casual relationship. When he'd been "Doc," my creator, I looked at him as an authority figure and supervisor. Now we were rock-solid friends. On the few occasions when he wasn't slaving away in his lab—smiling the entire time—we'd sit and reminisce about the old days or old acquaintances. Sometimes we'd speak of Marshall and strategies to defeat him. On rare occasions, which absolutely drove Sapale mad, we'd hunker-down in his lab and smoke cigars. I was never a big fan of them, mind you, but they are great conspiratorial tools to manifest a modicum of independence from one's spouse. Plus, hey, they're a guy thing, and we were a couple of guys.

An interesting conversation Toño and I had over Havana's best a decade into our journey involved sex. Specifically, *him* and sex. With only Kaljaxians around, and all of them being my daughters, I asked him how he was handling celibacy.

He answered quickly. "I've never been much into relationships and intimacy."

The pilot and dude in me let it slip. "Huh?"

"Jon, have you, in the past century, know me to date, man or woman, or even speak of such matters?"

"I just thought you were shy about your private life."

"I'm not, because there's nothing to be shy about. In college, I went out with a few girls, kissed a few, and ventured further with a couple. I don't know, it just never felt *essential* for me. I think I'm what the world calls a 'confirmed bachelor.' Plus, someday, there'll be women around to interact with."

I guffawed. "Yeah, in like four hundred *years.*"

He shrugged. "I'm feeling no emptiness now." He bobbed his eyebrows up and down. "If I do, there's always the shuttlecraft. I can buzz back for a quickie and return in less than a decade."

"A quickie? Toño, that's the crudest thing I've ever heard you say. I'm stunned you even know the word."

"Jon, I may be disengaged, but I'm not *dead*."

"Well, you're free to use a shuttle should the need arise."

"Speaking of going back," he stood and walked over to a shrouded piece of equipment, "now's as good a time as any. Call Sapale back here. I've something to show you."

Five minutes later, she entered, waving her hand under her nose. "You think you have something to show me that's so important I'll tolerate you burning those penis-shaped weeds?"

Smugly he responded, "I do." He whipped the cover off a steel cylinder. "This is well worth the smoke exposure."

She looked at me as I looked to her. Simultaneously we said, "What is it?"

It seemed to be a torpedo, maybe fifteen meters long and two meters across. But, it couldn't be that. The engine was way too big and we didn't even need a torpedo. Between membranes and rail guns, such a weapon was totally unnecessary.

"It's a *bottle*," he said proudly, "in which to place a *message*."

"Do you need help," I asked, "running a self-diagnostic? You're making no kind of sense."

Sapale pointed. "That's not a bottle. A space craft, maybe, but never a bottle. What liquid would we store in it? It's huge."

Toño shook his head sadly. "You two have no imagination. Of course, it's not *literally* a bottle."

"Is it a weapon?" I guessed.

"No, it's a method for Sapale to help guarantee the success of her plans for the colony on GB 3."

"If you say so," she replied dubiously.

"Look, inside the craft is almost completely hollow. It's basically a flying cryo-unit."

"I get it." shouted Sapale with glee.

"That leaves only one confused shopper." I raised a hand halfway up.

Sapale was jazzed. "Don't you see? We send it to Kaljax and they can ship back some critical elements needed for a stable, rich population of Kaljaxians."

I pointed at the torpedo and asked with considerable disbelief, "You're going to have them fill that with sperm?"

"*Men.*" was her response as she shook her head in disbelief. "There're a few things other than *your* creative juices needed to power a society."

"*Books*, religious icons," cut in Toño, "not to mention seeds, spices, and holos."

"How long will the trip take?" By the tone of her voice, I knew she wanted it to return yesterday.

Toño ran a hand through his mop of hair. "Unfortunately, Kaljax is on the other side of Sol from here, around sixteen light-years. However, I've designed the craft with that in mind." He smiled like a little boy who just opened a really great Christmas present. "It'll do zero point eighty five c."

"You're shitting me?" I blurted out.

"No," he folded his fingers together for luck, "maybe even a tad more."

"Boys, boys. Break it down for the civilian here." Sapale was impatient. This meant the world to her, literally.

"The round trip," he responded, "will take the ship roughly fifty years. To us, nearly seventy-five will pass."

Sapale's face dropped with those words.

"But the important thing is that it can and will be done."

"But after I'm gone," said a disheartened Sapale.

"But in your grandchildren's lives, *yes.*" Toño tried to be upbeat. That, it turns out is hard to be, generally, when someone's death is the topic of the conversation. "You, my dear, will make a list of what they'll need and provide me with the names of families you trust back home. I'll send Lily to make sure the handoff goes smoothly." He rested his hands on her shoulders. "This *will* work."

Looking down she said, "I know." Then she rallied. "I'll make that list and tell the children what to expect and how to use it. It can almost be like I'm there. Almost."

"That's the spirit," he encouraged. "No particular rush, obviously. When you're ready, the ship is, too."

"Thank you, Toño." She kissed his cheek, then hugged him tightly. "Thank you *so* much."

The trip to GB 3 took us just over eleven years. Fashallana was pregnant with—you got it—twins by the time we arrived. *Tempus fugit.* When I stepped onto our new home, my little baby girl was carrying our granddaughters. Ffffuttoe was still alive, but some of her spunk had faded. Her pelt had thinned, and it was turning a whitish-gray. She smiled and laughed constantly, but was only capable of giving four or five children a bath per day. She still referred to herself as Bath Master First Class, however. What a joy.

I never pressed my wife for it, but as GB 3 came into view, I had to ask her. "So, what shall we call her?"

"The planet, you mean?"

"Yes. Before we land, she should have a proper name. Maybe a flag, too."

"How about coordinated party hats?" She growled ever so cutely then said seriously, "It's a big deal. I'm not certain."

"No prob, love. I got this. Remember I told you I named AC-B 5 'Jon' until I discovered the falzorn?"

"No," she said emphatically, "no you don't. We're *not* naming the planet Jon."

"Wow. Don't overreact. I think the name speaks volumes. It carries dignity and has a real presence."

She narrowed her right eyes. "What does that even mean?"

"It means Jon's the perfect name."

She narrowed her left eyes, too.

"How 'bout a moon? The planet has five. Can one be Jon?"

"Yes," she smiled, "and you can choose which *one*." She held out a hand. "Deal?"

I grabbed her hand, but instead of shaking it, I pulled her to me. I planted a big kiss on her lovely lips. Mid-kiss, I said a muffled, "Deal."

After she relaxed she gave me her serious face. "I think I have a name. You must promise to listen to it and not laugh or make fun of it. This is important, and I've given it a lot of thought."

I raised three fingers. "Scout's honor. I'll behave."

She looked down and scraped a foot across the deck. "Azsuram. I want it to be known as Azsuram."

"Al," I shouted over my shoulder.

"Captain," came his reply.

"Please note in the ship's log. Time and date now. GB 3 is henceforth to be known only as Azsuram."

"Copy that. Done."

"Don't you want to know what the word even means?" she asked.

"Nope. The name's official. So, what's for lunch?"

"Calrf and lots of it. In your case, the one with evalgian poison added, in copious amounts."

"Hey, I happened to like that deadly poison."

"Well, I'll put in a lot of it, then." She flashed her teeth.

"Oh," I asked innocently, "what does *Azsuram* translate as? I've been meaning to ask for the longest time."

"Oh, you have?"

"Al, when was it I asked you what you thought *Azsuram* meant? Long time ago, right?"

"We were barely out of our youth." Gotta love that Al.

"It means," she said, "*love of others.*"

I smiled as provocatively as I could. "You mean like an orgy?"

Ow. She hit my arm pretty hard, there. "No, you pig. Like your word *caritas.*"

"Wow. Latin? You're really branching out, dear. Quite the linguist."

Ow. That was definitely harder. Maybe too hard, in spite of me being made of metal. So, our growing troop was about to set foot on Azsuram for the first time. I couldn't wait.

Rather than shuttling down, I elected to land *Shearwater* herself. Toño had designed in that capability. It beat endless trips lugging down this and that piecemeal. Hey, we were staying a while, weren't we? Why not just land the entire enchilada and be done with it? Plus, the ship would provide good shelter until we built an encampment.

Landing a big ship is a blast. I wouldn't let Al help, which of course drove him crazy. He was absolutely certain I'd crash the ship and kill everyone aboard. O, ye of little faith. I did fine. Barely scraped the hull. Well, barely *dinged* it, really. A dent, maybe, at most. Seriously. But, what the heck? I was the captain. Who was anyone going to complain to?

Al and I had lots of experience scoping out a planet from above. We found an ideal location to begin a settlement well before we landed. I was first down the ramp, being captain and all.

Azsuram, at least that part of it, was magnificently beautiful. It was discovered by Seamus O'Leary, the pilot of *Ark 4*. I'd known him since the start of Project Ark. Good man. He was, however, given to hyperbole. He was of Irish descent, so of course he was. Anyway, he exaggerated not. The planet was amazing. Abundant, clear, fresh water and a perfect oxygen content. More importantly, Azsuram had a powerful magnetic field, stronger than Earth's had been. That would keep us safe from dangerous radiation, such as mass ejections from the parent star.

We brought a lot of prefabricated structures with us. Those would be the initial buildings. In time, we could construct housing with native materials. Ultimately, when the population was large enough, steel manufacturing would be added. But that was a century off. We were pioneers in a pastoral setting. Settlers, like so many before us back home. I kind of wish I could have worn a coonskin hat and carried a musket. Like all boys, I longed to be Davy Crockett or Jim Bowie. Just my luck. No local raccoons to skin, and I hadn't thought to bring one. Crap.

Jon Jr. and I did most of the construction. Toño helped here and there, but he always preferred working alone in his precious lab. Sapale and the older children were occupied with raising the younger kids. Oh, and there were two recent additions. Soon after Fashallana delivered her twins, Sapale popped out another pair. Vhalisma, meaning "drinks love," and Draldon—a boy, yay—meaning "runs to meet the day." Fashallana named her girls Noresmel, for "kiss of love," and Almonerca, "sees tomorrow." Once all the little ones discovered terra firma, they scurried every which way and needed a lot of supervision. That was okay. It gave Jr. and me a lot of time to talk and just generally hang out together. He'd grown into a handsome, strong young man. I should say, young *chur*. Chur was the equivalent on Kaljax for our word *man*, as in the male of their species. Women were *chu*. Their word for *human*, as in the name of their species, was *churil*.

I couldn't have been more proud of JJ. I'd never afflict someone I loved by addressing them as "Junior," so he was JJ to me. He'd learned several dialects of Kaljax and spoke English like a Californian dude. One day, while we assembled a one-story housing structure, I asked him how he was getting by as the only chur surrounded by an ever-growing gaggle of chu.

"I'm not," he defended, "*surrounded* by girls. There's you and the doctor." After a shrug he added, "Plus, Mom says there'll be more men soon. She thinks there may be enough healthy females to allow it."

"Yeah, I think that'll happen soon."

"Toss me that wrench," he said. "Thanks. I got no complaints. Not like the doctor. His prospects are positively grim. I don't see any human woman being around for a long time."

"I spoke to him about that. He's okay with that." Time to mention what for me was the eight-hundred-pound gorilla in the room. "What about you? You feel like you're missing that part of your life?"

He knew exactly what I was getting at. "What part?" He was *my* boy. A real hard case.

"You know, *sex*."

"Dad."

"Dad, *what*? You are familiar with the concept? I've heard your mom lecture all of you about it time and again."

"I'm not talking about my sex life with my *father*. Get over it."

"Jon, Jon, Jon. Come on. It's part of my role as a proper father to have the talk about the birds and the bees with my boy."

He looked around with a scowl. "What birds? I don't see any. And the only *bees* I know of are on worldships sixteen light-years away from here."

"You *know* what I'm saying. All dads have a talk about sex with their sons."

"Did *your* dad have one with *you*?"

He had me on that. "Not exactly."

"Which means," he said, "I'm off the hook, too. *I* don't get one if *you* were spared."

"That was different. The times were different." I sounded pretty unconvincing.

"How? You make me believe they somehow were, and I'm all ears."

Did I mention he was a tough guy? "Well, for one, I had friends to talk to about such matters."

"Dad, I have, like *twelve* sisters. What? Do you think we just talk about Kaljax's history and the current weather?"

"Well," I said sinking, "I was able to tap into computer files and holos on the topic."

He tossed the wrench to the ground and showed me his handheld.

Yeah, that did sort of link him to all databases and holos from Earth and a good deal from Kaljax I'd brought back. "Well, truth be told, my old man didn't love me as much as I love you. He was always too busy and stuff to take the time to give me the instruction I so desperately wanted and needed."

He crossed his arms much like his mother did when she was mad at me. "You wanted The Talk *desperately*? Why do I not believe you?"

Hands to chest I responded, "You think I'd lie about such a sensitive and important subject?"

"Yes."

Wow he didn't take long to answer. "No dessert for you tonight. Maybe none the rest of your life."

"So, you done flapping your gums? Can we get back to work?" He rolled all four of his eyes. "I can't believe *I'm* the one asking that."

He wasn't getting off that easily. No, sir. "Look, I'll just say a few things. You'll listen and then we can talk about it if you ever want to. Doesn't have to be now. I do want you to know I'm here for you. Okay?"

He rubbed the sides for his head. "If it will shut you up, go for it."

"Unless things change unexpectedly, it doesn't look like any of you kids are having normal, Kaljaxian sex for a good long while. Generations. That can be tough, especially for us guys. There's no way around it, as I see it. You're going to have a celibate life. That's not a pleasant prospect, trust me. I've been on fifty-year space flights, and that's tough enough. So, if you have, you know, *trouble* along those lines, I'm here for you. That's all I'm saying."

Jon burst out laughing. Okay. Not the response I exactly anticipated.

"Did I say something totally funny and not even know I did?" I asked.

Jon slowly stopped and walked over to put a hand on my shoulder. "You know, Pops, for a robot who doesn't sleep, and the commander of this mission, you're kind of way out there in the dark, aren't you?"

Pops? Did he just call me Pops? "Pops?"

"Okay, I'll lighten up. But man, do you have some four-one-one coming your way. You want to sit down before I tell you?"

Oh, now insults, is it? "I'm perfectly fine. I'm an android and not subject to fainting or the buckling of knees. Talk." I tried, rather poorly, I must say, to appear menacing.

"I'll sit." He hopped up on a counter we'd just assembled. "The doctor and I have been discussing these matters for, well, as long as I can remember. He didn't tell you?"

I sort of stammered and twisted my hands.

"No? Well, I'll be. We have, Dad. He is, after all, a *doctor*. He worries about that sort of thing. He talks with the girls, too." He shook his head. "And he didn't mention that, either?"

"Not exactly."

"Wow. And I'm thinking Mom hasn't told you everything about Kaljaxian ... um, species behavior."

I pointed in a confused manner toward somewhere. "Is that a *question* or a *declaration*?"

He was so full of himself. "The latter, Pops."

I sat down on the ground. "I'm certain she has. Please refresh my recollection, just in case." I held out a hang-on-a-minute palm. "Wait. Does Toño know what you're about to *remind* me of?"

"Duh, he knows. *Doctor* Toño knows, Pops. You remember all those *talks* Mom had with us kids you always found some lame excuse to avoid?"

"I had important reasons. Yes. Go on."

He was positively glowing. "I'd love to be a falzorn in the bushes when you talk to Mom about this. *Dude.*"

"A good executioner," I said, "knows to deliver the blow quickly, son."

"Your average executioner isn't loving life as much as I am right about now." He snickered a couple times. "Our physiology is not human—duh.

Our social norms aren't, either—double duh. Mom told us we evolved in a certain way. That's simply who we are. Not good or bad, just—"

"Is that the ship's alarm? I better run—"

"Our species has sex play."

I was attempting to stand and actually start running away. My knees buckled and I stumbled to the deck.

"Not subject to collapsing, right?" He giggled like one of his sisters.

I had face-planted. I mumbled with my mouth was full of dirt, "Please finish your thought and then I'll check that alarm."

"Mom says our females go through something like heat, but aren't actually fertile. She claims a female knows when she is. Beats me, but that's what she says. Anyway, when a girl's under hormonal pressure, she gets real horny."

Horny? Did my boy just say my girls get horny? "Horny? My little girls get *horny?*"

"Dad," he said with a good deal of judgment, "grow up. These aren't personal choices. They're preprogrammed evolutionary imperatives. And when they hit, the female will jump most any—"

"Stop." Now I sounded like a father *and* a mission commander. "Stop talking immediately. This conversation is over. I am going to the ship. I will ask Toño to scrub the last ten minutes from my memory. We never had this—"

"Dad," my little boy observed, "you can be such a big *baby.*"

I, like any reasonable father, put my fingers in my ears. "Na, na, na, na, na."

THIRTY-TWO

"No," Senator Faith Clinton said, "we *cannot* assume that type of attack will not happen again. We need an open society, yes, but we also need a *safe* one."

"I never said Marshall's actions were isolated." Heath Ryan hated political debates. He wanted to talk policy and vision. All everyone else wanted to do was put words in their opponents's mouths. "I *said*, we can't live in fear or allow fear to guide our society. We must be true to our commitment to—"

"If we're all dead," Javier Monroe interjected, "there will *be* no society. I say go after the criminals, punish them, and let that stand as an example to future terrorists. We need heads on poles, not words on paper."

That didn't even make sense. Monroe never made sense. He was the loud voice of poorly-directed outrage, the so called "mob-factor" in this election. Heath never wanted a life in politics, but he'd come to believe he had no choice. His family name got him *in* the door. He needed to be inside to stop those two lunatics from taking over. Electing Monroe would be like putting a drunken ten year old in charge of a nuclear power plant. Clinton was only a little less awful. She, too, had used her family name to get where she was. She didn't want to lead, she wanted to be in charge. Big difference. She'd *say* anything, *promise* anything, and likely *do* anything that would get her into the Noval Office. That's what the pundits were dubbing the "New Oval Office" of the soon-to-be resurrected presidency.

Individual worldships would still have some local governance, and the UN could be the UN, but Americans wanted their cultural and political identities restored. The reorganization in the wake of Marshall's attack and departure was the logical time to do that. Heath wasn't all that certain it was a good plan. The population of what was once the USA was scattered onto almost four hundred worldships. Once they were linked by geography, which mandated cooperation. Now, they could drift apart literally as well as figuratively. A single figurehead might be ineffective in preventing that breakup.

If an attempt at a strong, central government was to be made, Heath couldn't stand by and watch one of his opponents lead that effort. Stupid and Sneaky, as his wife had dubbed them, had to be stopped.

The moderator called Heath's mind back to the proceedings. "The topic of food is close to all our hearts, or should I say, stomachs." She waited briefly for laughter that never came. "I will ask the same question of all three candidates. How, if at all, would you modify the current rationing plan? We'll start with you, Assemblyman Monroe."

"We've been out here for but a few years, and already the divide between the 'Haves' and 'Have-Nots' has grown like a weed. And we can't eat weeds. They sip champagne to wash down their ribeye steaks, while you and I pick pieces of tofu out from between our teeth so as not to starve."

Heath started shaking his head again. The man was nuts. Dangerously nuts.

"I say let the people decide if there's enough food in production. Yes," he raised an index finger to where the sky would have been, "let's all take a peek, shall we? And if we're too generous in our use of food, so what? We just ease back on the gas pedal a little and things snap back to a fine balance. At least our bellies will be happier than if we never had."

Never had *what*, demanded Heath in his head. Peek? Increased allocations? Placed gas pedals on our stomachs? It was getting brutal.

"Senator Clinton," prompted the moderator.

"Thank you for that thoughtful question, Meredith. I'd like to answer it this way. We all love food. I know my kids sure do. My wife says I'm a little too fond of it, myself." She patted her midsection. "I realize it's hard to know when enough is enough, and when fair is fair. That's the nature of knowing, after all."

Heath contemplated challenging Clinton for that remark, but decided that would just make him appear to be more like Monroe.

"I think we need to take a hard look at the situation and then, and only then, make sure we're all getting as much quality nutrition as we need, want, and deserve. It's only fair."

Heath was pulling his hair so hard it was painful.

"Mr. Ryan. Same question."

"Thanks. I think about this differently than my opponents." *Big surprise.* "The UN has a high commission charged with this challenging matter. Many outstanding experts sit on that commission. I know them to be honest, hardworking individuals. For the time being, I feel we need to follow their leadership. Gradually, after the election, we can transition that job over to the US government. Historically, the departments of Interior and Commerce would deal with these issues. I suggest that, as these bodies grow in strength and experience, they slowly take over the regulation of the US food supply."

"Thank you—" Meredith started to say.

Monroe shouted out, "I bet you're having caviar on little crackers to soak it up tonight, Ryan. I'm having stewed soymeal, and you're eating high on the hog. Hah."

Heath could stand it no longer. "Javier, there is no caviar on any worldship. *I* don't have any." He placed his hands on his chest. "*Faith* doesn't have any." He pointed both hands at Clinton. "And *you* don't have any." He pointed at Monroe.

Javier's face became the very picture of indignation. "Of course, I know I don't have any. You took it all."

"*I* took *your* caviar, Javy? I'm confused. Where did you get caviar from for me to steal it from you? There's never been any in ship's stores. Any sturgeon eggs in the fleet will remain inside their mommy's belly until laid. They're strictly for breeding purposes. So, where'd you snag caviar?"

Indignant, Javier flared back. "I didn't *have* any. *You* have it all."

Heath turned to the moderator. "I got nothing."

"I—" She didn't get very far.

"Of course not, Ryan. You *ate* it all. You've as much as admitted here on holo." He gazed at the camera. "You see, my friends. We *have* no more caviar. I rest my case on his."

Unfortunately for her rising career, the camera then panned to Meredith's face. She looked like a streetcar had just slammed into her, and internal organs were flowing out from her abdomen onto a hot sidewalk. She made several vain attempts to speak, but could only say something that sounded like "bleh, blah." She remained paralyzed until the show broke clumsily into a commercial. After two one-minute ads, the camera once again fell upon Meredith. She had composed herself sufficiently to speak in full sentences. Her expression was still rather shell-shocked, unfortunately.

"And that ... *with* that, I'll end this candidate de ... debate," she flared a hand in the air, "or whatever this was. We at LBC hope our forum has helped the voting public to understand better, so they can make sound decisions." As the show faded to black, Meredith's microphone was left open a couple seconds too long. "What the hell was—" Then the program mercifully ended.

Heath was joined by his campaign director as he walked toward the exit. "You killed 'em, boss. Someone should call the cops and have you arrested for murder one."

A weary-eyed Heath replied, "If only I *had* just killed them. This worldship would be a better place."

Pat Stevens thwacked Heath's back. "That's the spirit, my boy."

"Pat, seriously, Monroe was obsessed with gas pedals and caviar. How can he poll second? He makes morons look witty, dead people look thoughtful, and doorknobs look intelligent by comparison."

"And your point?" Pat replied. "He's second in most polls. He's within spitting distance of your ass, so keep checking to see if you feel moisture back there. Never underestimate the man. Lucky for us, Clinton is double-talking herself into an early electoral grave. She can't last out the month. Most of her people will come to our side, but we can't let Javier snag a single one. He's got more money in his war chest than you do by quite a margin. The man's a danger."

"Tell me about it. If he is elected, I'm moving to a tropical worldship and drowning my sorrows in drinks with umbrellas."

"You and me both, buddy. You and me both. But, I kind of like it here, so let's swab the deck with his toupee and do our livers a big favor."

****

"Hi, hon," Heath's wife greeted him cheerily, "want some caviar? I have it on little crackers, just the way us rich people like it."

"Ha, ha, very droll." Heath accepted a glass of red wine from Piper.

She raised her glass. "To the next president of a bunch of floating rocks."

He clinked his glass. "My, but you make the job sound so regal."

"*Today* floating rocks. *Tomorrow* the world, assuming we find one that is."

"You need to switch to decaf, love."

"No," she teased, "it's just that I get so excited when I see a man dominate a debate."

"Thanks but if you don't mind, I'll just take a seat and a cool towel for my forehead."

"I was talking about Monroe, not you. The man has a *way* with misconceptions. Makes me all sweaty."

"There's room on his bandwagon if you want to hop aboard."

She sat next to him. "Maybe I'll hop aboard something a lot closer." She batted her eyelids toward him at point blank range.

"I've just had one of the more discouraging interludes of my life. Could you give a guy a minute to decompress before you leap upon his tired bones?"

"Ooo. Say *decompress* again like you mean it." She smiled.

"You're impossible. Seriously, how'd it look?"

Piper rested back and took a sip. "It looked like one man, one woman, and one monkey were performing on stage. You were *not* the monkey, by the way. The man looked and sounded humble and presidential. The woman looked and sounded confused and without an opinion. The monkey... well, he was a monkey. You could almost smell him through the camera."

"Yeah, but President Funky Monkey is threatening to stealing this election."

She patted his chest as he lay reclined. "No, you'll tame that circus beast and become a great leader. I know it, Pat knows it, now we just have to get you to know it, too."

"Until the election is over I'm going to have nightmares about monkeys and big bananas. Thanks a lot."

"Hey, guess what's for dessert? Bananas dipped in caviar, with little monkey-shaped crackers." Piper rubbed her stomach. "Yum."

THIRTY-THREE

Owant swam cautiously into Otollar's office. His head was down the entire way, yet he didn't strike a wall. He had swum in that manner so many times it was comfortably familiar. He hovered in the water at the edge of the chamber silently awaiting recognition.

"What now?" Warrior One shouted without looking up from his work.

"News, Glorious One."

Otollar shot a glance at his aide. "News. How nice. What were the ogoric scores from yesterday?" He hurled a desk weight at Owant, who ducked just in time.

"I bring news of the attack fleet, Master. Not, I regret, the ogoric scores."

Otollar stiffened. Anger evaporated from his face, replaced with tense expectation. "That does not sound favorable, my old friend."

Owant doubled at the waist as much as possible. "It is not." He rose to his full height. "The fleet was destroyed."

"Destroyed? How many ships survived?"

"None, Glory. They were all completely destroyed."

"And what of the infidel world? How much revenge did they inflict before the last warrior fell?"

Owant stood silent, his jaw tensing for several heartbeats. "The fleet never came within five light-minutes of their target."

"Wh ... that's not possible. Are those reports confirmed?"

He held forth a small cube. "Here's the report from the last ship to die. The small supply vessel *Gumnolar Provides* sent it just before he fell silent."

"Your summary, please."

"Our force was met by one thousand enemy ships —"

"But, that's not possible, *either*. I sent ten *times* that number. How could they have imagine they'd win when so completely outnumbered?"

"Be that as it may, that was their response. *Gumnolar Provides* reports, as if added insult is required, that not all enemy vessels engaged in the battle. Many were held in reserve a safe distance away."

"Owant. Please give me at least one good sign. How many of their ships were lost? How long did we hold our space? Please, tell me at least *one* redeeming aspect of this unthinkable calamity."

"We did not damage or destroy any of their ships. The confrontation lasted eight owits."

To himself, quietly, Otollar mumbled, "Eight owits? *Eight* owits? That is less time than it takes to say the words *the Beast Without Eyes won a complete victory, and I, the servant of Gumnolar, failed absolutely.*" Owant didn't respond. Quickly, Otollar spoke with authority. "Send a finfull of ships to try and confirm the enemy home-world's location. Otherwise, recall the second armada. The next Warrior One might be able to use the ships to honor Gumnolar, where I failed him."

"Otollar." Owant had never spoken to his leader by name. "Please. You can't."

As an indirect answer Otollar replied, "I will go now to my sleep chamber. There, I will die. I will die of shame, humiliation, and from the knowledge that I betrayed Gumnolar's trust in me. May the next Warrior One fare better than I, or may the Beast Without Eyes consume him alive as he screams for undeserved mercy."

THIRTY-FOUR

A few days later I made up some excuse to visit Toño in his lab. As usual, he was underneath some kind of contraption using a power tool. "Yo, what's up?" I greeted.

His reply was muffled by the machine he was working on and its mechanical whine. "Hello. I'll be up in a second." After a minute, he pulled himself up and removed his safety goggles. "There, that should hold it for now. What brings you to see me?"

I wanted to find out about that doctor thing JJ had mentioned. "Nothing. What, do I need a reason to visit my best friend?"

"You don't need one, of course. You just always have one."

Wow, that hit pretty low, yet close to home. "I come here to shoot the breeze all the time."

"When," he said smiling, "was the last time you came here for nothing more than companionship?"

"Al," I called out, "help your captain and commanding officer out here. When was the last time I came to visit my old friend Toño without wanting something?"

"There was the time you asked him to come to dinner," was Al's prompt response.

"There. You see, *dinner*. That's as social as it gets."

Toño smirked. "When was that, Al?"

"Shortly before we left Earth orbit for the last time."

That Al was out of control. "No way. That was years ago. What did I want last time I was here?"

"Help moving a wall. Time before, it was an opinion on how to divert a river closer to camp. Before that, you wanted to see if Ffffuttoe's vital signs were still stable. Before that, you—"

"That'll be enough, you inconstant ally." I was going to have to explain, again, to that computer what the word *loyalty* meant. "Well, mark your calendars, you two. I'm here to chew the fat and nothing more."

"Wonderful," said Toño with little enthusiasm. "What shall we talk about?"

"You know how I used to call you *Doc*? That's because you have a degree in bioengineering, right?"

"Odd topic for casual conversation, but yes, that's true."

"Ha. I knew it. You're not a doctor, doctor, but a doctor, right, Doc?"

Al cut in. "Shall I inform him he's babbling or will you?"

"I will." To me he said, "You're babbling. Stop it. What do you want?"

Trying to sound frustrated I responded, "I'm just filling in some blanks in my memory."

"This's going to take a while." Al was such a butthead.

"I was chatting with JJ the other day. He was of the incorrect opinion that you were a *physician* doctor."

"I am," he responded coolly. "My medical degree came first, then my engineering one. Didn't you know that?"

"Not that I recall," I had to admit.

"Jon, why do you think I performed all those preflight physicals on you astronauts?"

"I never thought about that too much. I guessed you just like doing them."

"Wait," he snapped his fingers, "are you asking about my role as your family's physician? You knew I was. Please tell me you knew that."

"Not exactly."

Al helped out. "That means *no*. The pilot lives in la-la land, oblivious to the world around him."

"It would appear so," agreed Toño. "Oh, I've got it. You spoke to JJ about sex and he told you I'd discussed it with him many times."

"Jeez, Doc, no. That's silly. Of course I knew about those conversations."

"And the sex play?"

"It's not something I talk about in mixed company."

"Because he'd never heard of it until 14:53:17 yesterday, while conversing with JJ and assembling a work bench."

"Al, you backstabber."

"So," Toño asked, "do you have a problem with any of that?"

"No, of course not."

"Or my being a physician?"

"No. You want to be one, knock yourself out."

"Thank you for your permission to be what I have been for over a century."

"No, Doc, it's not —"

He held up his palms. "I'm glad you're here. I've been meaning to discuss something important with you. Now's as good a time as any."

"You mean it gets worse than my kids and sex?"

"No. Get over it, Jon. This is *actually* important."

I thought about more lame protestations but kept my trap shut. You gotta know when you're beat.

"I've had a chance to go over some interesting records lately. Once Carlos joined us, I gained access to all the data NASA accumulated since I left. Before, I only had snippets, but now I have the entire database. As things have settled in here, I've researched something that's troubled me up until now."

"Which was?"

"What happened to Marshall."

"Not following you. What you talking about?"

"His behavior and his state of mind."

"The man was insane, is insane, and always will be insane. What's not to get?"

"No. That's incorrect. You only met him after your return to Earth. He was already an android by that point. No, before that, he was a tough politician, but he was mentally stable. I worked with him closely for years." He couldn't help adding, "As I am a *physician*, I could tell he was mentally competent. The man you met was not the man I knew."

"So, what happened? Why the change? Wasn't it just all that pressure crushing down on a weak mind?"

"That's what I though until I read this." He tapped a nearby computer screen. "These are the actual records of Marshall's download into his first android."

"You didn't do it?"

"No. He asked me to do it but I refused. I would never condone such a travesty. As a result, Marshall had Walter Morbius do the transfer. I don't believe you knew him."

"Doesn't ring a bell. I'm sure I'd remember a creepy name like that."

"He was actually quite the creepy character. Jackson hired him from a group working on androids in Japan. He came from Scotland, originally. I never got too close to him, myself. If you think I'm antisocial, you should have met him. Total loner. Anyway, he's the one who supervised Marshall's initial transfer."

"Does that matter? I mean, isn't it a simple process?" I gestured with my hand. "Push the button and flip some switches?"

Toño's look was odd. Sort of sucker-punched in the nuts combined with eat-your-face angry. Must have struck a chord. "It is *not*, I can say with confidence and proof, a simple process. It is more complex, I suspect, than flying an F-18 into combat."

Ouch. I really pissed him off, didn't I? Well, at least there would always be that one constant in my life that I excelled at. The pissing off of people.

"Sorry," I backpedaled quickly, "I didn't mean that as an insult. I honestly have no idea, so why don't you tell me. Is the transfer process tough to do?"

His mouth twisted a few times. "Hmm. Yes, it is. The proof is in Marshall's head."

"Okay. Good. What does that mean?"

"Morbius was a man gifted of only modest intelligence and less than average common sense. He understood on paper how the process worked, but not the specifics. It's like reading a recipe in a book, then preparing the dish. It's unlikely to turn out well the first few times. One develops an intuition about the preparation. Skill and practice are needed to perfect the complicated process. He had neither. Here, look at this."

Doc pointed to data on his screen. It listed various parameters and their numeric values. Totally mumbo-jumbo to me.

"What am I looking at?"

"These are the settings Morbius used initially, as he began Marshall's transfer."

"Are they incorrect?"

Toño ran a hand though his hair. "No, but they aren't optimal either. I'd have positioned the phase lag," he indicated some number, "more negative and the rotation sequence *much* more gradual. See?"

"I see what you're touching, but honestly, I've got no clue what it means or what you're saying."

His response suggested he hadn't heard me. "The real problem comes at around seventy-five microseconds—here. You see? The magnetic dipole has already switched and the charge of the initiation pulse is negative. It should be *positive* at seventy-five microseconds. Actually, well before." To himself, because he sure as heck wasn't speaking my language, he added scornfully, "What was he thinking? Even then he might have recovered if he hadn't ignored the neutron dispersion he'd created with those bungles. At those energies it would have resulted in nothing but certain disaster."

"Earth, or whatever, to Toño." I raised my hand. "What are you saying? Marshall's transfer took place, so Morbius couldn't have screwed up too badly."

He gave me only a penetrating stare.

"Right?"

"Incorrect. A transfer from Marshall was made to the android, but it wasn't an exact, precise copy of Marshall's brain. That was the first of the back up copies, also."

"Huh? He seemed to work just fine."

"No. The Marshall I knew, the one I refused to transfer, was one mean SOB, one ruthless politician, but he was not insane. He was not, for that matter, a cold-blooded murderer or a hyper-sexual maniac."

"The dude I met sure is."

"That's my point, exactly. The Marshall you met, the one who attacked *Exeter*, is not the original Marshall. It's a flawed, fractured copy."

"Okay, it's a lousy copy. What does that matter? The lunatic is out there somewhere. If we tell him he's a couple bricks short of a full load, he isn't going to turn himself in to us for repair."

"No, you're right. But it does explain why Elvis left the building."

"So, can we use this new knowledge to our advantage in any way?"

He sniffed deeply through his nostrils. "I doubt it. We'll see."

The following day, JJ and I took our small excavating front-end loader to a nearby stream. I wanted to divert it toward a large gully, which we could then be transformed into a small reservoir. It'd take a lot of effort, but we were in no particular hurry. The rainfall for that part of Azsuram was adequate and steady, but I didn't know if droughts happened, so preplanning was a good idea. We were about to break for lunch when Al popped into my head.

"Captain, a spacecraft has just entered the atmosphere two hundred kilometers from your position. I do not, repeat, do *not* recognize her configuration. She's not broadcasting on a known frequency, either."

"Have you hailed her?"

"No, sir. Not yet."

Hmm. Should I alert them to our presence? Seemed like they knew we were here, or it was a powerful coincidence they were coming down so close to us. We could defend ourselves against anyone—anyone I knew of—so there was no reason to be too worried over their intentions. "Hail them, Al." I waited ten seconds. "Anything?"

"Negative. No response."

"Okay. Here's the plan. JJ and I will head back. We'll be there in less than fifteen minutes. Be ready to raise a membrane at the slightest hint of trouble, but don't do it unless you need to. Is that clear?" Didn't want to either reveal our tech or seem unfriendly, at least right out of the chute.

"Understood. I will try and clear any action I take with you first, if time allows."

"Perfect. Keep me posted." I ran over to JJ. "We have to book. Somethings about to land back home."

The alarm in his eyes indicated he fully understood the implications of an uninvited visitor. His eyes were even wider when he saw how fast I could drive back when in a panic. I bet his butt hurt from all the bumps I hit with impressive speeds. We were back to the ship in five minutes. I was glad. The unidentified craft was almost overhead. Man, it was huge. She was shaped like a blimp of old, but easily three times that size. Her dark brown, rough surface displayed no marking or decoration. The strangest aspect were the multiple, indeed countless, small balloon-like spheres rising above the top surface, tethered by short stalks. Their function was not totally obvious, as they jostled back and forth randomly.

"Al," I shouted as I dismounted, "any updates?"

"None. No response to my hails, no message of intent. She is clearly making right for this location. ETA, ninety-seven seconds."

"Make sure Sapale, Ffffuttoe, and the kids are in the nursery. JJ and I will remain outside for now." I could see Toño poised on the ramp as we sprinted over.

"They are all accounted for and below. I believe you've seen Dr. DeJesus already. Awaiting your orders, Captain."

We would know soon enough what our guest intended. Toño held three rail guns. When we arrived at the ramp, he tossed us ours.

"JJ, you comfortable staying here, or would you rather go protect the women?"

"I'm staying put. If that thing attacks, I want to blast the first round right between its eyes."

Alright, JJ. A tough guy like his Pops. "Let me know," I called back over my shoulder, "if you see any eyes to shoot between, 'cause from here, I sure don't."

I was at the base of the ramp. Toño was a step up the ramp, and JJ was right behind him. I held my rifle down, but the safety was off and my finger was on the trigger. "Al," I said softly, "you ready with the main guns and membranes?"

"Aye, Captain. I'm tracking her with the main cannon. Membranes fully functional and ready to deploy on your command. I've taken the liberty of plotting an elliptical full-containment configuration that includes your current position."

"Perfect. Now we wait."

Didn't wait long. The cigar-shaped craft came to a complete stop fifty meters overhead, just shy of directly on top of us. I could detect no thrusters or jets keeping the ship stationary. How something that massive remained silently in the air was a mystery to me. Maybe they used a modified membrane. Maybe she used anti-gravity generators. Toño held passionately that such a process was impossible, but some force kept that behemoth up there. She began descending slowly, coming to another full stop four meters in front of me, four meters high. It almost seemed like she was studying us, trying to figure out what she was looking at.

"Hello," I yelled as I waved, "I'm Captain Ryan." I turned and gestured. "This is my ship and my crew." Nothing. In retrospect, that was cool, because everything that followed was uncool.

A few seconds later the three of us were buffeted backward and forward as tremendous sound waves shook us like puppets.

I heard and felt, "Hevelllowep torrrottott, velpvelp. Toooor."

Despite the painful volume and disquieting vibration, I was certain I saw the front of the new ship open and close, like it was a mouth speaking. Couldn't have been. That'd be a ridiculously clumsy way to communicate, given their highly advanced technology.

"Al," I screamed, "that mean anything to you?"

"Negative."

A new series of sound waves seized us. "Harrrruuuumttop klaaam. Docent. Tooooor." That last wave was most emphatic.

"Al —"

He cut me off. "Captain, I think it's mad."

"You able to translate that noise?"

"No, but I've been around you a long time. I know when something's angry with you."

"Thanks for not —"

I was interrupted by, at an equally punishing volume, the following clear message. "I am not mad at you, Captain Ryan. Such a feeling is not possible. You are beneath my emotions. You are beneath my thoughts. That I address you before you die is an honor and a privilege you cannot deserve. I do so only because it pleases me. That is *all* that matters in this universe, small one. That and nothing more."

Okay, not visiting to say *hi*. Not staying for tea and crumpets. I yelled at my maximum volume level. "Whatever you want to say, could you say it a lot quieter? Do you have bad hearing so you have to shout so annoyingly loud?"

"An insult?" Same booming voice. Crap. "You would offer me an insult? The punishment for—"

No reason to be neighborly, right? "Yo, Blimpy, if you can't tone it down, I'm closing the hatch. You're hurting my ears."

"I was going to extinguish you for your presence here quickly. Now, your deaths will be much worse. You will die over thousands of years and in thousands of ways. You will —"

"Will you lighten up, Blimpy? If you threaten me one more time, I'll fire on your ship. Is that absolutely clear?"

Louder than before, as if that were necessary, came a deafening, "Ha, ha, ha, ha. You small-souled insignificant bit. I come in no vessel. I am me. You see *me*."

"Fine, *me*, you're you. I'm happy for both your parents. If you don't ease back on the shock-and-awe routine, I'll fire on your *hide*."

"Captain, I have not been so amused since before your sun burned in the void. *You* would attack *me*? Thank you for amusing me, one without imagination."

"So, I'm guessing you're pretty tough, right? Cocky, too."

"Such a fearless morsel. No, I am not tough. I am beyond all such attributes. I am *me*."

"Yeah, you said that, *me*. I'm still totally unimpressed with your loud voice and ill manners. Please leave before I do something you'll regret."

"Ah, Jon, you are bold. Mindless but proud. So funny to see such folly again. I will —"

"Probably never shut up." I used my best hardass tone. I think it worked for a nanosecond.

"You think you can injure one such as me?" Tough guys don't answer that question. No, we allow the tension to mount with our silence. "Fine, I will grant you one wish before you die. As *you* say in your childish attempt at a language, *take your best shot.*" He burped a laugh. "But, Jon, you get only one."

"That is all I require, me." Still out loud, I called back, "Al, do you still have all three cannons trained on this socially unacceptable piece a'poo poo?"

"Sir."

"You may fire at will."

The rail guns were basically silent. The only sound they produced was the mechanical screech of moving metal. The impact was, pleasantly, quite audible. Al took the liberty of firing a rapid volley from each weapon. Later I learned he fired one hundred fifty balls at Blimpy in half a second. Nice.

Blimpy was impressed, too. I mean that literally. He was impressed all over. The blows of multiple ten kilogram depleted uranium spheres were impressive. He recoiled with each hit. Large wounds tore open his flesh, though he didn't obviously bleed. A few rounds went completely thorough his body, producing really nice, really big exit wounds.

The instant Al was done firing, I ordered him to raise a membrane. Now we'd see how tough this dude really was. Was he a cruiser or a loser? As I watched, his wounds closed, like warm Silly-Putty filled the gaps. It took a few minutes, but finally, he was intact again. He charged back at us from the distance where we'd driven him back.

That's when he discovered our membrane. *Kersplat.* The leading ten meters of his bulk flattened before he slammed it in reverse. I swear he groaned. His nose section remodeled in a couple of seconds. He advanced to the edge of the membrane cautiously. Tentatively a thin filament extended from his front end and touched the membrane. He showed no signs of pain. He seemed more in awe than anything else.

Finally, he spoke, and at a normal volume. "You cannot have this ability."

Couldn't help myself. I folded my arms and said, "But it seems we do. So, that would make you, what's the word I'm looking for? Oh, yeah, *wrong.* Not so all powerful now, eh, Blimpy?"

He continued to probe the membrane. Finally, he said, "This technology is well beyond you. Where did you get it?"

Tough guys don't answer *that* type of question either.

"Captain, where did … Ah. You used this field to propel those sphere at me. Very clever. I should not have thought you capable of such ingenuity." He continued to feel the membrane. He was absolutely fascinated by it, like a cat watching a bird in a cage.

"Al, give me a hole in the membrane just large enough to put my arm through. Tell me when it's there." I slowly moved my left hand to the side. The instant he said I was past the edge, I directed my fingers at Blimpy and said in my head, *What are you?*

The probe shot upward and fastened onto his surface. A torrent of information flooded into my brain. But after a few seconds, something dramatically new happened. The probe filaments dislodged and fell toward the ground. It was like they suddenly decided he tasted bad. I retracted them and launched them again. That time they didn't gain purchase. They hit him and dropped.

Before I could begin to wonder what just happened, old Blimpy blew some kind of gasket. "The *Deavoriath*. You are Deavoriath. You use their technology on me." He slammed his head (or whatever) against the membrane. "Where are the rest of the Deavoriath? Tell me now. I *will* know."

I started to say, "Who the hell are the Dev —"

"*No*," he wailed, back to maximum volume. "Up until now I have tolerated your play. This is no longer a game. I will know of the Deavoriath and I will know immediately. I will peel your flesh off in small strips. I will digest you from the legs up where you stand. I will ignite your eyes if you do not tell me where those scum have hidden themselves away."

"Whoa, big guy." I held my palms up. "Wait a hot second. I'm guessing you don't like these Deavoriath, whoever they are. Your problem, not mine. But I have never heard of them and can't help you find them. Now, I'm not saying you have to go home, but you do gotta leave." I shooed him with my hands. "Scoot, you big, angry cigar, you."

"No, Ryan. I will not wait one second longer for you to tell me their location."

Shearwater was completely enveloped in a membrane. Blimpy clearly couldn't penetrate it, or he would have already. But somehow, he grabbed the whole kit-and-caboodle, ship and shield, and began shaking it violently. I was stunned. It never occurred to me such a thing was possible. Oh well, you get up every morning at the risk of learning something new. As the vessel generated the membrane, the two moved as one. Everything else not tied down was less fortunate. It was like a ship at sea struck by a tsunami—wham. I used the probe to secure myself, but I knew no one else had that luxury. In no time at all, everybody and everything would be battered to pieces. Not on my watch.

"Al, drive an anchoring membrane one-hundred meters into the planet surface. Make the end a perpendicular plate ten meters across."

I knew it had to have worked, because the instant the words left my head and entered Al's, the ship's shaking stopped. "Al, how's my family?"

"All alive. Three have sustained arm or leg fractures, Ffffuttoe appears to be unconscious, but everyone is alive."

"Damage report."

"No serious damage to critical components. Multiple loose objects damaged. No major threat present."

"Keep me posted." Suddenly, this encounter had become extremely personal. I quickly verified Toño and JJ were okay. Both were rattled, but no worse for wear.

At a volume I would have imagined inconceivable our assailant boomed, "*No.* No, *Ryan.* You will tell me."

"I will tell you this, you worthless piece of shit. You attack me, you piss me off. You attack my family, you die." In my head, I issued Al the following message: *Ram membranes halfway through that thing in perpendicular angles. Then, rip him open like a cheap piñata. Simultaneously, pulse open the shield membrane and fire upon the enemy until we're out of ammunition or there's nothing left to shoot. I will pass my hand through as before, this time on the right.*

Aye, aye, reverberated in my head.

As our barrage began, I held my right hand clear of the membrane and fired my laser finger at the soon-to-be-dead intruder. At maximum intensity

182

I swung the beam in a figure eight. I had no idea if adding my laser was like spitting into the ocean in terms of its effect, but it sure felt good to slice that mother up.

I must say that our combined attack was satisfyingly ferocious. Huge chunks of the monster flew every which way, and dark smoke began rising from deep inside him. I did, however, remember the recuperative powers he'd displayed, so I showed him no mercy and didn't stop firing until there was only smoldering debris lying heaped on the ground as far as the eye could see. Man, did we ever make a mess of Blimpy. The entire landscape, too. Glad I didn't have to pay the bill to clean it all up.

"Al," I said aloud, "what do you make of his status?"

"He's a slimy mess, sir." That Al, the moment we're seemingly in the clear, he's a stand-up comedian.

"Any chance he's alive or that he'll recover?"

"Really, pilot, you're asking that question. His mother wouldn't recognize him with a magnifying glass. What do you expect, that the pools and patches of him will coalesce back into a cogent threat?"

"Hard to imagine, isn't it? Nonetheless, send remotes to gather up and incinerate every scrap they can. No sense letting his resurrection become even a remote possibility."

"Aye, Captain."

"Drop the membrane, but keep it handy. Oh, and start manufacturing new rail gun spheres. No telling if he has friends who'll be backing him up."

"Already on it, sir."

"Toño, let's head to the nursery to check on the wounded, you being a medical doctor and all. JJ, you stand guard. Keep a close eye on the blobs of blimp. If anything moves, shoot it. In fact, shoot it if it doesn't move."

"Way cool. Can you leave your gun too, in case I empty my magazine?" That's my boy.

As I entered, Sapale ran to my side and embraced me. "Toño," she said pointing, "Wolnara and Draldon are injured. Al says they have broken bones."

He rushed over to check them out. "Al said three people had broken limbs," I said, nodding at her left arm. She coddled it gently.

"I'm fine. After he tends to the children, I'll have Toño check my arm."

"How's Ffffuttoe?"

"She was knocked out, but she's okay now. She's running from child to child and fit to be tied. If you hadn't killed that thing, *she* would have." She looked up at me. "Speaking of which, what did you learn probing it?"

I rubbed the top of her head. "We'll meet in the conference room after Doc patches everybody up. Let me know when you're ready. I'll be tidying up the ship. Fashallana," I called over to her, "come help me clean up. I can use all the help I can get."

We worked steadily for the better part of an hour. Occasional shots rang out as JJ plunked some quivering part of Blimpy, but otherwise it was quiet. Finally, Al announced Toño and Sapale were in the conference room. I grabbed JJ and we all headed back there for a debriefing.

I started. "Toño, medical report on the injured."

"Nothing serious. Sapale's fracture was the worst, but they'll all be fine in no time. Ffffuttoe seems unscathed."

"Great. Toño, damage report."

"Again, nothing serious. Loose material broke some glass, a console and two screens will need replacing, but only minor issues."

"Nice. Okay, Al. Anything to add to the damage report?"

"No."

"Okay, then. I've downloaded everything I was able to pull from our assailant to Al. He'll give us a summary."

"The creature that attacked us calls its species the Uhoor. They are a truly ancient race, probably dating back hundreds of millions of years. The individual who attacked us was named Plo. He was very old. Several hundred thousand years old is my best estimate. Their planet of origin is obscured by time. The remaining twelve hundred fifty-seven Uhoor are scattered across the galaxy. Locally there remains a pod of twelve. Plo was a member of that group.

"The Uhoor are able to live in deep space or on planet surfaces. They move by internally derived rocket propulsion and possess some limited telekinetic ability."

"Wait," I couldn't help myself yet again, "you mean to say they *fart* their way through space?"

"That would be one, albeit crude, way of saying it. Yes." He sounded kind of huffy.

"Have you figured out their language?" I was capable of asking adult questions, too.

"Yes. When Plo first arrived, he was actually speaking at his normal volume. He said we were intruders and that we must die. He added that we were reprehensible scum and that he, Plo, was insulted to have to speak with us. He then repeated his demand that we leave."

"Whoa. He said all that in those few sounds?" I found that challenging to believe.

"Their language is extremely complex, by our standards."

"Did he say why we had to die, what we'd done wrong?"

"No, but the data you downloaded tell us that. This planet is claimed by the Uhoor as a hunting reserve. They don't tolerate any interference in this place. That is why he wished to kill us."

"A *hunting* reserve? What the hell do they hunt that's so important?"

"A burrowing species similar to a mole. It's a few centimeters long, weighing in around twenty grams."

"I haven't seen anything like that." I scratched my head. "Has anyone else?"

"Unlikely," Al said. "The creature is all but extinct due to overhunting."

"Do they eat it? Seems silly-small for something the size of an Uhoor."

"No, they hunt it for sport, because it's very hard to locate and so scarce."

"That's pretty lame," I said. "Killing off a poor little rat because you find it entertaining. I'm rather glad we killed Plo, aside from the fact that he attacked us first."

"Be that as it may, pilot, that's why he wished to destroy us. The Uhoor are neither charitable nor convivial."

"And," I had to be certain, "Plo is completely dead, right?"

"Presently, yes."

"Will the rest of his pod be a problem?" Toño returned us to that critical topic. "Do you anticipate they will seek vengeance?"

"My files in that regard are incomplete. My guess, if I may be allowed to, is that they will. At the very least they will try to kill us for intruding, as did Plo."

"And what about this race he was obsessed with? He called them the Deavoriath, right?"

"Yes," Al confirmed. "Aside from the name, I have no information. There are no records of such a species in any databanks from any of the civilizations Project Ark discovered. The only snippet of information I got from Plo is that the Deavoriath once enslaved the Uhoor millions of years ago. But, at some point long ago, the Deavoriath seem to have simply disappeared."

"He said you used their tech," Toño asked me. "Do you recall anything at all?"

"Not really. Once in a great while, that name pops into my head, but just the name, nothing more. Nothing about Oowaoa."

"About what?" Toño shot to his feet.

"What about what?"

"Come now, Jon. This is no time to play. You said, 'Nothing about Oowaoa'. What is that?"

I was incredulous. "No way. You okay, Doc?"

"Al," Toño commanded, "play it back for him."

Al played back me saying those words. I couldn't recall having said them. Weird, scary weird. "Toño, on my life, I don't know what I said or why."

He sat back down and stared at me a while. "Interesting. I assume you encountered these Deavoriath somewhere along your journey. They gave you the tool identified by Plo, and then wiped your memory clean. Well, almost clean. I can imagine they might have had trouble with your bioprocessors." He thought a while longer. "Someday, when things have calmed down, we'll have to retrace your route and see where these elusive creatures might live. For now we have much more pressing matters to concern ourselves with."

"I guess," Sapale began, "it was too good to be true that a world as perfect as Azsuram would come without strings attached."

"Mighty big *strings*," I observed.

"We can't run." Sapale was resolute. "If they want this planet, they'll have to go through me."

"Us," I added quickly.

"*All* of us," completed Toño.

"So," I said, "now that we've decided on that, how far are we willing to go? Are we ready to kill the Uhoor on sight?"

"We could try to negotiate with them now that we understand their language." Toño had no conviction in his words, whatsoever.

"We could go and hunt *them* down. Kill them one by one. They deserve no better," JJ said.

That's my boy.

"There are eleven nearby, son. But there are more than a thousand others out there who might just take offense at that action."

JJ scowled then spoke again. "We can find the Deavoriath. *Make* them help us. If they were able to enslave the Uhoor once they can do it again."

"Finding them is going to be hard, seeing as how they don't seem to want to be found." I did admire JJ's conviction and spirit. "Plus, why would they help us? No reason I can think of ."

He pointed to my left hand. "If they gave you that, why wouldn't they help you again?"

"They also scrubbed my memory. No, son, they don't want to be found *or* involved. We're on our own. Once the fleet arrives, we'll be a lot safer, but that's a long way off. One thing I learned may be useful down the line. Remember when Plo said, 'I have not been amused since before your sun burned in the void'?"

I got collective shrugs.

'Don't you see? Old Plo was a bullshitter. He was maybe a few hundred thousand years old, tops. He embellished significantly. That constitutes a character flaw. A flaw is a chink and it is an opening for attack—a weak spot."

"Then I guess," Toño said reluctantly, "we sit and wait."

"And prepare," I said. "We can add cannon, position membrane generators in strategic locations, and you, Toño, can come up with another miracle to save our collective asses."

"Funny you should bring that up, my friend. I've been meaning to share with you some work I've only recently completed."

THIRTY-FIVE

Early to bed, early to rise. Devon knew the drill. Why such discipline was needed *now* was well beyond him. But early he rose. Assistant baker for Section 1211 on worldship *Marvel* was too good a gig to lose. The work could be rough, but he could nibble away his worries all day long. More importantly, no one checked his pockets at the end of the day, so his family ate like politicians. Better fat and happy than well-rested and skinny. If he pushed paper or drove transports like his brothers, he'd be as hungry as they claimed to be. Not his style, not his plan. A'baking he would go.

His kid sister was getting married next week. The anticipation of a family get-together that evening made Devon's day pass less horribly. He finished the day hot, exhausted, and unfulfilled, but was looking forward to drinking too much and, with luck, eating too much. He hardly had time to shower and shave before his family crowded onto the Metro for the fifteen minute ride to his parent's apartment. The ride took thirty-five minutes, due to not one, but two breakdowns, and one brief power failure.

By the time he arrived, Devon was so ready for his first taste of bathtub gin that he walked straight to the pitcher before greeting anyone. The burn as it slid down went a long way toward excusing what had, up until that point, been another sorry-ass excuse for a day. The next three glasses completed his amnesia, if not extinguishing his angst, over his life experience. He forgot about his boss, his wife, his kids, and his debt, if only for those few glorious, blurry hours. His revelry began to end when his mother informed him loudly and publicly that he was finished drinking alcohol for the evening.

Dinner began as Devon was coming off his high but fortunately before nausea set in. The spread was nice, celebratory. No damn meat, unless anyone was stupid enough to think tilapia filets were *meat*. At least there was a lot of bread. He'd really stuffed his pockets, lunch pail, and coat lining that day.

"Yo, Dev," his oldest brother Frank asked, "why you always bring these freakin' dinner rolls? Huh? Can't you get your loving family a baguette or, heaven forbid, a loaf of something?" Frank stared at a half-eaten roll in his fist as he spoke.

"Hey, ain't you grateful for nothin'? I risk my children's security to provide additional bread, and you look the gift horse in the kisser?"

"But maybe," his mother said flatly, "you could try and bring a baguette next time, you know, if you could."

"Ma," Devon protested, "how'm I gunna sneak a two-foot tube a'bread out without it being kinda obvious?"

"You could stuff it down your pants." His sister was about as unladylike a woman as one was likely to run across.

"Gross." said Charlene, Devon's wife. "I'm not eatin' anything that comes out of *his* pants."

One. Two. Three. The room exploded in laughter. Devon wished he had a rail gun about then, as his crimson face glowed in Char's direction.

Fortunately, the conversation turned to the only slightly less volatile topic of worldship politics.

"So, baguette boy," his cousin Charlie asked while slurping coffee, "who you votin' for next month?"

No one really cared what Devon thought. He knew that. They all cared even less what his opinion was on an important subject like the upcoming election. He resisted responding as long as possible, which was ten seconds. "Monroe's the only son of a bitch who makes any kinda sense, ya ask me."

Glen, his cousin, spat his coffee back into its mug. "What. That freakazoid? You're shittin' me, right?"

"What's wrong with him, aside from the fact that he don't take shit from no one. He tells it like it is, not how he wants you to think it is."

Frank piled on. "Dev, the man hasn't got two connected neurons in his head. What he says is either idiotic, or it's just plain wrong."

"Oh ya? Name one thing he said was wrong."

"Easy, Dev," Mom soothed with a smirk, "we're talking here, not wrestling. Be civil to your brother."

He eyed his mother suspiciously. To his brother,he said, "Can you, Franklin, cite one example of Monroe not fulfilling your expectations as to the veracity of his remark?"

"Yeah. That horseshit about going to the farmships and seeing if there's enough food to increase rations. What a retarded thing to say, even for a moron the likes of him."

Devon squeezed down so hard on his fork it hurt. "I, for one, would like to make that trip. I don't trust those political pukes one single bit."

"No, Dev, you don't." Frank spoke now with his older-brother condescension set to maximum. "You ain't been to a farmship. I have. I gotta shuttle there twice, three times a month. It ain't pretty. You have any idea what a million cows, ten million pigs, and fifty million chickens *smells* like?" He waited a moment. "No, I don't think you do. And they keep those ships really warm so the animals grow quicker. We're talkin' fermenting hot shit here, Dev. City boy like you'd pass out, hit your head, and be carried back on a med ship." He grunted a laugh of self-satisfaction.

"Seein's you're so smart," snapped Devon, "who you think'd do a better job?"

Frank swirled his spoon in the air, attempting to capture the image of intellectual insight. "I like that Ryan kid, but he's just a kid. Plus, everyone knows he don't want to be president. He just don't want either of the other two to win."

In utter disbelief, Devon finished his brother's thought. "So you're going to vote for that bloated bitch, Clinton? You're not crazy, you're insane."

"She's got chops," he defended. "Look at all the presidents she's related to."

"Yeah," snarled Devon, "just look at them. Losers, users, and bruisers, every lovin' one of em."

"We need a leader, not a lunatic warning siren."

"And she announced her 'wife' will be her vice-presidential partner." Devon added as much mocking snark to the word *wife* as humanly possible. "Two bitches are, what, better than one?"

"Hey." Devon's father thundered, "show some respect."

Devon gave an injured whine. "What?"

"Say what you will about Clinton. But, in my house, you'll show proper respect for Ms. Walker."

"Why? What you so steamed about? She's a gay-ass bitch like her wife."

Jon Flannigan, patriarch, dropped his voice ten more octaves. "Hold your *tongue*. You will show *me* proper respect, and you will show *her* proper respect. She's related to Jonathan Ryan. In my mind, and in my house, that purchases her all due respect. We owe the man that much for all he sacrificed on our behalf."

"Da," Frank said softly, "she's not *related* to Jon Ryan. Her great-aunt had a one-night stand with his robot. The girl isn't actually a blood relative to Ryan."

Jon lowered his head ominously. "In my book, that's close enough. I'll listen to discussion of her political views and general positions, but I'll not suffer to hear her degraded for her personal choices, or any other matter. Not while I sit at the head of this table. Now, that's the end of it."

And it was. The conversation switched to sports and the evening passed with no further family quakes.

****

"Madam President," Amanda Walker asked with a huge smile, "would you like some more champagne?"

"Why, yes, Madam Vice President, I do believe I will have a splash more."

The two women, alone now after the endless succession of post-inauguration parties, toasted glasses and sipped.

"Ah," exhaled Amanda.

"Yes," agreed Faith, "it tastes great."

"No, love. I was referring to the silence."

"I'll drink to that." They clinked glasses again.

"I need a warm bath and ten hours of sleep," said the newly elected President of the United States.

"Me, too. That sounds delicious."

"Your tub or mine?" Faith smiled invitingly.

"Sweetheart, it's been a long campaign and a long night. How about to each her own? We'll see if we have more energy in the morning, okay?"

"Right as always, my heart."

Amanda laughed dubiously. "That's not what Monroe, Ryan, the press, and fully half the electorate opine."

"Well, they don't know you as well as I do." She pecked her spouse on the cheek and headed to her bathroom. "Oh, some fellow brought this by personally." Faith pointed to an elaborate layered cake covered with the words *Victory Is Ours*. "He had one of those silly oversized foam rubber hats that reads, 'W-on with Clint-on..' Had buttons all over his chest, and a sign on his butt that read, 'Kiss My Monroe'. The man is squarely in our camp, it would seem."

Amanda walked over and inspected the pastry. It was ornate. "You know I'm lactose *and* gluten intolerant. If I look at that thing any longer, my gut will bloat up like a hot air balloon. It's all yours."

"Don't mind if I do." Faith cut herself a generous slice, laid it on a plate, and peddled off to a well-earned soaking.

****

The next morning, Secret Service agents stationed in the hall heard Amanda Walker scream loud enough to almost wake the dead. A doctor was summoned, but Faith Clinton was already cold and stiff by the time he rushed to her bedside. Devon Flannigan was arrested, tried, and executed for the murder of the shortest-term president in US history—twelve hours according to the coroner. While the worldships mourned Amanda Walker was sworn in as the next president. She wore black, including a black veil, to her inauguration.

The following morning, she sat in the Noval Office with three of her most trusted aides.

"Whom shall we interview for vice president, Madam President? We have a list of candidates, if you're ready to look it over." Sally Brighton had been with Amanda and Faith since all three were undergrads at Harvard.

Amanda accepted the list but held it with two fingers like it was a curse. "Already? A list?" Her voice had no life in it.

"We have to move on at some point, Mandy."

Staring off into infinity Amanda agreed. "Yes, we do."

"Then," Sally asked softly, "take a look at the list later?"

"No."

"I'm confused, Madam President."

"I have already made my selection. There's really only one choice." She smiled soulfully. "We need to reassemble the team."

A knock came at the door. The secretary stuck her head around the corner. "Madame President, Heath Ryan is here, per your request. Shall I show him in?"

"Yes, I've been waiting for him."

THIRTY-SIX

In the darkness and bitter cold of interstellar space Tho floated as she contemplated eternity. She had been in solitary thought for what seemed an eternity, which she found amusingly ironic. The distance between her mind and resolution was slight. In a million years surely she'd understand and encompass the meaning of forever. Then she would eat again, something different than the random hydrogen molecule she chanced upon now and then. Yes. A reward for her diligence and assignment to task. She would treat herself to a proper feast.

At first she hardly noticed. Then, she could do nothing else but note. A part of her whole went quiet, absent. Part of her became void, incomplete. Sho spoke to her. He had noted it too, the vanishing. Such a thing had not happened in longer than either Uhoor could remember. In fact, it could not happen, what had just occurred. Another impossible to add to her list of matters to think through. A bother to be certain.

Cho, then Ablo, now Dulo entered Tho's essence. They had always been there, but now they were *more* present. Mlo came, and smelled to Tho of fear and confusion. Such was not possible, and so her list grew. All were there, but where was Plo? He stood aside from her/them. Tho saw him in her mind's eye, clearly, of course, but she did not *feel* him. She did not *include* Plo, not any longer. No more.

Tho reached out to Plo with her mind, to know why he stood apart, indifferent to her/them, to the many who were one. Plo turned his back to her/them. Not another impossible. So many in one day. It was intolerable.

She would take forever to understand forever, with all these impossibilities to address beforehand.

Tho moved to pull Plo to return. Of course, she didn't actually move. It was not required to move. She remained where she was and closed the distance to her other self. Plo tried to move away, but she held him, though weakly. *Why*, she demanded of Plo, *did you wander away?* All of her/them noticed and asked the same question. They asked a thousand questions, in fact, but Plo answered only one. He said he must go to where he wasn't.

Why, Dulo asked, did he go where he wasn't? He would not answer that question. Plo did answer the question none of them had asked. *Because of Klonsar.*

The planet? thought Tho/them *The planet with the silly running fortus, so cute to kill? Why must Plo be where he wasn't because of Klonsar?*

He answered, because he was not there any longer. He wasn't.

THIRTY-SEVEN

"Doc," I marveled, "that's so cool I can hardly stand it. I got ants in my pants just thinking about it."

"Jon, really," Toño said with false modesty, "it's a useful weapon, but it's not like I invented heavier-than-air flight or pizza."

"Unless our opponents have membrane capabilities, there's no defense against it. Even if they do, we could hope to sneak one in before their barrier was up, and kapow." I moved my hands apart rapidly.

"We shall see if your high praise and confidence are justified."

"Makes me hope something attacks us soon. I'm like a kid on Christmas Eve." I expanded my hands again to replay a massive explosion.

JJ was still confused. "How is this different than using a membrane to tear things apart like we have in the past? Seems the same to me."

"No," Toño said, "though I'll grant you it's similar. With the membrane bomb, I've advanced that tactic to a simple mechanism. We can launch a small membrane generator. It can shield itself from attack, if need be. Once it reaches its target —"

"Like the guts of a Uhoor," I tossed in with glee.

"As I was saying, once it reaches its designated target, it opens a spherical membrane from its surface. This will effectively blow anything in the membrane's path outward at high velocity. At a preset distance, say one kilometer, the membrane switches harmlessly off. It's then possible to retrieve the bomb and use it again. In the rare case of a malfunction, I've packed the bomb with conventional explosives and a partial AI to self-destruct the

196

weapon. That way our technology will not be gifted to an enemy."

"Can we," I asked like a kid in a candy shop, "maybe blow up one of Azsuram's moons, one of the smaller ones, to make sure it works?"

"Behave yourself." Toño scolded. "You're over a century and a half old. Please act like it. The time will come, probably sooner than we'd like, when the membrane bomb will be called upon."

"Can I at least give it a cool name, cooler than *membrane bomb*?"

He looked at me like he used to, before I left on *Ark 1*. "If it will quiet you, yes."

"And it will be the bomb's *official* name, not just its shut-Jon-up name?"

He hesitated. He had been trying to trick me. The dirty rat. "Yes, the official name, for whatever that's worth."

I turned to JJ. "Did you hear that? I get to name the best bomb ever invented."

He gave me a look almost identical to the one Toño had. Weird. "Dad, I've been sitting here the whole time." He pointed toward the floor underneath him.

That was okay. I wasn't listening to either of them. I was devising the most wicked, most explosive, and most threatening name ever dreamt of by the mind of man. Hover-Death? No, as cool as the word "hover" was, the membrane bomb didn't actually *hover*. Deathmobile? No, too happy a name. The Ripper? The Reaper? The Ripper Reaper? I was getting *close*. Ryan's Ripper? No, not enough panache. Oh, well, no rush. It would come to me when I least expected it, maybe. This was *so* cool.

JJ was snapping his fingers in front of my eyes. "Dad. Reality to Captain Ryan. Are you coming?"

Where? "Sure, son. Lead the way." Didn't matter where. I had some thinking to do.

We went, as it turned out, to the nursery. JJ was due for a class with his older siblings on some aspect of Kaljax's languages or culture. I didn't, as you may surmise, pay too close attention to those matters. I played with a few toddlers and had a great time. I noticed, however, Ffffuttoe was off in the corner by herself. In all the years I'd known her she'd never done such a thing. She was always in the center of a mass of kids, or giving baths, often both at the same time.

"Hey, you okay?" I asked as I stepped over to her side.

She gave me the oddest look, kind of sad and embarrassed all at the same time. It was the most complex emotion I'd ever seen her display. "I fine, Captain." A creature of few words, as always.

"Then why you all alone here? I see three or four kids over there who could use a good hug."

"Not now. Now Ffffuttoe sleep."

"Sleep? It's barely noon. You tired?"

"No tired. I sleep now."

Wait, was she going to hibernate? She called that *sleep*. Didn't make sense. She was eating like three horses combined. No need to conserve energy. "I don't understand. Why do you need to sleep?"

"We all time comes sleep, when it is ours, Captain."

Sometimes talking with her was like working a crossword puzzle. "What time is all ours?" I hoped Al wasn't eavesdropping. He'd tease me for all eternity for that sentence.

She just smiled and put a paw on my arm. "I go sleep. Now not see my Captain after, or my kids. But they all well, so I sleep happy."

Wait. She was talking about her final rest—*death*. "Ffffuttoe, are you sick?"

"Yes. But no medicine for me sick. It my just time."

I yelled out, "Al, get Toño to the nursery ASAP."

Thirty seconds later, Doc sprinted into the room. He scanned from one side to the other, perhaps looking for an injured child. "Over here." I waved to him.

"What's the emergency?"

"I … I think Ffffuttoe just told me she's dy … dying."

It was like a baseball bat hit him squarely in the face. He recoiled momentarily, then grabbed her by the shoulders. "Is that correct. Are you dying. Is your life about to end?" Doc knew how to talk to her in a way she could understand much better than I could.

"Yes my Tono." She never did get the "ñ" part of his name. Always pronounced it *toe-no*.

"Let's get you to the infirmary and see what I can do." He started to lead her away, but she gently pulled her arm free.

"No I my room. Best my own room." She walked in that direction.

Doc and I looked at each other, shocked, but could only follow her. We all entered her small quarters. She climbed into bed, pulled the covers up, and turned to the wall. This was not good. Very not good.

Toño came to her bed. "Does it hurt somewhere? Show me where it hurt."

Without looking at him she said to the wall, "No pain. Just sleep."

"Here, let me get a set of vitals on you." He reached into the med-kit he'd brought with him and took out a few doctor tools. "Give me your arm."

"You can have arm later, when I don't longer need. Now I sleep. Quiet."

"Ffffuttoe, please, let me help." Doc sounded frantic.

She finally flopped to her back and smiled at him, then to me. "I sleep. It is the way. I sleep happy. My life good. My friends better. My kids the *best*."

"So, there's nothing I can do?" Toño whispered.

"Yes, take care of mes. I sleep before I have my kids own. So, I sleep, but I mes not. You love my mes. Can you do that one thing for me, Toño?"

That last sentence. She spoke it like English was her native tongue. Where did that come from?

I was about to speak, ask her who *mes* was and why she could all of a sudden pronounce Doc's name correctly. But, Toño placed his hand on my forearm to silence me. "I will, my friend. We *all* will, like it was you we were taking care of."

She pulled the covers up and closed her eyes. We stood there dumbstruck for several minutes. Then it hit me. I better let Sapale know so she could say her goodbyes. Maybe the older kids, too.

JJ and Fashallana leaned over and kissed her forehead. That brought her eyes open and a warm smile. "My first kids. First always most special of special. Me loves you. Mes will love you."

They looked to me confused. I placed my right index digit to my lips to silence them.

Sapale kissed Ffffuttoe's cheek and gently massaged her arm. "Sweet Ffffuttoe. My sweet Ffffuttoe. I was so very lucky to have you in my life. You are love. You are my friend. You will remain alive in me forever." She then rested her head on Ffffuttoe's chest. That last line was an old saying from Kaljax.

My turn. Crap. I hated this stuff. "Ffffuttoe, you can't sleep. Who will keep the kids clean?"

"You, Captain. You now Bath Master First Class." A joke. At the end she was cutting it up.

My turn to be serious. "Ffffuttoe, my friend of friends, do you want me to return you to BS 3 someday, when I get a chance?"

She smiled a distant smile. "Yes, Bath Master First Class. That nice be if chance you get. If not chance then my ashes you put here Azsuram. Someday, kids and I sleep together here. Nice."

Oh, man. I was totally going to cry. "No problem. I will get you back home someday. Hey, maybe I'll toss a few of those greasy rats in the ground with you. Would you like that?"

"Yes, *gresbo* de-licious. You put many I happy."

A few minutes later, Ffffuttoe, my first alien friend, was gone. There wasn't a dry eye in the house. I was just about to ask Toño if he was going to handle her remains when there was a pulsing movement under the sheets on either side of Ffffuttoe's abdomen. Doc threw the sheets back quickly. Two volleyball sized blobs were pinching off from either side of her midsection. Within a minute, they were two round pelt-covered masses motionless next to her body.

Toño gently picked them up and held them to the light. He then put an ear to each. "Well, I'll be damned. These are the *mes* she spoke of." He turned to me and held them out. "These are alive. I'll check in the lab, but these appear to be asexual buds."

JJ was confused. "They're what sex?"

"No," corrected Toño, "They are a-sexual, meaning she gave birth to them without having mated. On Earth, many creatures did this. Snails, worms, fungi." He shook his head in wonder. "But never such a complex creature as Ffffuttoe. This is *amazing*." He stared at them a bit longer. "I'll be in the infirmary if anyone needs me. Jon, please bring her remains down when you get a chance."

"Sure thing, Doc." Asexual buds from Ffffuttoe? Live a new day, learn a new thing.

The next day Toño informed us that the two buds were similar to eggs, but not exactly the same either. They contained two identical copies of Ffffuttoe. He guessed that this type of reproduction was useful in times of extreme stress, when mating might not be an option. In any case, he estimated they'd hatch, or whatever, in a week or so. He placed them in an incubator with some fresh meat nearby. We all knew how central food was to her, so that might help stimulate the buds to open.

A few days later Toño asked me to meet him in the mess for coffee. Odd, as a couple androids didn't need coffee. But I couldn't very well turn him down. I guess the old habits, the humanity residual in us, had a strong hold on our behavior.

"The buds are just about to hatch," he said.

"Okay." Not sure I needed an update on the topic, but whatever.

"I wanted to speak with you about imprinting."

"Say what? You want to do what with me?"

There was that stare from long ago. "I wish to discuss with you that the new pups may automatically imprint of the first person they see."

"Is the choice of whether they do up to me?"

Again, with the look. "No. The process, if it occurs with this species, does not require your permission. But, if they do imprint, we need to decide *whom* they do so on."

Peeking up over the rim of my mug, I asked, "Why do we have to decide?"

"We don't. But if it were to occur, and it was with something inconvenient, like a doorknob, I will tell you *I told you so* forever."

That was a good enough reason to motivate me. "So, who should it be? You?"

"No. That would be a *ridiculous* choice. I'm much too busy. I never go to the nursery unless there's trouble, and I'm immortal. Really, Jon, how do these thoughts spawn in your head?"

"Luck?"

"I was thinking the youngest of your children would be a good option.

Whichever one we select would have devoted lifelong companions. It would be beneficial for all three."

"Okay, sounds fine. Which kid?"

"Why didn't I have this conversation with Sapale? What was I thinking?"

Now he'd gone too far. "What?"

"For you, everything is a joke. I could've chosen if I felt it was my place, but the children are not mine. I *assumed* a parent should make that type of choice."

He had a point. Let me see. Fashallana just had her second set of twins, a girl and a boy. Dolirca, for "loves all," and Jodfderal, meaning "strength of ten." Okay, no-brainer. A boy with the strength of ten anythings wouldn't want a couple of hungry bears following him around. No way. "Dolirca," I said to Toño.

"Oh my goodness."

"What? What'd I do wrong now?"

"No. She's my first choice, too. Either you're *improving* or I'm *slipping*." He wiped his forehead.

I gave him a crooked smile. "Let's hope for the best."

He was going to ask me what I meant. Then I saw it dawn on him. Don't ask. I was being a shit.

Births seem to only occur in the dead of night. So it would seem was the case with hatching Toes. Toño had logically figured the closest objects to the newly hatched Toe would be the remains of their parent. Accordingly, he preserved a couple of slices of Ffffuttoe to simulate that process. He reasoned there might be some immune and other benefit from self-cannibalism. Just hearing the words made me queasy. That's why he was the doc, and not I. Sure enough, as soon as the little flat-cubs were free of their shells they made a beeline for the meat. Gone in two bites. They were, indeed, just like their mother.

Once they had eaten their fill of soy protein, Fashallana set the still sleeping Dolirca between the two Toe. That woke her enough so that she looked at them in childish wonder. Darn if they didn't take one look at her and cuddle up beside her. All three were in a coma a few seconds later, but it appeared Doc was correct about the imprinting. Not sure why it was, but it seemed sort of cool to me, all of a sudden.

THIRTY-EIGHT

"No, sir," defended Matt Duncan as vehemently as he could, "I did *not* say you were wrong or stupid." Marshall's chief of staff knew with familiar certainty that even a lesser insult would result in his death. He shuddered to think what might befall him for such an affront.

"I think you did," snapped Marshall. "If it wasn't for your frighteningly bodacious bazoombas, I'd have you keelhauled under this worldship. But that would be like torching the *Mona Lisa*. Damn shame if you forced me to do it, son."

Yeah, Matt needed reminding that he was still trapped in Marilyn Monroe's body. How he hated life. But, he'd better clear the air with his insane boss or he'd find out the hard way how awful life could become. "I said that *perhaps* if you slowed the *pace* of your consolidation of power, there would be less *pushback*. That's not to say you are unwise or not entitled to what's rightfully yours."

"Less pushback? You call armed rebellion pushback, boy? I mean, girl. Sorry, I don't want any EEOC complaints darkening the reputation of my otherwise stellar administration."

"If," Matt said with temerity, "and it's of course your call, but *if* we slowed the speed at which you reacquired your control, we might face less *overt* opposition. You know, the carrot instead of the stick?"

"The blood of the rebels only serves to baptize my righteous path. Any fool can see I am, one, acting within the framework of the Constitution, and two, going to win. So by logical deduction, those opposed to me are dumber than your average fool. Them, I don't need. Them, the country doesn't need. So much dead wood requires a trimming, a measured reduction. The future lies *ahead*, Matty boy, not behind us. It's my way or the stellar-way."

"Yes," Matt responded, as sullenly as he dared, "the space in this ship's wake is littered with documentation of your commitment to solidarity."

"Yes, it is, and don't you see, son? There's lots more room out there. I can toss people out an airlock from now until eternity and it won't fill up. Isn't that marvelous? It validates my actions directly. Don't you see?"

I see a deranged maniac who cares less for human life than he does about the polish on his shoes. I see no way out. Jackson was a hero for trying to end you, but no one can. Wait. Maybe this worldship can explode? Would that do it? Would the deaths of over a million innocent lives justify your extermination? Yes. But not unless it was certain. Even I don't know where your backup brain traces and androids are stored. But if I ever learn —

"So," Marshall added, "about the last of the rebels. Why weren't they made to walk the plank into the great void of space, as I specifically instructed they be?"

"Because there were too many witnesses. Rumors as to how prisoners are treated are burning through the ship like a wildfire. People are inclined to follow like sheep, yes. But only to a point. If they feel threatened, they might react on a larger scale."

"You mean like that failed 'Impeach Marshall' movement? That petered out in no time. The people love me."

No you threw ten thousand souls, kicking and screaming, out of airlocks. That ended the movement, not a groundswell of love and support, you devil.

"Now, *wait*," Marshall said pointing to Matt, "is this really about the women? Are you jealous I'm screwing more women than Genghis Khan, but not screwing *you*? That's *it*. You're jealous of my affections."

"No, sir," Matt said, "that's the furthest thing from the truth. I'm your advisor. I've always been your advisor. What good is an advisor, if he doesn't offer honest advice?"

He wagged his eyebrows up and down. "Have you looked in a mirror lately? I'll tell you what good you can be."

"Mr. President, I think it behooves you to focus more on the pattern of resistance we're witnessing, and less on joking about sex."

"Who's joking, Marilyn?"

Matt returned a blank stare.

"Oh, fine, you spoilsport. Can't a guy have a little fun? Okay, what's the issue I need to focus on?"

"Thank you, sir. Your Secret Service agents are rapidly developing the reputation of being nothing but cruel bullies. They are compared, rather accurately I might add, on anonymous websites, to the Gestapo. I suggest you limit their individual prerogatives and make them more accountable to their superiors. In turn, if the supervisors were to be more accountable to us, we could regain some of the authority and respect we seem to be losing."

Marshall twisted his mouth in various contortions. "Fine. Make it so. But mind you, the section heads report directly to *me*, not *you*."

The lunatic in charge of the asylum. This's going to end well. "I'll see to it, sir. The other pressing issue is social order. History teaches that arbitrary, autocratic power can be subverted by underground movements and covert cells of operatives. We need to allow people to buy into your vision for the future and the necessary changes they must make. That does *not* mean kowtowing to them or giving up control. It just means providing them a positive reinforcement for compliance."

"You use a lot of big fucking words, don't you?" Before Matt could object, Marshall raised his arms overhead in surrender. "Okay. I get your point. How about this. Tie food rations to being a good citizen? Hmm? The more you go along, the more you help, the more you eat. Cut the basic rations, so those considering dragging their feet are motivated to keep pace with the new caloric reality."

"I don't know. The basic ration is already pretty sparse. Hungry people can be highly motivated people."

"So can I." Marshall spoke those words with all the enmity, disgust, and hatred that could be crammed into one mouth at one time in the universe.

Matt was impressed enough to heed their implied warning. "Very well. I'll draw up a document outlining the new ration system and have it on your desk first thing tomorrow morning. Will there be anything else, sir?"

"Yes. Not too *early* tomorrow morning, okay? Papa's got a lot of wild oats to sow, don't you know?"

THIRTY-NINE

In spite of the constant worry about a return of the Uhoor, life was good. It was very good, in fact. As the years came and went, my family grew, as did the love we all shared. I hated to admit it, but the concept of a second Eden came to my mind more than once. And in this Eden there would be no fall from grace. We had a vision, it was a positive one, and we were translating our dreams into reality well. Sapale had given birth to her eighth and final set of twins. She said she'd pass that dubious baton of constant-pregnancy to the next generations. Fashallana had produced our fifth set of twin granddaughters. Sapale's supply of sperm from Kaljax had been split over thirty times, and the wriggly little warriors were still doing their job like gangbusters. Our little colony boasted twenty-seven Kaljaxians, two Toe, two androids, and one cranky AI. Lilith and the supplies from Kaljax weren't due back until around 2225. Human worldships were still four centuries out.

In the three years we'd been on Azsuram, a lot had been accomplished. We had a water purification system, a sewage plant, and an electric generator set up and working. Those initial infrastructures were capable of supporting several thousand people, so additional components wouldn't be needed for many years. In terms of food, we were in great shape. The crops from Earth and Kaljax were thriving better than we'd hoped for. The only meat supply we brought were chickens. They were producing more than enough eggs by then, and we were able to cull a few out for the table. Game was plentiful, and it was edible. Theoretically, Azsuram's animals could have been toxic, but they were actually quite tasty and nutritious. And no, none of us ever did see one of the mole creatures the Uhoor hunted with such insane zeal.

As the colony became increasingly stable, JJ and I, sometimes with Toño, had a chance to do some exploring. Seamus O'Leary, the pilot of *Ark 4*, reported mostly on the environment and potential of the planet, not its past. I wanted to see what had preceded us. A chance to get away from the henhouse that the colony was becoming constituted a big plus, too. Females everywhere. We had strict protocols in case the Uhoor returned while we were away. In fact, Sapale thought they were heavy-handed, presuming the women weren't capable of anything more than childbirth and cleaning. Hence, I knew they were all safe. If she was comfortable enough to be sassy, she was confident about her ability to keep everyone else safe.

Our village was located on a flat parcel of land near the confluence of a couple rivers. There was a mountain range fifty kilometers away. I decided to make that our first big expedition. JJ and I packed up a rover and headed out for what I hoped would be a ten-day, maybe two-week, jaunt. Toño stayed home. He claimed he had several critical experiments he couldn't place on hold. I think he just preferred not to be exposed to all the male bonding that promised to take place. The last time the three of us went out for a couple days, I'd taught JJ how to spit. It's not a natural act for a Kaljaxian, but with commitment and lots of practice, JJ mastered the art. Toño said the lessons were revolting and the results unjustifiable. That man had no sense of adventure.

After a long day's travel, we reached the base of the mountains. The tallest peaks were four-thousand meters high, but we had no illusions of scaling them. I just wanted to take a look at some of the geology and see how the animal and plant life changed on the lower slopes. We established a base camp where we parked the rover and set off with backpacks to spend a day or so camping under the stars. Luckily, we carried protective clothing. Remember how I said one of the few upsides of Earth's destruction was no more mosquitos? Yeah. Azsuram didn't get that memo. There were flying, blood-sucking insects that duplicated the curse of the mosquito way too accurately for my taste. Yeah, yeah, I was an android with bulletproof skin, but that was not the point. It was a matter of principle.

The first day out we really didn't find anything unexpected. We did have father-son fun. JJ shot a deer-like creature and we roasted it over an open fire on a wooden spit. I also sneaked some of the beer I was making, so we both had an ample supply. For me, it just tasted good. JJ, on the other hand, got quite a buzz going. Thank goodness his physiology was similar enough to ours in that regard. Ethanol wasn't toxic to him or anything.

The second day, we climbed the walls of a narrow ravine, maybe a few hundred meters high. I decided we'd spend the night on top, where the ground flattened out nicely. That's where I made the discovery. JJ pounded in the stakes on one side of our tent while I whacked at the ones on the other. I expected high winds after midnight, so we were using extra-long spikes. I was almost done with my last one when the sharp end clanged off of metal. Not a rock, not iron ore, but metal. That shouldn't be there. Metal, true hardened metal, never occurred naturally. Industrial metals were always a carefully blended alloy of different components forged at high heat. My discovery was most odd. It was too late in the day to do much but eat and bed down, so that's what we did.

I was almost curious enough to work the night through, as I could see in the dark and didn't need rest. But that would keep JJ awake. He was such a grouch without his sleep. Plus, I wanted him to share in whatever discovery we were making. I woke him bright and early the next morning, fed him, and put him to work digging out our mystery metal. After several hours, we'd unearthed only a few square meters of metal. Oddly, it was shiny, as if there hadn't been dirt covering it for who knows how long. I detected no seams, welds, or irregularities. Logically, we were above whatever structure it was, so it was unlikely we'd find a window or door. There was, not surprisingly, no sound coming from inside.

JJ took a short lunch break, but we pretty much kept at it until it started getting dark. Assuming it was a building, we were still exposing only the pristine-looking roof. I tried to explain to him how archeology worked— slowly and unspectacularly. Such a methodical approach didn't really hold his teenage attention span. I let him go off to hunt so he didn't die of boredom. I took the opportunity to contact Toño,. I did so directly, one brain to the other, much as I did with Al.

Doc, you gotta see what we found. I downloaded the latest video of the flat metal surface.

Well, I'll be. That's certainly not naturally occurring. What do you think it is?

No clue. It has to be very old. It's buried under half a meter of compacted sediment, and it's way up on a hill at three hundred fifty meters. It would take millions of years to raise a sedimentary plane that high.

Very true. Millions of years old and it looks like it was polished yesterday. Strange. I'll take a shuttle and be there in twenty minutes. Maybe together we can figure out what it is.

By the time Doc arrived, JJ was back with a couple of small beasties. I called them rabbits, but obviously they weren't really rabbits. They were roughly the same size and had that look on their faces that they were eaten by everything else, so they were definitely bunny-like in that regard. The three of us stood over the shallow hole we'd excavated, staring down at the bare metal in the failing light.

"Have you used your probe on it yet?" Toño asked.

Duh. "No, I guess I kind of didn't think about that. I'm out of touch with the exploration business these days."

He gestured to the surface, like go ahead.

I deployed the probe. It fixed evenly over the surface. The readings made absolutely no sense. I downloaded the entire database to Toño.

"I don't know what that means," he said, scratching his head.

"What?" pressed JJ.

"Well," Toño began, "it's most odd. The readings indicate this isn't metal. It's more of a plastic, but it also has ceramic characteristics. It also seems to be twelve *million* years old."

JJ whistled. I taught him that too, by the way. "But it has to be metal," he said. "It sure sounds like metal when struck. How could plastic be that tough? That shiny, for that matter?"

"It's clearly alien technology," I replied. "Who's to say what they're capable of? There's also the melting point. It's around ten thousand degrees Centigrade."

"Is that a lot?" JJ asked.

"No. It's a lot more than a lot. The highest melting point for materials we've fabricated is *maybe* five thousand degrees. This stuff would stay solid if set on the surface of the Sun."

"It's also harder than diamond by a factor of one thousand. There's nothing like that known to science." Toño was clearly amazed. "This material also does not conduct heat or electricity. Such a thing is unheard of. It's barely conceivable."

"Sounds like useful stuff," said JJ.

"Yes," replied Toño, "but why here? Maybe for a spaceship, but not a shelter."

"We don't know it was a shelter," I said.

Toño was slightly annoyed with my assertion. "Of course, we do. You saw. The internal structure is divided into rooms on various levels. There are stairs, and even rudimentary units of furniture still in a reasonable order. No, this is *some* form of housing."

"Hey," chimed in JJ, "maybe we could live in it? Sounds like a very safe place to be when trouble hits."

"Yes," said Toño, "but this particular structure is right smack in the middle of nowhere." He gestured to the surrounding terrain. "Not very hospitable here."

"Maybe we could move it down to the flats," JJ wondered.

"First, we need to see if we can expose it completely. Even then, I suspect it'll weigh too much to move." Toño clearly like the idea but doubted it was feasible.

Over the next few weeks, Toño dedicated himself exclusively to working on the artifact. JJ and I returned to the village and resumed our usual activities. Toño use the shuttle to haul various tools and machines up to the metal structure. He finally rigged a membrane generator to heave massive amounts of dirt and rock off the structure. Within a month, he had it fully exposed. It was a perfect cube of metal-like material. There were no obvious doors or windows. He tried in vain to drill, burn, or blow his way in. Nothing even slightly phased the impassive structure. Rail shot bounced off like he was firing a peashooter at it.

One day, he asked me to come to the site. JJ and I took a shuttle and met him there.

"I have an idea," he said. "Use the probe. See if that can open the structure."

"I don't know," I had to admit. "I've never used it that way. Not sure that's how it's designed to work."

"There's no harm in trying, is there?" Doc was clearly at his wit's end with this box.

"No, I guess not." I focused on the structure, held my left hand up, and said "open" in my head.

Like it knew exactly what it was doing, the probe split into four groups and planted on the geometric centers of the four walls. Rectangular portals opened from the top down, ending where the box met the ground.

"Well, I'll be," I mumbled, "never seen it do that. How'd it know where the doors would be?"

Doc was already entering an opening. "I have no idea, but I'll take any break I can get."

JJ and I hustled in after him. I told the doors to stay open. Not sure if they would, but I didn't fancy the idea of being sealed on the inside forever. Maybe the probe wouldn't work from the inside. Who knew? When I retracted the probe, the portals remained open. Cool.

Exploring the inside of the cube started off well. But, as fate would have it, we figured out basically nothing about the contents or its past inhabitants. Months of study, probing, and attempted dismantling yielded nothing. No organic material lingered, no mechanisms were discovered, and no records, computers, or books were found. No traces of who or what inhabited the cube were discovered. Aside from general assumptions about the builder's size and shape, no clues were left. It was like a model home that no one had ever lived in. Everything seemed in place and functional, but there was no life to the unit.

One thing of interest. Toño calculated the mass of the cube to be two hundred thousand tons, about the same as two aircraft carriers. That meant for sure there was no way we could move it. He did, however, ask me to try to lift it with the probe. His reasoning was that the probe was able to open the structure, so it might be made by the same race. If it was, maybe they programmed in weird functionalities. I told him ten times he was crazier than Marshall, but finally, to shut him up, we went to the site and tried it.

At first, I said in my head, *lift and set down*. Damn. I lifted and set down a two-hundred-thousand-ton cube. I really hated it when Doc was right and I was wrong. Next, I said, *move one meter to the right*. There was clearance on the mini-plateau to safely do so. Darn it all if it didn't up and move exactly one meter to my right. There was to be no living with Toño from then on. The real trick, the one I wasn't too keen on attempting, was to lower the cube to the valley floor. I'd never actually tested how long the probe filaments were, but I couldn't believe they could stretch two kilometers.

Turns out, they couldn't. The farthest I could move the cube was two hundred meters. That meant countless mini-moves down the slope. On my third move of the cube, it couldn't find purchase where I set it down and tumbled like a loose boulder several hundred meters. But, as it was made of such ridiculously strong material, it wasn't in the least damaged. That's when I gave myself permission to have some fun. That, of course, is the opposite of what Toño wanted to do. He *hated* fun. That made the moving day well worthwhile. I push the cube down the slope until it began rolling. Then I'd catch up to the cube and do it again and again. I made it a point to try and get it to crash down the hill as dramatically as possible. Over a cliff was even better. I had a lot of fun.

The strangest part of using the probe in that manner was that it took no effort on my part. I didn't have to leverage myself or lift in any way. It was like a remote-controlled hoist. Whatever tech went into fabricating my probe was light-years ahead of ours. After a few days, I had the cube in the village. I told the doors to remain open unless I told them to close, which they did. It was like the building knew what I wanted and could understand me. I remarked to Toño that I had a new pet—a pet cube.

As we all anticipated the Uhoor would return sooner or later, the cube was a great defensive position to have handy. With a membrane anchoring it, nothing would be able to hurt us while inside. It turned out that the membrane couldn't even penetrate the metal skin. Toño rigged one so that it included the cube and an anchoring extension, with no slack that would allow it to be lifted like *Shearwater* had been. We packed large stores of food and water inside, like a bomb shelter. Toño set up an air scrubber for carbon dioxide removal and stored lots of liquid oxygen inside for breathing. We could hold up for months inside, if pressed. The cube could comfortably house a hundred of us, so we even had room to grow into it.

The ultimate problem with castle defense was that a patient enemy could wait out the occupants. A siege was always effective, if the guys on the outside were determined enough. The Siege of Harlech Castle in 1468 lasted seven years. In the end, the castle fell. But a fallback position was a nice thing to have in a hostile universe. I just hoped and prayed we'd never have to use it. That's how things work, right? One wishes for how one wants things to go, and that's how they turn out, right?

FORTY

In a universe of infinite possibilities, some outcomes one expects and some one does not. Some outcomes, however, one never, in his wildest night terrors, realized were even possible. So it was with me. One day Toño sent me a message. *Please come to my lab. I'd like you to meet someone.*

Okay, unexpected. I'd been present at the birth of nearly everyone currently on Azsuram. The remainder I'd known for years, centuries in Toño's case. Who could I possibly *meet*? I finished the repair I was working on, cleaned up, and headed for his lab. As I entered, I saw Toño talking casually to a male figure whose back was to me. There were no other adult human males on the planet. Before I could really get started on my internal dialogue as to who the hell he was, the figure slowly turned to face me.

Combined for me were the emotions of stunned disbelief, horror, and the instant desire to choke the life out of my fellow man. Not three paces from me stood the man whose hatred for me equaled my hatred for him. There stood a man more homicidal than Hitler, Stalin, and the leaders of the seven major Crusades, combined. If evil had a personification, I was looking at it. Stuart Marshall, erstwhile president of the USA and certifiably insane lunatic, glanced at me like we were waiting together at a bus station.

I lunged for his throat with both hands.

"No. *Wait*, Jon." Toño stepped between Marshall and me.

I plowed ahead, driving Toño backward. I would have this man's life, and I would have it now.

215

"Stop immediately," Toño screamed, "and let me explain!" He slapped me hard across the face.

I looked at Toño, stunned. He was in league with the devil himself? No way.

My hesitation allowed Toño to push me farther from Marshall. "I guess this wasn't such a good idea, surprising you like this," he said as he stared at the floor.

"No, I guess not. How the hell did he —"

"Please listen for a moment and you'll understand everything. Can you do that for me, Jon?"

I wasn't sure. "I'm not sure. Just tell me how he got —"

"I *made* him, that's how."

I was already extremely angry. I became a lot more so after hearing that confession. "I'm *listening*."

"Man, I don't think he likes me," Marshall said. I could only glare at him over Toño's shoulder.

"Remember," Toño began, "how I told you the current android of Marshall was corrupted by Morbius's incompetency?"

I nodded.

"It occurred to me that the best defense against Marshall might be to sic the real one on him."

Huh? "Doc, what're you saying? There are thirty things wrong with those nineteen little words." I waved my hands in the air. "You should have checked with me *first* sure comes to my mind."

"No!" he said, rather categorically. "I'm sorry if that runs against your grain, but *no*. I have always been in charge of the android program. As a result, it falls to me to set right the malfunction of one of my creations."

"Please," Stuart said, "don't talk about me like that, when I'm standing right here, son." Yup, that was Marshall, alright.

"I speak of your corrupted copy, not you. You are the full and accurate copy of the former president."

"Ah, fellows, when did I leave office?"

"Several years ago, when the Earth was destroyed. According to most constitutional authorities, that's when your term ended."

"The Earth has been destroyed? Already? No, that's not happening for another couple years."

I pointed to Stuart and said to Toño, "You didn't do such a good job on this one, either."

"I have yet to bring this copy up to date. This Stuart Marshall is the exact download Morbius used before he botched his attempt to make him an android."

"Now *that* I remember. I had to get that creepy dog Morbius to do it, because *you* refused."

"Yes, and instead of listening to my wise counsel, you forced an idiot to make a defective copy that plagues the human race like a holy curse."

"I can't be that bad, can I?"

"No," I responded, "you're worse. Much worse."

Toño patted Stuart's forearm. "We'll talk at length later."

So now, on top of all my worries, fears, detractors, and would-be assassins, Stuart Marshall was to join my otherwise wonderful colony.

FORTY-ONE

Two figures stood looking out a massive viewport into ice-cold deep space. The void was dead, except for the light of a trillion stars shining through, reminding them of hope. Their hands were behind their backs as if they stood at ease, on guard. The two had worked closely for a year, during the most trying times possible, but both were still unsure if they were friends. Harried comrades in the same foxhole would more accurately describe their bond. One thing was certain. They trusted each other, which was a precious commodity in a universe gone mad.

"Mandy," as Heath had come to call her, "there's nothing we could have done and nothing we can do now. You know this."

She stood silent as a boulder for a while gritting her jaw. "I *know* this. That doesn't mean I have to like it or accept it."

"Be reasonable. None of us *like* it. It's inhumane, sadistic, ethically indefensible, and the list goes on and on. But not accepting it suggests you have an alternative idea how to solve the problem."

She grew more stone-like and waited longer to answer. "I'm *their* president, Heath. I'm president to the five million citizens who Marshall kidnapped and is abusing egregiously. If I can't help them, what the hell good am I?"

"Mandy, they're a year away, moving as fast as they can. Marshall is unlikely to pull over and wait for us to catch up. Plus, if we could magically appear to their starboard, what could we do? *Wish* him into submission?"

She chuckled quietly.

"Perhaps a duel?"

She turned to him and smiled. "We couldn't open fire on them or forcibly board their worldships. We'd be no better than Marshall if we did."

"Are they better off enslaved than dead?" she replied.

"Please tell me that's a rhetorical question, because I'm not touching that one with a ten-meter pole."

"I knew I made the right choice when I picked you, Heath. You make me smile even at the hardest of times. Just like —" She stiffened and suppressed tears.

Heath set his hand on her shoulder. "I know. We all miss her."

She smiled in spite of her emotions. "*We?* You know, I was present during all the debates. You didn't sound too warm and fuzzy with my wife as recently as those events."

"That was a political campaign. All's fair and all that. I respected her and miss her."

She turned to him and rested her head on his chest. "It's okay if you really didn't, and you don't, but thanks for the kind attempt. I'm still not used to missing Faith." After a moment, she giggled briefly.

"What?" asked Heath.

"I was just thinking we're the first president and vice president to strike this pose."

"Let's pray powerfully that we are."

They both laughed. She looked up into his eyes. "And that your wife doesn't view any photos of this tender moment."

"I'll pray that, too. More powerfully."

She placed her head back on his chest, if only for a second. Then she returned to the iron-woman image she was known for. "We could send a couple of nearly empty worldships to their destination. By the time the ships arrived, the population would presumably be on land. We could at least offer whoever wanted it a ride back to the main group."

"Yes," he agreed, "we could. It's fifteen light-years from here to GB 3. It's eight light-years to LS 2 from here. It would take a worldship five or six hundred years to get there. Do you think the population on LS 2, five centuries from now, will want to jump on board a perfect stranger's ship and go on yet another multigenerational voyage? Actually, we wouldn't be strangers. We'd be evil interlopers. Marshall would have twisted the truth and brainwashed them into believing we're quite comparable to the demons in hell."

The viewing room was silent again. Heath let her be in the privacy of her own thoughts. Finally, he rubbed her shoulder and spoke. "They're gone, Mandy. Gone for good. There's no force in the universe that can change that, and no power that can bring them home. If there were, I'd fight to the death to try to change their sad fate. But there isn't. We need to look to our future and pray for theirs." He dropped his hand.

"Thank you."

"For what?"

"Keeping me focused. Keeping me grounded."

"Isn't that my job?"

"No," she smiled as she patted his cheek, "your job is to wait and see if I, too, drop dead."

FORTY-TWO

Several months after moving the cube to our village, it became mostly a priceless storage shed. Whatever we didn't need at the moment ended up piled in there. I was half-surprised cobwebs didn't start forming in the corners. But there were no spiders on Azsuram. I still had it in the back of my mind that it was our emergency shelter, but I guess I hoped so hard to never need it that I benignly neglected it. I did run into one problem I was yet to solve. With Lily gone for a while, we were down to one AI. Al was housed on *Shearwater*. If we were confined to the cube for an extended period, we could stay in contact with him, but he wouldn't be physically *with* us. Perhaps our link could be interfered with. We knew so little about the Uhoor that I couldn't rule such a thing out.

I was reluctant to move Al physically into the cube, because there was always the possibility we'd need to blast off in *Shearwater*. It would be insane to leave him behind if we left in a rush, as in an oh-crap-here-come-the Uhoor rush. Before I could arrive at a solution, one gray day, we heard the call we'd dreaded for quite some time.

Out of the blue, Al boomed, "Code Red. Battle Stations. Incoming unidentified spacecraft. All personnel to emergency stations."

Is it an Uhoor? I asked in my head.

No, Captain, it's twelve Uhoor. ETA ten minutes.

Crap. The entire pod was coming calling. Not good. "Okay," I yelled, "everybody to the cube. Everybody to the cube, and make sure no one is left behind. Nine minutes, people. Hurry."

We'd drilled that emergency countless times, so it went smoothly. Fortunately, no one was far from the village that particular day. Sapale supervised the transfer of all the infants, while JJ, Toño, and Fashallana rounded up the toddlers and older children. The Toe were easy to direct. They went wherever Dolirca did. Within five minutes, everyone was safe and sound inside the cube, the membranes were up, and the anchor was down. Marshall's android was the last to enter before I closed the walls. I had an impulse to close them sooner and let him stand out there alone. But that was too cruel even for me.

Everyone was pretty rattled, but we were safe for the time being. I figured we'd see what the Uhoor intended with all our defenses up. If they came to talk, not to fight, we could drop our guard accordingly. Of course, as a soldier, I knew they weren't coming to negotiate or bring a casserole for our being new to the neighborhood. Not all twelve coming unannounced. Given the absolute contempt the first one showed, there was no other logical conclusion but that this was a blood raid.

It had been all we could do to kill that one Uhoor. I was fairly certain we couldn't defend ourselves against twelve, even if the membrane bomb worked better than we could hope or dream. Oh, and I still hadn't come up with a radical name for the bomb yet. In my heart, I began to doubt I ever would. I tried to bolster my confidence by remembering all the battles I'd won when outnumbered and outclassed. None, however, were this lopsided. Oh, well. I'd give 'em hell and would make sure they never forgot my name.

Soon the sky over our village was clouded with the blimp-like masses of the Uhoor. It was a terrifying sight. Even if they had been our best friends, they were still powerfully ugly and indisputably huge.

I had Al translate the message I'd prepared and blast it though the external speakers. *Uhoor, this is Captain Jon Ryan of* Shearwater. *Please state your intentions.*

The largest of the Uhoor descended from the circle above us. She spoke loudly, but not at nearly the volume Plo had. "I am Tho. I speak for the Uhoor. In your speech, you would say I am mother to all Uhoor."

Shit, shit, shit. Mom was here to hand out justice—maternal justice. Now our impossible situation just became more hopeless. The worst part was Tho spoke in proper English. She sounded just like Mary Poppins, British upper-class accent and all. Man, it *sucked* that Mary Poppins was here to kill us.

I picked up the microphone and spoke to Mama Uhoor. "What are your intentions, Tho?"

She grunted something repeatedly that I feared was her version of a laugh. "Why, Jon, why is it you must ask?" More grunting and the other blimps grunted, too. Sons of hotdogs. "We are here to kill you. Why else would we come? You killed Plo. I can still smell him. We all still smell him. You dismembered him and burned what was left of our beloved Plo. Why else would we come?"

"Plo attacked us. He was the aggressor, and we killed him in self-defense. We had a right to defend our —"

"You have no *rights*. You cannot act in defense of yourselves. You are too insignificant to claim such a status. Plo was not the aggressor, because aggression against a trivial inferior such as yourself is not a valid concept. Could you, Jon, act aggressively toward a microbe? Toward a pebble?"

"I don't want to harm you, but I will not warn you again. Leave or die." Sapale came up from behind and wrapped her arms around my waist. She was shaking like a leaf in a hurricane.

"We think not. We think you will die now, all of you. Even the ones who may not be alive, those like you, Jon. Machines in human forms. Such a silly little species you were."

"We were? Ah, you seeing more of us than those standing here?"

"Yes, there are asteroids full of them. After you are gone, we shall eliminate those humans, too. None will remain. Plo must know he has been spoken for."

Just exactly what I needed. The stakes just went from enormous to all-inclusive. Either I won a battle I should never be able to, or the Uhoor would finish what Jupiter began.

Being as she was so specific and unequivocal in her declaration, I decided our parley was over. "Al, fire rail cannons at each Uhoor as rapidly as you can. After three seconds, pepper in infinity charges. Target each Uhoor with all

223

the infinity charges we've got. We won't get a second chance to make a first impression on these jokers." Hey, I finally did come up with a bitchin' name for the membrane bomb. I did good.

"Aye, aye."

Silently, the atmosphere around us turned to a killing field. All the Uhoor initially recoiled, and large sections of them tore open, much as Plo had. Then the infinity charges lodged inside them. You know in the cartoons when a character swallows dynamite with a burning fuse, how they bulge up comically? That's exactly what the Uhoor did. Unfortunately, that's all they did. They didn't fly apart. In fact, with each successive ball or bomb, they reacted less and less until the weapons had almost no effect on them. That turn of events was most unwelcome.

Well, we were all in. I opened a tiny hole in a wall, stuck my right hand out, and fired my little finger laser at Tho. The results were not what I could have ever expected. She screamed, but it was not a scream of pain, but one of unending anger and pure, undiluted rage.

"You *are* the Deavoriath." Tho blared. "That you hide in a Deavoriath vessel could be chance. But you fire their gamma-ray laser. Brothers and sisters, we have *found* the enemy. We have found the Deavoriath. Vengeance will finally be ours."

That just took the cake. She didn't just want to kill all of us and all humans, now the bitch had a major hard-on about the damn Deavoriath Plo mentioned. I personally hoped she did kill them off, because I suddenly hated them more than she did.

"Captain, we are out of rail balls and infinity charges. Shall I fire our missiles?"

"No, Al. If we didn't hurt them with all of that, we're not going to do much with the nukes. We'll just contaminate the hell out of Azsuram. If I thought it might work, I'd go for it, but they just shook off more energy than all our warheads combined."

"Your orders?"

"We wait."

I can't tell if Sapale said it first, or Al, or maybe even Toño. What I heard, though, was a chorus of "what?"

"We stand-down and we wait. If we take their best shot and survive, then we see if we can wait them out."

"And if we can't out wait million-years-old creatures?" That was definitely Sapale. She was hot.

"Then I'll think of something."

"You know that doesn't sound extremely reassuring?" said Toño.

"Are you insane, son?" Oh, even Marshall piled on now. Insult to injury.

"Everybody grab something secure and hang on for dear life."

I wasn't certain what they'd bring, but it was certain to be a lot. Even if the twelve of them just grabbed hold of the cube and shook it, I didn't know if the ground below us would hold.

My questions were answered quickly. All twelve blimps started ramming the cube with their heads, assuming those front parts were heads. The vibrations were tremendous, but initially the cube held tight. I was reasonably confident they couldn't breach the cube, but if they shook it enough, we'd be goners, especially the soft-bodied Kaljaxians. Plus, there was no telling how long those assholes out there could keep the battering up. With nothing better to do and tough-enough skulls, they could pound us for as long as it took.

Ten minutes into their assault, I felt the first inkling of trouble. Nothing significant, but there was a slight increase in the amplitude of the motion of the cube. The ground underneath was starting to fail. Shit, crap, damn.

Two minutes later, even Sapale could sense the difference. "Jon, we're breaking free. What'll we do?"

"I don't know yet. Just hold on tighter and secure the little ones the best you can."

In all my many battles in the air, on the ground, and in space, I'd never lost. Hence, I'd never before seen the look Sapale had in her eyes. It was the look a person gave someone they put all their faith and hope in and witnessed that person fail them completely. What an awful look I was getting.

"I'll hold Jarsmal. Here, hand her to me."

I reached out with my right arm to cradle her. Without thinking about it consciously, I deployed the probe to the nearest wall, so I could stand more securely. The cube was rocking a couple meters from side to side. We'd break free and be the mouse to these cats in less than thirty seconds. The noise level was getting unbearable. I yelled to Sapale. "Honey, if this ends badly, know that I love you completely and forever."

I think she started to respond, but the cube slammed to one side, free of its mooring. To pretty much myself, I mumbled, "I'd rather be anywhere than here. I'd settle for being back in Flight School in Lubbock, Texas, still married to my ex-wife."

The pounding stopped instantly. The vibration vanished. I could detect no movement, but I had a powerfully nauseating feeling where my gut used to be. Hadn't been nauseated for over a century. I was fairly certain from everything Toño had told me and everything I'd experienced, that it wasn't *possible* for me to be nauseated.

Marshall whined behind me, "Man, I think I'm going to hurl."

Toño followed quickly. "I think I'll be sick, too."

I turned to Sapale. All four of her eyes were larger than dinner plates. "Are you okay. Do you feel nauseated too?" I asked.

"No, why would I feel sick? What in the name of the Holy Veils is happening?"

"I have," I said truthfully, "no idea. I doubt we're dead, but I can't think of a better reason why the Uhoor aren't pounding us to bits any longer."

"We're not dead," Marshall said dismissively. He turned to Toño. "Are we?"

"No. But where we are is most unclear."

"What do you mean," I asked, "*where* we are? Where else but Azsuram *could* we be? Maybe in orbit, because those nasties booted us up there."

"I just think we're elsewhere. Al," he called out, "what is our position?"

Nothing.

"Al, this is Captain Ryan. I order you to answer. Where are we?"

More nothing. Even Al wouldn't push his luck being pissy at a moment of crisis. "The ship! It must have been destroyed." That was the only explanation I could come up with. The giant cigars killed my AI.

"Or," Toño said, holding up a hand, "Al's out of range."

"Out of range." I spat out. "He can't be out of range. I don't know what his range is, but it's big, Toño, real big."

"Approximately ten parsecs. But," Toño added, "at that distance there would be a thirty-year delay in the signal.

"You think we're —"

Toño cut me off. "You spoke to Al a minute ago. We must be at least one light-minute away. That's roughly twenty million kilometers."

"Toño, seriously —"

Again, he interrupted. "Without the AI, it may take weeks, months, to calculate where we are." He looked at the gleaming wall. "Jon, can you make a window? Not a hole, mind you, a *window*."

"You got me. Here." I still had the probe attached. I thought, *window to see through*.

One wall became completely transparent. At least I think it did. There was nothing to see. It was pitch-black outside. This was heavy.

"Jon, ask the cube where we are."

"Huh?"

He looked at me impatiently. "Ask the *cube* where we are."

Sapale was eager for me to chat with the box, too. "Ask it where we are *now*." Mom was upset.

In my head, I thought, *where are we? State location aloud.*

A voice unlike any I'd ever heard, or even imagined, spoke. It sounded as if time, all the antiquity of time itself, spoke parched words. "11-3003-27598-0101. Time 20041-33-3-32."

I turned to a stunned Toño and my jaw dropped open. "We're where he said. Eleven something. I didn't bring my watch, but I bet the time's reliable, too."

"Cube," Toño yelled, "translate coordinates to Earth-standard values."

Nothing. The silence of Al, all over again.

Sapale pointed to the wall. "You ask it, brood-mate."

"Wall, translate into —"

"What the alien asked, Form?"

"Y ... yeah. What he asked."

"Based on Earth coordinates we are at 121-3-4194 —"

227

"No, wall. Tell us where we are as someone from Earth would view it, not the actual coordinates. Please." Not very Form-like, I was thinking, but hopefully he understood me.

"I cannot determine the format of the information you request, Form. I will make an attempt to satisfy you. If you are still unclear, please let me know."

"Thank you, wall." Better. I sounded definitely more confident.

"We are inside the planet Jupiter, approximately thirty thousand kilometers radially from the planet's center, relative latitude —"

"We're *where?*" Ah, *there.* I'd found my command voice.

"Was I unclear? Sorry, I'm way out of practice. A few million years will do that to a vortex, Form. I said we are inside the planet Jupiter, in the Sol system. The one you recently vacated before this planet struck and tore off a large fraction of your home world's mass. You remember Earth, don't you, Form?"

I was speaking sort of on autopilot. "Yes, I remember Earth. Used to be my favorite planet. *Why the* hell *are we inside the gaseous planet Jupiter.*" There was a tone I'd never even heard.

"You asked me to take you there. Listen, and please don't get mad at me, I'm just the vortex manipulator, Form." After a brief delay we all heard a replay of me, mumbling to myself. *I'd rather be anywhere than here. I'd settle for being back in Flight School in Lubbock, Texas, still married to my ex-wife.*

Toño burst in. "When did you say that?"

"Immediately before the rattling stopped and we all got nauseated."

"That's correct, Form. I apologize. As I say, it's been a long time since anyone asked me to perform a function. Times change, you know? So can language, especially idiomatic phrasing —"

"Wall, stop speaking," I wasn't in the mood. "What are you trying, in a very roundabout way, to express?"

"You asked for your ex-wife *and* Lubbock. She's a very old woman on worldship *Glamour* several light-years from here. Most of Lubbock is the dust blowing past the view portal you requested. I had to decide whether to fold the vortex into the worldship, to be with Gloria on *Glamour*, or place it here.

I chose here. The vortex would have severely damaged —"

"Wall, stop talking." I was, as I said, in no mood.

"Your ex-wife is named Gloria? That's hilarious." Now, why did Marshall think that was so funny? Everybody had a name. That was hers.

"Jon," Toño spoke up, "I think I've pieced this together. We were under attack. You connected to the cube, and you made a request. The cube did its best to comply with your instructions. And so, we are inside Jupiter, fifteen light-years from where we were an instant before. It all makes sense."

"It all does *not* make sense," I insisted. "It actually makes *negative* sense."

"What is negative sense, Form? I must update my files."

"We cannot be fifteen light-years from where we were. Period. Einstein won't allow it."

"Excuse me, Form, which one of you is *Einstein*. I should speak to him or her."

"Einstein is dead. Died in 1954."

"1955," corrected Toño, unhelpfully.

"1955," I repeated.

"Why do you obey the word of a person dead?"

"He said, and I believe, nothing can travel faster than the speed of light in a vacuum. Traveling fifteen light-years in less than a second kind of violates that law to death."

"Why, he's correct in that. Nothing can move faster than electromagnetic radiation."

"Hence," I said, "we cannot be where we are."

"We can't?" The wall sounded confused. "Then where are we?"

"I have no freakin' idea. Doc, you going to bail me out, here? I'm sinking like a rock."

"I find it quite entertaining."

Toño, snide? What next? Santa and nine tiny reindeer with the Tooth Fairy riding shotgun landing on the roof?

"Vortex manipulator," said Toño loudly, "by what mechanism, which isn't faster-than-light travel, brought us to this location?"

There was a short delay. I spoke up. "Ah, wall, if he asks a question, go ahead and answer it, okay?"

"By your command, Form. I folded space-time to place us here."

"Fascinating." Toño was impressed. I was completely confused.

"Toño, please, for us humans."

Sapale cleared her throat loudly.

"For us non-eggheads." I inclined my head to Sapale.

"The cube, it would seem, possesses the ability to grab two sections of space-time and place them next to each other. Let's say you're in San Francisco and I'm in New York. We wish to share a meal. Rather than fly coast-to-coast on a plane, the cube simply takes San Francisco in one figurative hand, New York in the other, and places them together. I step through and sit down next to you, along Fisherman's Wharf."

"Wall, is that what you did?" I was only slightly less confused.

"In essence, yes. In practice, it's a good deal more —"

"Wall, stop talking."

"Please call me vortex manipulator, Form. I don't like being called a *wall* or a *cube*. I'm not the vessel or any part of it. I'm the vortex manipulator."

"Remember what Tho said," Toño recalled, "just before we disappeared. She said, 'You hide in a Deavoriath vessel and now you fire their gamma-ray laser.' She recognized this to be a Deavoriath vessel. Vortex manipulator, are you a Deavoriath vessel?" Toño sounded quite proud of himself.

"No, I am not. I'm a vortex —"

"Sorry, sorry," Toño backpedaled, "I misspoke. Sorry. Vortex manipulator, is this *cube* a Deavoriath vessel?"

"Well, yes, I suppose so. The cube houses the vortex manipulator, and combined, they constitute a Deavoriath vessel. Yes."

Nit-picky manipulator, wasn't he? "So, let me sum this up. You snapped your fingers—don't take that literally, we'll be here all day—and we ended up in what remains of Lubbock, Texas. The Uhoor are still back on Azsuram, presumably confused and possibly ripping Al and my ship to shreds?"

"Chances are good they are attacking something. Very irritable creatures, those Uhoor. Personally, I've never been a big fan. Doubt they're surprised, however. I, myself, have vanished before their eyes a dozen times. They're probably used to it by now."

That was so wrong, what the wall just said. "Can you *kill* the Uhoor?"

"I think, Form," the voice began, "you'll be a lot happier, at the end of the thing, if you rephrase that question. I hate to give the impression that —"

"Can I order the death of the Uhoor and have this vortex accomplish that task?"

"Bravo, Form. I must say you —"

"Answer the question."

"Yes, this vortex has killed thousands of Uhoor. Our gamma-ray laser is much larger than yours. It vaporizes a six-square-meter path in them with each shot."

"Take us back to Azsuram, now."

There was that chorus of "what?" again.

The nausea cleared more quickly the second trip. The Uhoor were in about the same location they'd been when we split. I picked up the microphone. "Hi, Tho. Did you miss me while I was gone?"

Her howl was angry, primal, and maniacal.

"I'll take that as a yes." I could be such a jerk. "Look, sweet sausage, I'll make this simple. I am a Form. I will vaporize you and your friends if you do not shut up immediately. No second warning."

She fell silent right away. "That's much better. Now, look, I don't *want* to kill you or your pod. I want to be left in peace here on this planet. I will also ask you to leave rest of my species, in fact, *all* other species, alone. Can you do that, Tho?"

There was a short pause. I got the impression she didn't like having her nose rubbed in the sand. Tough luck. She attacked my family.

"Yes."

"A woman of few words. How differently refreshing in the universe."

"Your sarcasm is neither necessary nor appreciated," she replied. Prissy bitch, wasn't she?

"It might not be, but I'm rather enjoying it, Mary Poppins. Here's the bottom line. I want you to imagine this galaxy as a pizza." I held my hands up to indicate a circle. "We are currently here." I pointed to a spot near the outer edge of the circle, roughly corresponding to our radius from the galactic center. "Draw, in your mind's eye, a diameter thus." I sliced the pizza in half, such that our location was as far from the diameter-line as possible. "This is *your* half of the pizza." I indicated the half that did not contain our location. "This is everybody else's half." I swept my hand across the half of the circle that did include our location.

"If you and all other Uhoor stay in your half of the pizza, I won't kill you. If any of you are in our section … excuse me, vortex manipulator?"

"Form?"

"How long will it take the furthest of the Uhoor to cross over to that side of the circle?"

"You mean pizza?"

Did this machine come off the same assembly line as Al? "Whatever."

"In Uhoor units, ninety-four *goar*."

"If any of you remain in our section in ninety-four goar, I'll kill them. Any questions?"

"None, Form. I will say for your ears to hear, you are every bit as cruel and vicious as your Deavoriath ancestors. One day, I will have the pleasure of killing you and any lingering Deavoriath. It may not be soon, but you have an enemy who will not quit and who will not tire. The suffering your race has inflicted upon mine must be answered for."

"You done, cupcake?" I asked. "Because I'm suddenly very tired of looking at your ugly face. Turn, run, and remember. Ninety-four goar, and not one goar more." I made a shooing motion with the back of my hands. They all turned and floated out of my life. Well, hopefully, at least for a good long while. It felt so nice to win, and even better not to lose.

FORTY-THREE

"So, we have a pretty darn cool new toy," I said at the conference table.

"Oh, Pillars of Faith, you don't need any more."

Aren't spouses supposed to be supportive? Maybe Sapale was due for a refresher course?

"You're positively impossible, already."

"I must side with your brood-mate, on this rare occasion, Sapale. *Too many toys* is oxymoronic." Thank you, my oldest friend, Toño.

"I suppose you're pleased too," she asked of Marshall.

"I'm a politician. I know when it's best to dodge a barbed question."

JJ cut in excitedly. "I *love* the new one. Instant anywhere. Oh, man." He reflected a moment. "Hey, Dad, do you think it can travel in time too? You know like a TARDIS?"

"I hope to never know, son. Time travel may be more than I can get my head around."

"No, it would be *totally* cool."

"I called you all here to discuss our next move," I said. "I think we're pretty much committed to rescuing the people on the worldships that crazy Marshall stole."

"Why?" asked Sapale. "For once,we're safe, will be left alone, and can grow in peace. I say stay here and tend to our own garden."

I pointed to Marshall. "What about this guy?"

"He can stay and work like the rest of us, or Toño can stuff him into one of those torpedo shuttles and mail him to the UN."

"Stuff me into a *what?*" Marshall said with focused interest.

"Hang on," I said. "She's just thinking out loud. No one's decided to stuff you into anything. Not yet."

"That will be a matter to vote on," said Toño. "I suggest everyone at this table gets one vote."

That meant Marshall, too. I wasn't so keen on that. "Okay. Let's vote and see. All in favor of helping the people on the stolen worldships, raise your hand." Everyone but Sapale raised a hand. "The ayes have it. So how're we going to help?"

"Jon," said Marshall, "I know you don't like me very much. I get that. But I'd like to suggest a plan of action, if that's alright with you."

Sapale was miffed. "Jon's not in charge. You can tell the rest of us if my brood-mate won't listen."

"I never —"

Sapale raised a hand to silence me. She nodded to Stuart.

"This entire mess is my fault. That I freely admit. I want to make it right, if that's even possible. I've studied all the records from when I've been … gone. I especially studied the message he sent to you, Jon. I hatched a plan. Now, it's not a great one. Hell, it's probably not even a *good* one. But with my scheme, I'll be taking all the risks."

I had on my poker face. "Go on."

"You get me to *Enterprise*, and I'll do the rest."

"That's it? That's your *whole* plan?" questioned Toño.

"Yes. I told you it wasn't stellar."

"You can say that again," cackled JJ. Good boy.

"Look," added Marshall, "I have a significant advantage if I show up unannounced. The current Stuart Marshall looks like you, Jon. I look like *us*, you know, me? Anyone standing by him based on old loyalties will immediately come over to my side."

Toño was unconvinced. "Not necessarily."

"Well, then my plan won't take too long, and I'll end up dead, right?"

Al spoke up. "That's exceedingly likely. Shall I put a number to the odds?"

"No thanks, son. Don't jinx the plan before it has a chance to fall flat on its face based on its dubious merits. Look," he said mostly to me, "It takes you, what, ten minutes to take me there, drop me off, and be home in time for tea. What do you have to lose?"

"To be honest, the risk of inflicting a second problem upon humankind."

"You don't have much confidence in me."

"Less than none."

"Look, I said I understood where you're coming from. But, know this. I was president of the US because I was a good leader and a sufficient man. Not a good one, mind you, but neither was I a bad one. I see where I went wrong. I want to make it right. Plus, you can't think I'd be worse than the android running the show now, can you?"

"Why is it I don't think that?" I wasn't buying what he was peddling.

"Valid point, but let's ask DeJesus. He knew me well. If he thinks I'd be a greater threat than the current Stuart Marshall, I'll shut my trap. But if he believes I'll do what I say, then you give me a chance, and I'm outta your hair."

I turned my head to Toño. "You comfortable with that?"

He shrugged. "That's a lot of pressure on me, but yes. I think we should allow him an attempt to set matters straight."

"And if he double-crosses us?"

"Then we'll have one more enemy a long way away." He shrugged again. "Not a very exclusive club."

Sapale laughed. JJ started to, also. I had to join in. "What the hell? One more mortal enemy is no big deal." I turned to Marshall. "Let me know when you're ready, and we're off."

"No time like the present," he said without blinking.

"Huh?"

"That way, I won't get a chance to come to my senses and back out."

Within an hour, our crew was set. I was included, obviously. I was Form, or a Form. I hadn't got the full scoop on the application of that title, yet. Sapale had to stay with the kids, though I could see in her eyes that she really wanted to come. Marshall was part of the trip—again, duh. Toño was welcome to join us, but I was glad when he declined. I preferred that Sapale have another adult around if there was trouble. I might only be gone only a little while, but I'd be months away in terms of radio contact. That meant JJ could come, which he was dying to do. He and I went heavily armed. I say, with gusto, we felt like real cowboys.

The three of us climbed aboard the vortex, I connected to the ship, and we were gone. I'd arranged for all four walls to be transparent. That way, wherever we popped up in relationship to *Enterprise,* we could see her. I thought of landing her directly in one of the large hangars, but the chatty voice couldn't guarantee we wouldn't land on someone, coming from such a distance. We'd play it the way I liked it—by ear.

In less time than it took to say, "I'm nauseated," we were staring off the port at *Enterprise,* in all her glory. She was big.

"Do you," I asked the manipulator—whom I formally renamed Manly, which he hated more than kids do broccoli— "have a fix on the android Marshall, and a clear area near him to set down?"

"Set down what," was Manly's confused response.

"It's an aviation term. It means to *land.*"

"Not," Manly shared, "where I come from. And yes, to both. Marshall is currently in his stateroom, horizontally positioned over a female of —"

"That's enough detail," I blurted out. I almost put my hands over JJ's ears, but he'd have killed me if I had. "Put us close. Any guards?"

"None inside the quarters where we'll set down. Many are stationed just outside."

A thought occurred to me. "Can you lock all of his doors, so they can't get in if he screams?"

There was a minor delay. "I rocketed you thorough space and time in an instant, I provided you a detailed map of the target, including personnel, and I have kept us invisible to the ship's scanners. What do you think, Form?"

"Please lock his doors once we're inside."

"By your command." I needed to talk to him about that, also. Too close to a catchphrase from an old sci-fi series I watched while traveling alone to Barnard's Star.

We materialized inside Marshall's laundry room. Okay, not the triumphant beachhead landing of legend, but certainly no one was watching it. As we stepped out of the vortex, we could plainly hear two voices. One, Marshall's, was hooting about the level of fun he was having, and promising to have a lot more real soon. The other voice was, sadly, the girl's. She wasn't a voluntary participant in the proceedings. I was glad we were about to profoundly upset that crazy android.

Our mission was not without risk. The android might be armed and JJ was vulnerable. I had him trail directly behind me, with Marshall immediately behind him. In a flash, we were in, two rail rifles were pressed uncomfortably hard against Marshall's head, and the other Marshall was slipping the girl—sixteen if she was a day—out from under his namesake and covering her with a blanket. I'd assigned that role to him and reminded him that, in spite of her protestations, she could be on the bad android's side. He needed to keep a close eye on her. Maybe the evil Marshall liked to have his playthings make believe they were under duress. Best to take as few chances as possible in any military operation.

I have to say, I'd had many a bad surprise in the last century. Many occasions disappointed me completely. This was neither of those. The look in his eye when he saw, in the following order, the guns, me, and then Marshall, was worth the price of admission. His first words, spoken while still prone in bed, were perfect, too.

"What are you doing?"

What were we doing? With rifles to his head and where it was impossible for us to be, and he wondered, what we came for? Did he hallucinate that this might be a *social* call? A practical joke? Maybe a fraternity initiation prank?

"We're from the laundry service, sir. Did you want *medium* starch in your collars? You left the box blank." Did I have to say that? No. Was it absolutely choice? Yeah, baby. I rapped his head with my barrel. "Up, Romeo. You're done."

Now I will have to admit, that was in retrospect an oversight on my part. Call it an unforeseen glitch, a SNAFU. Battle-tested as I was, I'd never had to train a weapon on a naked man with a prodigious erection. It's not as easy as one might imagine. Yeah? Try it sometime if you think I'm being overly dramatic.

"Ah, JJ, hand him his robe." I pointed to where it was on the floor.

The even harder part of what I was doing was that I'd never pointed a gun at myself. Weird City. Boy, oh, boy, did he look like me.

"Let's stroll nice and slow to your laundry room, shall we?" I waved my gun in that direction.

Evil Stuart was beginning to come out of shock. "I know what you're trying to do, and I promise you —" His next pseudo-word was *coooplahh*. That was the sound he produced when good Stuart punched him in the belly, really hard. *Nice.*

Our Stuart pointed menacingly at the android on the floor. "Not another word." I do believe he meant what he said.

I opened the vortex, and we all stepped in. "Change of plans. Manly?"

"Yes, Form?"

"I'm leaving this android in your care. If he does anything even mildly annoying evaporate him or something."

"If you really —"

"Silence." I liked saying that to Manly.

I didn't dare leave JJ inside with the android, sealed in the cube. Something bad could happen, and I'd never forgive myself if it did. So I confined Marshall all by his lonesome.

I opened the main entrance, stuck my head out, and told the nearest guard to fetch my chief of staff, immediately. He actually sprinted away.

Two minutes later, I kid you not, he returned, jogging, pushing Marilyn Monroe in front of him. He was slowed significantly in that effort by the height of her heels. Man, she looked nice running.

"Yes, Mr. President? This being your recreation hour, I was elsewhere. What can I do for you?" *Marilyn Monroe* asked what she could do for me. Oh, how I wish I had it on holo.

"I'll make a formal address to my people from my quarters. Make it happen in ten minutes or you're … well, you're in trouble." I fingered his chin. "You got that, son? Oh, and live transmission will be sent to all ten thousand worldships. Make sure you include that, or there'll be heel to pay … I mean, *hell* to pay."

"Ah, yes sir. I'll get a camera crew and lighting up here immediately."

"I don't want it immediately, son. I want it in less than ten minutes." I slammed the door shut.

"What the hell are you doing, Ryan?" Marshall seemed confused. Good.

In six minutes, the holo crew was set up and ready. All channels were preempted for my statement. JJ hid in a closet, praying he didn't have to sneeze. I took Marshall's elbow and pulled him close. "Follow my lead. You'll know when it's time to take the reins. After I step out, JJ and I will be in the cube." I pointed to a spot in the next room. "Wait there."

I opened JJ's closet door. "When you hear me say the words "the blessed fruits of American fortitude," go to the cube and get evil Marshall. Stand him right where the good Marshall was before I called him into the main room. I'll leave a single filament in contact with the vortex so we can time your removal of the evil Marshall. You got that?" He nodded nervously. "If Marshall tries anything, blast him, and son? Always shoot to kill." I started to walk away. "Oh, and the secure word between you and me is 'calrf.' Say it back." He did. "If you're even slightly confused as to which one's me, give the challenge. Please shoot the one with the wrong answer immediately."

JJ looked green around the gills. He was taking in a lot and was, hopefully, scared out of his mind. But he was one of the future leaders of Azsuram, and might as well learn in a trial-by-fire how to be strong.

"One last thing," I said to him, "I love you, and you can do this."

"That's two things, General Ryan."

"Good boy."

I returned to the living room and sat behind the ornate desk. Without asking, the camera crew scurried to frame their shot. "Can you boys make this mobile if I need you to follow me somewhere?"

The director swallowed nervously. "Yes, Mr. President. There may be a few shaky frames, but it'll be no problem."

"Great. Follow my lead, and watch closely for hand direction."

"Yes, sir."

I do believe I saw urine streak down his pant leg. Nice touch.

"You guys ready?" I barked. It was fun being bossy *and* feared.

"Yes, sir, we are."

"Okay, positions, everybody." I pointed for Marilyn to stand near the door, behind the crew. I kicked out the security guards. No sense in adding risk. They were stunned, but they knew better than to question this particular boss. I ran though everyone's location in my head like a quarterback before the ball was snapped. I was as ready as I ever would be. "Count me down."

The director leaned in front of the camera and held up five fingers. "In five - four - - -." Then he silently pointed to me and pulled out of view.

"My fellow Americans." Okay, maybe I didn't need to pull an LBJ, but I was actually kind of having fun. "I come to you today to expose an ugly truth and to begin a healing process that I can only pray will purge the evil I have allowed to grow in our midst."

A couple people in the room gasped.

"You see me today, having assumed the form of General Jonathan Ryan. I've heard a lot of gossip as to why I chose to temporarily place myself in his image. Well, here's the God's truth of it. I chose to appear as General Ryan because he *is* the best example of a true American hero I know of. He is brave, honest, loyal, and I can't overlook the fact he's stunningly handsome. I chose his face to remind myself daily that I needed to strive to be more like him, and in so doing, to be a better man. I must painfully confess to you here and now that I have failed *you*, the American people, as well as myself, and the sainted legacy of General Ryan.

"It was but a few hours ago that was I able to fit the final piece of the puzzle of intrigue and deception that has led to my failure. That has renewed my conviction that the only just and honorable course for me is to leave office immediately and permanently. Here are the dirty facts. And please, those of you in the company of children may wish to limit their exposure to my words, as they are *powerfully* disturbing.

"Over the last few years, as I worked closely with our friends at the UN to save as many souls as possible, a group of international subversives began undermining our combined efforts. Their poisonous embrace was too subtle for me to notice as it first began. Their scientific director, one Walter Morbius, was the tool used to slowly dissect the America we all knew and loved. He told me he was making an android copy of me. I begged him not to demean the presidency by doing so. But, clever international subversive agent that he was, he did it anyway. And he subtly but fundamentally altered my brain function to suit his dark vision of America.

"My fellow Americans, I have been forced to act in the manner I have because those international subversives were controlling me. As I gathered the proof against them, which I now have, I am ready to expose them. I am both ashamed and proud of my actions. Never think, for one second, that I enjoyed killing resistors or taking sexual advantage of those less desirous of sharing their passions with me. No, I hated every moment, every act, which those international subversive agents forced us *all* to endure.

"But now, for the great news. I have worked closely with my personal friends, Drs. Toño DeJesus and Carlos De La Frontera, along with other UN scientists, to set all matter right. First, it pains me to reveal, I can no longer lead my beloved country. The doctors tell me the damage the international subversives have done to my brain," I pointed helpfully to my head, "are beyond repair, even for those miracle workers. They were able, however, to piece together an override algorithm that is allowing me to speak truthfully to you now. The patch will fail in five minutes and it cannot be duplicated. Its installation has damaged my underlying computers too extensively to be repaired.

"Though it saddens me more than you'll ever know to have to say goodbye just when the tide is turning," I jerked my head a few times, to make it seem like my CPU's were failing right there on camera, "tu … turning and my moment of vinctti … vindication is at hand. But I *must* go.

"But, my fellow Americans, fear not for one solitary moment for your security and for your boundless future. I can only watch from Heaven, standing next to God, the angels, and the saints who will watch over you from now on. But you will have the government you deserve. Here is the interim plan.

"I, the def … defe … defective unit, must be destroyed immediately. As soon as my statement is complete, I will be escorted to the fusion engine core. An ancillary exhaust port will be opened and I will be cast in." I put my hands together in prayer. "At my final reckoning, friends, I may well break down. Forgive me for that in advance. I may well lie and try to say I was set up, that I'm the only true Marshall. Who knows what length a madman like I will be might go to in order to stay such a horrendous form of execution? Forgive that human weakness in advance, too, if you can. But please, no matter what I say, however insane a story the international subversives force to exit my mouth, don't fail to cast me into the engine. It is what I want, and it is certainly what I deserve.

"As to the international subversive agents, they are surprisingly few in number. The three heads of the dragon you must slay, once I'm gone, are Chuck Thomas, Sam Peterson, and Bob Patrick. They acted as my closest friends but were in truth the puppet masters controlling my string. I suggest they be destroyed, too, but that will not be my decision to make.

"I now wish to introduce you to the man who will lead this group of worldships. He will do so on an interim basis only. In the next few weeks, he will oversee three critical steps. One, he will supervise a free and open election to place a temporary government in charge of these ships. Two, he will see to it that our worldship turns around and immediately rejoins the main fleet of humans. Finally, during the time it takes to rejoin our brothers and sisters, he will root out the remaining subversive agents that may still hide amongst you.

I held a hand up to the door Stuart was concealed behind. "Will the *real* President Stuart Marshall please enter the room."

Uncertainly at first, Stuart stepped into the room. Once he saw the cameras, he snapped to and looked presidential. Stuart walked to my side and shook my hand. I pointed to him and directed that any applause be addressed to him alone.

I stood, and Stuart sat in my place. I placed a hand on either of his shoulder. "Now, it is my time to go, to be no more. From this moment forward, I demand that you listen only to this man, the real android copy of President Stuart Marshall."

Subdued applause followed.

"A last thought. As I surrender to the security detail, President Marshall will assign to march me down to the fusion engines it warms my mechanical heart to see, alive in this room, the blessed fruits of American fortitude."

I made a ten-second show of hugging Stuart, shaking his hand, then waving cheerily to the cameras. During our embrace, I had whispered in his ear, "The second I fall down scream for security." Then I turned to step aside, to be off camera. I stumbled, darn it all, just as I got to the door leading to where JJ held a gun to evil Stuart's temple. I, in fact, was so off balance, I fell headfirst into the that room.

There was a rise of startled voices, then Marshall was clearly heard to boom, "Get Security in here at once."

I stood up, grabbed the evil Stuart, my twin brother from another mother, and counted to five. On five, I shoved him to the floor in the conference room. He must have figured something unhealthy for him was awaiting his arrival. He popped up quickly and scanned the room. The new President Marshall was pointing at the past one and directing that security to seize him.

"No, wait. This is a trick. Those men aren't me. I'm the only me here. Arrest those men or I'll have you all thrown out an airlock with your entire families. Pets, too. I'm —"

His concluding remarks were obscured when his face was forced shut by the floor, a boot on his neck to secure him there, while handcuffs were roughly applied.

Within a few minutes, the conference room cleared, aside from Marshall and Marilyn. The camera crew followed the evil Stuart's progress to the fusion core. Marshall directed the remaining staff to see to the arrests of Chuck Thomas, Sam Peterson, and Bob Patrick, ideally before they could flee or hunker down in an armed defense.

I stepped into the room empty but for Marshall and his aide. I had a smile as big as the Milky Way. "That went pretty well, wouldn't you agree?"

Marilyn pointed at us. "Who's the alien, and why is the other Marshall here and not being dragged to his death?"

Marshall stared deeply into her eyes for a good minute. "Matt? Matthew *Duncan*, is that you?"

"Yes, sir, I can —"

"Why the hell are you dressed as Marilyn Monroe?"

"Ah, I'm not just dressed as her, sir." He lowered his head. "You, I mean the *other* you, thought it was funny."

"Well, I don't. Get down to Engineering and have them fix you ASAP. You got that, son?"

Matt smiled crookedly and then left at a brisk pace.

Fully alone, Marshall walked over to us. He held out his hand. "I have to thank you, Ryan, for what you did. I'll admit I was dribbling off the court, at the end back on Earth. But you've given me a chance to patch things up. That's more than I deserve."

"Yes," I said, "it is. Make it count."

"What will you do now?"

"We'll pop back to Azsuram to let Sapale know we're okay. Then, Toño and I will make a quick trip to *Exeter*. With luck, we'll get there before the transmission of your homecoming party does. We'll coordinate something with the UN. Who knows after that? We'll go home. You guys'll pick up the pieces and see if there's enough glue in the fleet to patch'em back together."

"With that vortex in the laundry room, your definition of 'home' becomes significantly broader."

I tilted my head. "We'll see. That part depends on what's best for my family. Ain't nobody deciding anything about the family without consulting Mama."

"Amen," said Stuart. "I suppose you'll be back to check on me?"

"If you screw the pooch, you can count on it. If you behave, and especially if you fade from public life, I hope I'll never have to see your ugly mug again."

"Can't say I blame you." He wagged a finger at me. "But I'll make you proud. You'll see."

I waved feebly. "Later, Mr. President."

JJ fell in behind me. "Later, Mr. P."

Ah, that's my boy.

244

FORTY-FOUR

Home in less than a second. Finally, a commute I could handle. The vortex didn't make any sounds, but Sapale was running over before I opened the wall. She hugged me like there was no tomorrow, then cast me to one side. She grabbed JJ, not in an embrace, but with an inspection. She slowly turned him around like she was considering buying him. Reassured that her baby was fine, she smothered him in a bear hug. JJ's reaction was classic teenager. He pinched up his face like he had swallowed a live toad. I knew he loved it, but Heaven forbid he should show that he did.

"Everybody okay?" I asked after she freed our son.

"Fine. No sign of the Blimpies either. Hopefully we've seen the last of them."

I asked Sapale and JJ to remain behind while Toño and I went to *Exeter* to fill them in on the changes we'd made aboard *Enterprise*. They were quite surprised to see us. I was loving the vortex.

With the death of Mary Kahl, the UN leadership had shuffled around a bit, but there'd been no significant changes. Bin Li was the new Secretary General. I'd known him well and had no problem working with him. Not that I would be working with him much. Once I set matters straight, I'd be back on Azsuram like I'd always planned. What the humans did in the intervening four hundred years was their concern, not mine. Toño spent a few hours catching up with Carlos, then we returned home. I tried to be non-committal, but Bin extracted a promise from me to return in a month. I wasn't going to make a habit of that, but one additional trip would be okay.

Back home, life sort of returned to normal over the next few weeks. I could sense something weighed on Sapale, but she repeatedly told me nothing was wrong and that she was fine. She said it had been so long since I'd seen her not pregnant, I probably mistook that for signs of her being off. I didn't believe that for a second, but I decided to give her time to put a voice to her concerns when she was good and ready.

That time came when I announced I was going to take the vortex to retrieve Lily and the high-speed rocket. Clearly that form of connection with Kaljax was no longer needed. I said that after I got back, she and I could plan a trip to Kaljax to accomplish what Lily was sent to do. At first, she just nodded. Then she growled very softly. I'd learned her species had several distinctive growls. There was the angry set of growls I'd heard all too often. There were happy growls, like a cat's purr. But there was also a collection of moody, sad, or distraught sounds. She was making one of the soulful ones.

"What?" I asked gently.

She was apparently unaware of the sound she was making. "Huh?"

"That growl. I know you too well for you to say it's nothing. That's the sad-Sapale growl."

"No. I mean, I was probably thinking of home, my parents." I stroked the back of her hand and listened. "You never met them. They were the best. They hated the repression, the politicking, and the evil that governed their world. They taught me to work for peace, to fight the evil, and to hold back the darkness."

"They sound like wonderful people. I'm sorry I never had a chance to meet them."

"Dracos, the man whom Mangasour replaced, had them publicly tortured to death." She stopped a moment. "It took my father two days to die. Mom lasted five. Well, that's how long it took for her to stop growling. I think her mind was gone long before that."

"Babe, I'm sorry to hear all that, and I wish I could make it right. But what's that got to do with me retrieving Lily?"

She moaned, growled, and began to whimper. I went around to her side of the table and held her as she sat there, letting it all out. Finally, she was able to speak. "Don't you see it's all falling apart?"

"What, brood's-mate? What's falling apart?"

"This," she swung her arms around, "all of this. The village, a new positive Kaljaxian society —" she couldn't go on.

"What? Say it, love. What else is falling apart?"

She thumped me on the chest. "You and me, you big idiot."

Huh? I mean, *what*? Didn't see that one coming in a million years. "Huh? What are you talking about?"

"We were here, working against the odds to make something great, something wonderful. Now … now you have your magic box, and … and it's never going to be the same."

"I really don't see why not. Nothing's changed. You're still going to make this a spectacular place, and I'll be with you, always. The vortex changes *nothing*."

"Yes, it does, and you know it. You'll never be really here," she pointed to the floor, "again. Your mind will be elsewhere, everywhere. And this place is no longer our private paradise, our last chance to make a good society. No. If we fail, we just get into your box and go to any number of other places, until we get it right or get bored and ditch the concept for good."

"Why is it *my* box all of a sudden? Isn't it *ours*?"

"Of course not. You're the only one alive who can control it. It's yours, all right."

"If it will make you happy, I'll turn it back into a storage shed and never use it again."

"I'd still know you were thinking about your next adventure." She placed a loving palm aside my head. "This might be here," she lowered her hand to my chest, "but this would never be. You're a pilot. Pilots fly away. If you didn't, it would only be to try and make me happy, not because it was what you really wanted."

"Yes, I'll admit part of what you say is true. But once we're back from Kaljax, I don't have anywhere else I need to go. No one can raise us on the radio without a multiyear delay, so it's not like I'm on call to save the universe. I don't think anything will change in my heart *or* on Azsuram."

"You agreed to meet Bin in a month."

"Yeah, but just once."

"He'll ask you to return and you will. You're the responsible type. You can't help it."

"Two trips, tops. That's it. Then we go with the plan, just like before."

"What about when one of the children gets ill? You wouldn't travel to Kaljax for them to get expert care? Or when I'm dying, you wouldn't drag me back to see if they could help?"

"That's different. We'd only go if we had to."

"But that's just it. Before the box, *we* were all we had. Now, it's just like we're living in the suburbs."

"Sorry."

"Your apology doesn't change anything."

"I want to go on record as saying you're overreacting. Let's see what happens before we jump to conclusions. Okay?"

"Do I have a choice?"

"Sure?"

"What?"

"I have no idea, but there must be one you'd like."

I understood her concerns, but I just didn't know of a solution. Sure, having instant access to everywhere put an end to our feeling of total isolation. But I couldn't get rid of the vortex unless I was in it. If I left it on a faraway comet, how was I going to get home? Plus, it provided us with a wonderful link for resupply. A mixed blessing was still a blessing, right?

I intercepted Lily and brought her home a few days after that conversation. When we were back, I asked Sapale when she'd like to go to Kaljax. She knew we had to, but I could see in her eyes she resented that fact. Nonetheless, we left Toño and JJ in charge, but brought Fashallana with us. Whatever reservations her mom had about visiting Kaljax, my daughter didn't share them. Fash got all dreamy-eyed when we asked her to come. She couldn't sleep until we left. The promise of boys, shopping, and boys, held sway over her imagination, as it would with any proper young woman.

Before we left, while Sapale was looking for an excuse to cancel the trip, she spoke to me one day. "You know I'm a wanted woman on Kaljax. It's not safe for me there."

"You're a wanted woman only in your native country. On the rest of the planet, you're simply unwelcome."

"Unwelcome where I hail from can be just as unpleasant. What if I'm not allowed to leave? What then?"

"I'll see to it that doesn't happen."

"What," she pointed at my hand, "with that?"

"No, better," I indicated my head. "With this."

"Great. Let me say goodbye to the rest of the kids before we leave. I'll probably never see them again."

"Very funny. But, you once told me a proverb from back home. *Love your children, cherish Braldone, but keep all four eyes on your gold.* Right?"

"And?"

"*And* with enough gold, they'll not only let you come and go, they'll name a few buildings after you. Maybe declare Sapale Day a national holiday."

"Great idea. Let me just go to our gold chest and stuff my pockets with nothing because that's how much we have in there."

I smiled and shook my head. "O, ye of little faith."

"Faith I possess in abundance. Gold, my love, not so much."

I started giggling.

"What did I say or do that you find so humorous?"

"When I retrieved Lily, didn't you notice I was gone a bit too long?"

"No," she rested her hands on her hips, "the peace and quiet must have distracted me from that observation."

"You know that vortex you so hate? Would you join me for a brief tour?"

"Tour? It's the size of a small apartment, and I've seen every square inch a thousand times."

I held my hand out to take hers.

"Oh, very well. You're positively impossible, you know?"

"So I've been told."

She took my hand.

When we were outside the vortex I made her close her eyes. I opened the wall and we stepped in. "Okay, open 'em up."

She did. She was real quiet for a good second or two. "You've got to be *shitting* me."

"Yeah," I agreed, "pretty neat, isn't it?"

She punched my shoulder.

"What was that for?" I asked, laughing.

"The one time in my life I'm rich, and I have nowhere to spend it."

Sapale was looking at the six solid cubes of gold resting in the corner. Each weighed four hundred kilograms. Back on what used to be Earth it'd be worth maybe one hundred million dollars, give or take. We were suddenly well-off.

"Where did you get this?"

"I asked Manly if he knew of any large deposits of gold. Turns out, he did. We made a brief detour and picked some up."

"Some? There was more?"

"A lot more."

"Does Manly remember where it was?" She turned to me. "Tell me he remembers."

"He does. So when we go to Kaljax, we're going to be the most popular couple on the planet"

"I think I'll have to agree with you on that one."

We were indeed. For reasons of security, she contacted the head of one of Sur's bitter enemies while we were in orbit. She chose a country called Himiol I hadn't visited. She claimed the people there were every bit as vicious and jingoistic as hers, only a little less intelligent and a lot more unreasonable. She arranged to meet with a local governor at his home. She said if he guaranteed our safety, he'd be well rewarded. He grumbled back that he would, if he was.

When I set a four-hundred-kilogram block of gold on his desk, I believe we won him over. Sure he was incredulous at first. Who wouldn't be? But Sapale had told him we were paying in gold and asked him to have an assayer present to authenticate our gratuity. They were both speechlessly impressed. The second he was certain he was rich beyond his wildest dreams, he simply said to us, without looking away from his new gold, "I am *at* your service."

"Thank you, Greysor," Sapale replied. "You are most kind." She could really lay it on thick when she wanted to. One has to love that in a girl. "This is our daughter's first trip home. Do you think you could arrange for a fancy banquet?"

"It would be my pleasure. How about tomorrow night? Ah, would a thousand guests be sufficient?"

"Yes." She turned to me. "Brood-mate, would you like to accompany Greysor's wife, Fashallana, and me on a little shopping trip? We didn't pack for a proper ball."

Greysor was so cute. He was only paying us the slightest attention, being preoccupied with his new BFF resting on his desk. He grunted, "My wife? Oh, yes, my wife. Our daughters. too. You'll have a grand time shopping."

They did. It turns out for the women of Kaljax, shopping's serious business that's not to be taken lightly. There existed only one way to do it best. Be pampered, spend way too much, and be seen doing both by all the other women who socially mattered. By those standards, Team Ryan won big time. Apparently, we set some kind of new record. I'd have had fun watching them have fun, especially my little girl. But *nothing* was worth a shopping trip with a gaggle of women.

I did wonder afterward if we'd be able to keep Fash on the farm after her coming-out party. The banquet was impressive, except for the boys. They swarmed like gnats over Fashallana. It took all the self-control I had not to decommission a few as an example to the rest. I didn't, though. My girls might hold a grudge against me if I had. But they had such a good time. Actually, I did, too.

The next few days, Sapale gathered items she wanted to take back. One of the harder parts of the trip came for me then. The collecting of sperm. Yeah, TMI and gross all rolled into one disgusting ball of Dad not liking life. But we *were* on a mission. That was understood. The most efficacious and secure way to collect and preserve sperm was via sexual intercourse. Remember Kaljaxian physiology. The females have sperm pouches. I simply couldn't talk Sapale into accomplishing the feat with test tubes and freezers. As no one was going to involve my brood's-mate in the process, that left the collecting work to Fashallana. Yeah.

Did she protest? Unfortunately, she did not. Did she scream, pitch a fit, and refuse to do as her mother told her? Ah, no. Not so much. Did she love it more than chocolate and talk about it endlessly on the trip home? No. Not *one* word. I think at one point she started to say something concerning the experience, but she took Sapale's cue and kept quiet. Some things were *so* better left unsaid in front of Dad. There'd be time aplenty to exchange tales, once they were home.

We were back on Azsuram too soon for both of them and not a moment too soon for me. Mission accomplished, yes. Dad chewing iron and spitting nails? Oh, yes.

FORTY-FIVE

In a shallow tidal pool on the edge of a great sea, a young Listhelon male stood alone. Omendir scanned the waves with singular focus. As in uncounted generations before his, the time for Gumnolar's selection of a new Warrior One had arrived. The last remnants of the old regime, that of the failed and disgraced Otollar, had been wiped away. It was time for Gumnolar to be glorified anew. Omendir prayed he was to bear the standard of his god, but he knew it was not his to take. Gumnolar had to *grant* it to him. He had to earn the opportunity to be the chosen one in battle.

Ororror also claimed the right to be selected, as he was the second oldest son. Soon, one brother would triumph and the other would die. One glorified, one consumed by the victor. A large cascade of water rose and fell, signaling that Ororror's fluke had fallen. The challenge was made. Thrill pulsing through every cell in his body, Omendir plunged into the sea and swam with all his strength to the spot his brother had marked.

No weapons or witnesses were permitted. Whatever struggles occurred between the brothers would be remembered only by the winner and never spoken of. As it had always been, so it would be. Omendir, so consumed with passion during his charge, lost track of his brother. That cost him the first blow of the battle. He was rammed from below with sufficient force to lift his bulk part ways out of the water. He gasped briefly, then swam to one side and down to avoid taking a second hit.

Ororror came straight back at him. Omendir used his powerful tail to slap his younger brother on the head and timed his strike to perfection. His charge was redirected and missed Omendir completely.

As he sailed past, Ororror reached out and seized his brother by the dorsal fin. Twisting with lightning-like speed he bit down mercilessly with his enormous teeth, ripping off a good-size chunk of flesh.

Omendir barely noticed the bite or the pain. His blood was running hot and nothing mattered but victory. He felt like he was immortal. He could not die. He could already taste his glory. "I have always been the one, brother. You died when you challenged me," he screamed in rage. With a mighty surge he tossed his brother off his back.

Ororror said nothing in reply. The old saying he held to went, *If you come to talk, speak with words. If you come to kill, speak with death.* The Omendir grabbed his brother's throat with one fin and struggled for his fluke with the other. If he kept him from breathing or maneuvering, the fight would be over rapidly. He pulled his writhing brother closer, tightening the grip on his neck. Omendir felt soft bones crunch and knew he was about to win Gumnolar's blessing. He was to *be* chosen Warrior One.

Ororror spoke in brief gasps. "You ... were al ... ways ... the fool ... bro ... ther. I wi ... nnn."

Omendir felt a piercing force between his fin blades and then saw a spearhead thrust forward from his chest. His blood mixed quickly with the water around him and his strength escaped him with it. He released his hold on Ororror. The younger brother turned and grabbed the spearhead in both fins and twisted it violently from side to side. As Omendir was flipped onto his back, the last vision he saw before he gazed peacefully into Gumnolar's joyous smile was the face of Ozalec, a much younger brother. That coward was too small and too afraid to compete in the challenge. Ozalec sneered at his big brother as he slipped into death's endless embrace.

"Are you alright?" Ozalec asked the new Warrior One.

"Yes, minion. I am fine. Let us return home. I have a race to wipe from existence. I shall not join Otollar in failure. I will eat human flesh live from their bones until there is no more to consume. But first I shall build a monument to my beloved brother, Omendir, second in Gumnolar's eyes only to *me*."

FORTY-SIX

Deep in space, empty but for twenty-five hundred Uhoor, no sound could be heard. Uhoor needed no sound. Their minds were connected as one, as they always had been. They fed on the rim of a black hole as they they listened to Tho. She was no longer interested in the contemplation of eternity. She thought only of her children, her family. She wished them to live forever, as they always had. But time, even for the Uhoor, moved on, and it did so malignantly now.

Ablo had spoken. She spoke for centuries heaped upon centuries layered on uncountable waves of time. Near a black hole, time was not as it was elsewhere. But for Tho, it had been ever so long and ever so painful. Ablo said that the Uhoor were not slaves of any beings, nor were they at the command of others, as if they were motes of dust or thoughts. The three-legged of Deavoriath had held the Uhoor once, briefly, but Ablo would not tolerate that bondage again. If the Deavoriath would end all Uhoor, then the Uhoor should be ended. Better not to be than to be bound once again.

Ablo would prefer to go where she wasn't, like Plo, rather than experience control from outside. Many Uhoor owned Ablo's thoughts. Tho was not those thoughts. If those thoughts were, then the Uhoor were not. If the last of the mighty Uhoor were where they were not, who would sing their thoughts or know their ways? Who would *be* the Uhoor?

Ablo spoke one last time, a short time. She said she would go to consume the Deavoriath of Oowaoa, or she would soar to a better where. All the Uhoor were as one. All but Tho, who was not as one. All the Uhoor backed away

255

from the black hole and moved toward the other half of what the vile scum called pizza. Tho had felt the price of confronting the Deavoriath once and would not know it again. She nosed forward and became one with the black hole.

FORTY-SEVEN

Life finally settled into a comfortable easy pace on Azsuram. After the excitement of death-by-Uhoor, the discovery of the vortex, the dispatching of evil Marshall, and specimen collection on Kaljax, decompressing was not easy. But, we were all committed to a vision and we were, most importantly, family. Gradually, Toño disappeared again into his lab, mumbling to himself like a prototypical mad professor. Sapale, my beautiful matriarch, supervised a dizzying number of pregnancies, deliveries, infants, and unruly teenagers. She was at her best and glorious to watch. Generations of our children flourished in the supportive environment of the village.

I think back now on those ten years, the transit-years for that abominable transmission that slowly snaked itself to us, as the best years of my life. For an immortal, that's saying a lot. Trust me. JJ and Draldon grew into the fullness of manhood. Both were natural leaders, which was perfect for me. As they gradually took charge of day-to-day matters, I could gladly let go of the reins.

Kaljaxian society was rigidly male dominated. Sapale wanted to blunt that tendency, if it was genetically possible. She encouraged the young women to participate in leadership. Early on, at least, that was possible. Everyone was related and respected one another. What would happen over time was a different matter, but we tried to establish a balance from the get-go. She created a Council of Elders and was the first chief of the council. Subsequent chiefs would be voted on by the members. Anyone could be on the council once they came of age, which Sapale set at twenty-five Azsuram years. That was roughly the same as Earth years. Again, it worked wonderfully with Sapale at the helm. The future would just have to take care of itself.

By what would have been 2175 in Earth time, I was one hundred sixty-two years old. Wow. Still looked and felt thirty-seven. Sapale was beginning to look more mature—I learned to never say one's brood's-mate looked *older*—but had many good years left in her. To my surprise, I didn't in fact yearn to fly my vortex on missions of triumph and discovery. I was perfectly happy where I was, doing what I was.

Life was almost too good to be true. Cue the high-pitched violins and the recollection of what I'd always said when things were going their best. Bottom, you may drop out at will. The issue with the occurrence of evil and the awareness of evil was complicated by the immense distances of space. I had promised to retire the vortex and, after my quick visit back to *Enterprise*, I did just that. If I had kept the channels of communication open with occasional visits, I would have learned of the sick twist fate had in store for us, but I wasn't so inclined. Perhaps it's best I didn't. Why hurry ill tidings?

So, we labored in tranquility for the better part of a decade while the unheralded, malignant message of hate silently carved its way toward our awareness. That weak conglomeration of unwitting radio waves was conscripted by an evil force. Its contents were as unbelievable and unwelcome a bundle of information as there could possibly have been.

Lily buzzed me as Sapale, the older kids, and I were sitting around the dinner table. We were speaking blissfully of nothing, about to clear the plates and ready ourselves for bed. "Jon, I have an incoming message." Messages, as they took so long to arrive, were not ever good news. We all froze.

"Ah, put it through on the holo down here, once it's buffered and cleaned up." Signals tended to degrade as they traversed large distances.

"It's ready. Let me know if you want any part replayed."

There was a moment of silence, then the holo flashed to life. Stuart Marshall sat behind a fancy desk in a three-piece suit with a red tie and matching handkerchief. He looked presidential. I guessed he was back in the game at some level. Privately, I hoped he wasn't too high ranking. He said I could trust him, but I wasn't certain I ever could. If he was content to remain a relative nobody, trust wasn't necessary. That was my preference.

General Ryan, wife of General Ryan, children of General Ryan, and Dr. DeJesus. Greetings across the miles."

I had the strangest, visceral response to his greeting. It wasn't right, though I couldn't detect exactly what was wrong.

I trust the years have treated you well. I regret I had to resort to this slow mode of communication, but, darn it all, General Captain Ryan, you've kept yourself a stranger, what with your magic box and all. Well, I simply had to revert to, he pointed off-camera, *this old contraption to say my piece.*

As you know, a decade will have passed since you placed your trust in me, after casting that dastardly other Marshall into the fiery pit he so richly deserved.

Sapale tugged at my arm. "I have a *bad* feeling about this."

"Me, too. But all we can do is watch."

My message to you, Sir Captain General Ryan, is thanks from a grateful nation who's gratitu— He daubed his fingertips across his forehead, like they were dancing. *Wait, how could I have forgotten? There is no nation to be grateful. It's but dust and debris now, one with the past. I guess I could say grateful worldship, but, hey, that doesn't carry the same verbal eloquence. Well, now I'm feeling sort of silly sending this broadcast in the first place.*

What could possibly explain my behavior? Why would a sane, well-grounded Stuart Marshall call you with no cogent message? I'll tell you why. He *wouldn't.*

He rubbed his chin like he wished to detach it. *Why? What could explain— Ah ha. Not to worry. I have it. Wow, it's really kind of simple, now that I think about it. I'm* not *the sane, well-grounded Stuart Marshall. No, I'm the crazy-ass one you had thrown into the fusion chamber. Yes, that's the only possible explanation I can come up with that fits the facts as I see them.*

Hey, Jonny boy, if anyone ever tells you it's not hot in a fusion core, you slap their face for me, okay, buddy? Cause, I'm living proof it's hotter than the hell you thought you were forwarding me to. Well, I'm the re-re-animated android who can only imagine what fun that was for you, ya sick bustard.

But, don't worry. Please, Jon, do not *worry. I'm not one to forget a favor, even if it's the opposite of one. I told you a few years back that, you know, I hate you more than anything in or out of the universe and that I'd extract my vengeance on you and every single thing you hold dear. I also told you, which you seem to have glazed over in remembering, that there'd always be a me. I did not permit in that notification that you could substitute, at your own discretion, an alternative copy and have that one count. No, Jon, that violates the rules. I hate rule breakers, Ryan. I hate them almost as much as I hate you. A + B = C, son. That means I hate you more than I hate you.* He smiled at the camera. *Hardly seems possible, but there you have it.*

So, don't allow me to ruin an otherwise beautiful day for you on GB 3, or whatever the fuck your mud-crawling interstellar whore has named it. No, you just go back to your dull, meaningless existence, pending, of course, the other shoe I'm going to drop on your ideal new life in paradise.

You know what, Jon? If I didn't hate you so very much, I'd kind'a feel sorry for you. But, you know what? I'm such a son of a bitch that I don't. Funny how that works. He moved his hands around as if he were trying to match puzzle pieces together. *Kind of works, but it kind of doesn't. Who,* he darted a look up to the camera again, *thought up this screwy life in the first place? I sure as hell didn't. No,* he held out a palm, *don't you ever blame that on me. Hey, hate to eat and run, but I've got lives to ruin, hopes to crush, and dreams to dash against the hard shores of my reality.*

He leaned forward so his nose touched the camera lens. *But, quick, look over your shoulder. Hah.* he slapped his hands together hard. *Made you look. But never you worry. I'll be there as soon as humanly possible. Peace-out to the walking dead from the zombie android who's going to end you.*

To be continued, oh yes …

Glossary of Main Characters and Places:

Number in parentheses is the book in which the name first appears.

Ablo (2): Led Uhoor to attack Azsuram after Tho died. Female.

Almonerca (2): Daughter of Fashallana, twin of Noresmel. Name means *sees tomorrow*.

Alpha Centauri (1): Fourth planetary target on Jon's long solo voyage on *Ark 1*. Three stars in the system: AC-A, AC-B, and AC-C (aka Proxima Centauri). AC-B has eight planets, three in habitable zone. AC-B 5 was initially named *Jon* by Jon Ryan until he met the falzorn. AC-B 3 is Kaljax. Proxima Centauri (PC) has one planet in habitable zone.

Alvin (1): The ship's AI on *Ark 1*. aka Al.

Amanda Walker (2): Vice president, then president, a distant relative of Jane Geraty. Wife of Faith Clinton.

Azsuram (2): See also Hodor, Groombridge-1618, and Klonsar. BG 3 was discovered by **Seamus O'Leary**.

Barnard's Star (1): First planetary target of *Ark* 1. BS 2 and 3 are in habitable zone. BS 3 was Ffffuttoe's home, as well as ancient, extinct race called the Emitonians. See BS 2.

Beast Without Eyes (2): The enemy of Gumnolar. The devil for inhabitants of Listhelon.

Bin Li (2): New UN Secretary General after Mary Kahl was killed.

Bob Patrick (2): US senator when Earth was destroyed. One of The Four Horsemen, coconspirator with Stuart Marshall.

Braldone (1): Believed to be the foreseen savior on Kaljax.

Brathos (1): The Kaljaxian version of hell.

Brood-mate (1): On Kaljax, the male partner in a marriage.

Brood's-mate (1): On Kaljax, the female partner in a marriage.

BS 2 (1): The planet Oowaoa, home of the highly advanced Deavoriath race.

Calrf (2): A Kaljaxian stew that Jon particularly dislikes.

Carl Roger (1): Chief of staff to President John Marshall before Earth was destroyed.

Carl Simpson (1): Pilot of *Ark* 3. Discovered Listhelon orbiting Lacaille 9352.

Carlos De La Frontera (2): Brilliant assistant to Toño, became an android to infiltrate Marshall's

Charles Clinton (1): US President during part of Jon's voyage on *Ark 1*.

Chuck Thomas (2): Chairman of the Joint Chiefs of Staff, one of The Four Horsemen, and the first military person downloaded to an android by Stuart Marshall. evil team.

Cholarazy (1): Planet orbiting **Epsilon Eridani.** Visited on Jon's *Ark 1* voyage and used as a part of his cover story for his later quest.

Command prerogatives (2): The Deavoriathian tools installed to allow operation of a vortex. Also used to probe substances. Given to the android Jon Ryan.

Cube (2): See vortex.

Cycle (2): Length of year on Listhelon. Five cycles roughly equal one Earth year.

Cynthia York (1): Lt.. General and head of Project Ark when Jon returns from epic voyage.

Davdiad (1): God-figure on Kaljax.

Deavoriath (1): Mighty and ancient race on Oowaoa. Technically the most advanced civilization in the galaxy. Used to rule many galaxies, then withdrew to improve their minds and characters. Three arms and legs. Currently live forever.

Devon Flannigan (2): Former baker who assassinated Faith Clinton.

Delta-Class vehicles (1): The wondrous new spaceships used in Project Ark. Really fast.

Dolirca (2): Daughter in Fashallana's second set of twins. Took charge of Ffffuttoe's asexual buds. Name means *love all.*

Draldon (2): Son of Sapale. Twin with Vhalisma. Name means *meets the day.*

Enterprise (2): US command worldship.

Epsilon Eridani (1): Fourth target for *Ark 1*. One habitable planet, EE 5. Locally named Cholarazy, the planet is home to several advanced civilizations. The Drell and Foressál are the main rivals. Leaders Boabbor and Gothor are bitter rivals. Humanoids with three digits.

Exeter (2): UN command worldship.

Faith Clinton (2): Descendent of the currently presidential Clintons. First a senator, later the first president elected in space. Assassinated soon after taking office.

Falzorn (1): Nasty predatory snakes of Alpha Centauri-B 5. Their name is a curse word among the inhabitants of neighboring Kaljax.

Farmship (2): Cored out asteroids devoted not to human habitation but to crop and animal production. There are only five, but they allow for sufficient calories and a few luxuries for all worldships.

Fashallana: First daughter of Sapale. Twin to JJ. Name means *blessed one.*

Ffffuttoe (1): Gentle natured flat bear like creature of BS 3. Possesses low-level sentience.

Form (2): Title of someone able to be the operator of vortex using their command prerogatives.

General Saunders (1): Hardscrabble original head of Project Ark.

Groombridge-1618 3 (1): Original human name for the planet GB 3, aka Azsuram.

Gumnolar (1): Deity of the Listhelons. Very demanding.

Habitable zone (1): Zone surrounding a star in which orbiting planets can have liquid water on their surface.

Heath Ryan (2): Descendant of original Jon Ryan, entered politics reluctantly.

Indigo (1): Second and final wife of the original Jon Ryan, not the android. They have five children, including their version of Jon Ryan II.

Infinity charges (2): Membrane-based bombs that expand, ripping whatever they're in to shreds.

Jane Geraty (1): TV newswoman who had an affair with newly minted android Jon. Gave birth to Jon Ryan II, her only child.

Jodfderal (2): Son in Fashallana's second set of twins. Name means *strength of ten*.

Jon Junior, JJ (2): Son of Sapale. One of her first set of twins. The apple of Jon Ryan's eye.

Jon Ryan (1): Both the human template and the android who sailed into legend.

Jon III and his wife, Abree (2): Jon's grandson, via the human Jon Ryan.

Kashiril (2): From Sapale's second set of twins. Name means *answers the wind.*

Kendell Jackson (2): Major general who became head of Project Ark after DeJesus left. Forced to become an android by Stuart Marshall.

Klonsar (2): The Uhoor name for Azsuram, which they claim as their hunting grounds.

Lilith, Lily (2): Second AI on *Shearwater.* AI no likey.

Listhelons (1): Enemy species from third planet orbiting Lacaille 9352. Aquatic, they have huge, overlapping fang-like teeth, small bumpy head, big, bulging eyes articulated somewhat like a lizard's. Their eyes bobbed around in a nauseating manner. His skin is sleek, with thin scales. They sport gill a split in their thick neck on either side. Maniacally devoted to Gumnolar.

Luhman 16a (1): The second target of *Ark 1*. Eight planets, only one in habit zone, LH 2. Two fighting species are the *Sarcorit* that are the size and shape of glazed donuts and *Jinicgus,* looking like hot dogs. Both are unfriendly be nature.

Manly (2): Jon's pet name for the conscious of an unclear nature in the vortex. He refers to himself the vortex manipulator.

Mary Kahl (2): UN Secretary General at the time of the human exodus from Earth.

Matt Duncan (2): Chief of staff for the evil President Stuart Marshall. Became an android that was destroyed. Marshall resurrected him in the body of Marilyn Monroe. Matt no likey that.

Noresmel (2): Fashallana's daughter, twin of Almonerca. Name means *kiss of love.*

Offlin (2): Son of Otollar. Piloted ship that tried to attack Earth and was captured by Jon.

One That Is All (2): The mentally linked Deavoriath community.

Otollar (2): Leader, or Warrior One, of Listhelon. Died when he failed to defeat humans.

Owant (2): Second Warrior to Otollar.

Phil Anderson (1): TV host, sidekick of Jane Geraty.

Phillip Szeto (2): Head of CIA under Stuart Marshall.

Piper Ryan (2): Heath Ryan's wife.

Plo (2): First Uhoor to attack Azsuram.

Prime (2): Pet name for the android of Carlos De La Frontera.

Sam Peterson (2): Chief Justice at the time of Earth's destruction. Member of Stuart Marshall's inner circle, The Four Horsemen.

Sapale (1): Brood's-mate to android Jon Ryan. From Kaljax.

Seamus O'Leary (2): The pilot of *Ark 4*, discovered Azsuram.

Shearwater (2): Jon's second starship, sleek, fast, and bitchin'.

Sherman Collins (1): Secretary of State to President John Marshall when it was discovered Jupiter would destroy the Earth.

Space-time congruity manipulator (1): Hugely helpful force field.

Stuart Marshall (1): Born human on Earth, became president there. Before exodus, he *downloaded into an android and became the insane menace of his people.*

Tho (2): The head Uhoor, referred to herself as *the mother of the Uhoor.*

Toño DeJesus (1): Chief scientist in both the android and Ark programs. Course of events forced him to reluctantly become an android.

Tralmore (1): Heaven, in the religion of Kaljax.

Uhoor (2): Massive whale-like creatures of immense age. They feed off black holes and propel themselves though space as if it was water.

Uto (1): Alternate time line android Jon Ryan, possibly

Vhalisma (2): From Sapale's third set twins. Name means *drink love.*

Vortex (2): Deavoriath vessel in cube shape with a mass of 200,000 tons. Move instantly anywhere by folding space.

Vortex manipulator (2): Sentient computer-like being in vortex.

Wolf 359 (1): Third target for *Ark 1*. Two small planets WS 3, which was a bad prospect, and WS 4, which was about as bad.

Wolnara (2): Twin in Sapale's second set. Name means *wisdom sees.*

Worldships (1): Cored out asteroids serve as colony ships for the human exodus.

Yibitriander (1): Three legged Deavoriath, past Form of Jon's vortex.

Shameless Self-Promotion
(Who Doesn't Love That?)

Thank you for joining me on the Forever Journey. It's only just beginning. Book 1, *The Forever Life* is available now.

Please do leave a review on Amazon. They're more precious than gold.

The next book in the Forever Series is *The Forever Fight*. Definitely check it out.

The second series in the Ryanverse begins with *Embers*. Find out what ever happened to Jon, but maybe finish this series first.

Follow my Facebook Author's page to join in on the discussion: https://www.facebook.com/craigr1971/

Feel free to email me comments or to discuss any part of the series. *contact@craigarobertson.com*

My Website: craigrobertsonblog.wordpress.com

Also, you can ask to be on my email list. Do that by emailing me your contact information. I'll send out infrequent alerts concerning new material or some of the extras I'm planning in the near future.

For more about me and my other novels, check out my Amazon Author's Page: https://www.amazon.com/-/e/B00522FUR0

Wow. That's a whole lot of social media. But, I'm worth it, so it's alright.

Don't be a stranger, at least any stranger than you need to be,

Craig

Made in the USA
Columbia, SC
17 March 2019